12 BEFORE 13

ALSO BY LISA GREENWALD

11 Before 12
TBH, This Is SO Awkward
TBH, This May Be TMI

A FRIENDSHIP LIST NOVEL

12 before 13

LISA GREENWALD

KATHERINE TEGEN BOOKS
An Imprint of HarperCollins Publishers

Katherine Tegen Books is an imprint of HarperCollins Publishers.

Friendship List #2: 12 Before 13
Copyright © 2018 by HarperCollins Publishers
All rights reserved. Printed in the United States of America.
No part of this book may be used or reproduced in any manner
whatsoever without written permission except in the case of brief
quotations embodied in critical articles and reviews. For information
address HarperCollins Children's Books, a division of HarperCollins
Publishers, 195 Broadway, New York, NY 10007.
www.harpercollinschildrens.com

Library of Congress Control Number: 2018021526
ISBN 978-0-06-241177-8

Typography by Aurora Parlagreco
18 19 20 21 22   PC/LSCH   10 9 8 7 6 5 4 3 2 1
❖
First Edition

In loving memory of Helen Feiler Greenwald—
my Bubbie, my cheerleader, and my friend

12 BEFORE 13

ONE

"WHAT DO YOU MEAN YOU made a list?" Alice asks me. We're at the water fountain in center camp, and I'm refilling my water bottle. My green West Brookside Middle School V-neck tee is getting drenched in the process.

"Kaylan and I made a list of eleven things we had to do before we turned twelve, to kind of like prepare for middle school, and now we're making a new one of twelve things to do before we turn thirteen." When my water bottle is full, I snap the cover back on and take a sip.

Crinkling her nose, Alice says, "But why? Just, like, for fun?"

I laugh a little. "Um, kind of, yeah, but it really helped calm us down before middle school. And now it's a tradition, and we don't break traditions."

Alice throws her head upside down and pulls her

skinny braids into a low bun. "Cool. I like it." She links arms with me. "Seriously, how have I only known you for two weeks? I feel like we've been friends our whole lives."

"I kinda do, too," I say. "I should've come to camp earlier."

"Lamey McLamerson," she says. "But wait, I'm confused—how much water do you really have to drink?"

"Just enough to keep our glowing complexions." I turn my head to show her both sides of my face.

"You're hilarious. And your shirt is soaking wet, B.T. Dubs."

I shrug. "Whatever. It'll dry."

"What's the next thing you're—"

"Girls!" we hear someone yell behind us. It's Sari, one of our counselors. Her voice is pretty much unmistakable—high-pitched and squeaky. "You're going to be late!"

"Sorry!" Alice yells out. "Come on." She grabs my hand, and we run to the *Beit Am*. It means "house of the people" in Hebrew. "We are so getting in trouble."

"It'll be fine. Don't worry," I reassure her, almost out of breath.

We get there just in time and plop down on the wooden floor. Most of our unit turns around to look at us, and we shrink down, laughing behind our hands.

"Can I see the old list and the new list when we get back to the bunk?" Alice whispers once we've stopped laughing. "Do you have them at camp with you?"

I nod. "Of course. I take them everywhere."

"So." Jake, our unit head, talks with his hands on his hips from the stage in the front of the room. "What does it mean to be a leader?"

Alice and I look at each other, rolling our eyes and groaning as quietly as possible.

"Haven't we already done this, like, a hundred times?" Alice asks under her breath.

"Alice Kalman!" Jake yells out. "You seem to have an answer. Come on dooowwwnnn . . . ," he says like he's a game show host, gesturing with his hands.

In a way this kind of feels like school when you get in trouble, but not exactly. Here it just feels funny and laid back, and people are laughing but they're not really laughing *at* Alice. They're more laughing with her. I make mental notes of all the things I have to write to Kaylan later. We've been trying to write every day. She's way better at it than I am, but in all fairness she has more time.

Maybe we should've added *write each other every day* to this year's list, but I guess that would've been too much. At least I've been keeping up with the *doodle a day* thing. It doesn't take very long, and it's fun.

"Um, hi," Alice says from the front, her arms folded across her chest. "A leader is someone who gets things done."

Jake nods, drumming his fingers on his chin. "Nice.

Good job. Now call someone else up."

Our eyes lock, and I'm almost positive she's going to pick me.

"Okay." She looks out and raises her eyebrows, and I nod to let her know it's okay to call on me. "Arianna Nodberg, come on dooowwwnnn. . . ."

I hop up from the floor, dust off the butt of my shorts, and think about what to say as I walk up to the front. I'm not sure I've ever really thought about this before.

"So . . . ," I start, looking out at all the kids in front of me. "A leader is someone who can organize other people and get them excited to be part of the project or work or whatever is, um, happening. And also, like, bring out everyone's strengths." The list pops into my head. "Ya know, help others shine. That kind of thing."

"Excellent!" Jake says, high-fiving me. "Your turn to call on someone."

I could pick someone from my bunk or one of the girls in the mindfulness elective, but this feels like an opportunity, a chance to do something different. And that's the thing about camp—you can be whoever you want to be here. Even risky things don't really feel all that risky.

"Um, I pick Golfy." As soon as he stands up, I run back to my seat and Alice pulls me in for a squeezy hug.

"That was a fab answer," she says.

I watch closely as Golfy walks up to the stage. (His real name is Jonah Malkin, but everyone calls him Golfy

4

because of an answer he wrote on a camper question-naire when he was seven. That golf was his favorite sport, or something like that.)

He stands with his hands in the pockets of his gym shorts. His brown hair is sticking up in a million different directions.

I feel like my heart could explode through the V-neck of my T-shirt.

"A leader is someone who thinks about the greater good. And makes things happen. And generally just crushes it every single day." He shrugs and half smiles.

Golfy. It's like there are tiny little red hearts all around him.

I am the embodiment of the heart-eye emoji right now.

He may be the most perfect boy in the history of the male species.

I've only known him for two weeks, but I think I love him.

Really and truly love him.

TWO

AT REST HOUR, WHILE WE'RE waiting for our counselors to hand out the mail, I read over the list Kaylan and I made. It feels kind of daunting at the moment since I'm so far from home and most of the things I can't really do here. The water thing is under control. The handstand thing is within grasp. The doodle thing is going great.

But the tell-a-boy-how-we-really-feel thing feels impossible.

I love Golfy. I know I do. But I can't exactly tell him that. Not yet, anyway. I've only known him for two weeks.

Twelve Super Incredible Things to Make Us Even More AWESOME Before We Turn Thirteen

(When Ari becomes a woman in the eyes of her people. Kaylan will be half woman, half girl. Maybe. Who knows.)

1. Keep our friendship strong.
2. Drink enough water (for a glowing complexion).
3. Make our mark.
4. Master the art of mac and cheese (from scratch!).
5. Perfect our handstand.
6. Help someone else shine.
7. Stay up long enough to watch the sun set and rise.
8. Find the perfect man for Kaylan's mom.
9. Draw a doodle a day.
10. Tell a boy how we really feel.
11. Pursue a passion (first find one).
12. Break a bad habit.

"This is the new list." I show Alice after she hops up onto my bed. "And here's last year's."

Eleven Fabulous Things to Make Us Even More AMAZING Before We Turn Twelve

1. Make a guy friend.
2. Do a Whole Me Makeover.
3. Get on TV for something cool we've done (not because we got hit by a bus).
4. Help humanity.

5. Highlight our hair.
6. Do something we think we'll hate.
7. Fulfill lifelong dream to kayak at night to the little island across the lake. (First step, find a kayak.)
8. Kiss a boy.
9. Get detention.
10. Have a mature discussion with our moms about their flaws.
11. Sabotage Ryan.

"The old one seems way harder," Alice declares, still eyeing both of them side by side. "I mean, get on TV? You did that."

"We both did." I beam, looking at her while also staring at the front door of the bunk, hoping our counselors come back soon with the mail.

"Although the new one is, like, bigger, grander things, I think." She laughs a little bit. "You guys are hard-core to do this, and also kind of weird, no offense."

I laugh too. "None taken."

"Both lists started in summer and had to be completed when?" Alice pulls her knees up to her chin.

"Yeah, we start them in the summer and have to finish by our birthdays. Oh! That's another thing. We almost have the same birthday. Kaylan's is November first, and mine is November second, so that's the deadline," I explain.

"Oh! That makes so much sense. Like New Year's resolutions but for the school year!" she yells.

I ponder it for a second. "Yeah, you're right. I never thought about it that way, but totally."

Alice looks at the list again. "This one is all soul-searchy. It feels like you're trying to figure yourselves out."

I pause to think. "I guess we are. Kaylan is always like a mega-anxious girl, and she says I'm all chill, a go-with-the-flow girl." I shrug. "But who knows? No one really has themselves figured out. No one knows who they are."

"No?" Alice asks, picking at her chipping blue nail polish.

"I don't think so. Better to just do what feels right and not think too hard about it."

Alice laughs. "See! You *are* go-with-the-flow, then." She looks down at the list again. "I'm confused on the doodle thing. Why is that one on there?"

"We both have a mini calendar, and we doodle in each box at the same time every day, 9:04 p.m., and that way we're, like, together, and at least thinking about the other one for a few minutes." I stretch out my legs. "Apart but still together, ya know?"

"OMG." Alice cracks up. "That is so super cheesy, but also cute, and—"

We're interrupted when Sari screams, "Mail!" as she walks into the bunk.

Alice and I hop off my bed and go to stand around her bed as she hands out the envelopes.

"Zoe. Alice. Miriam. Hana. Ava. Eloise. Sara. Rebekah. Miriam again. Zoe again. Tovah. Ari. Rachel. And Zoe again."

"Ari, earth to Ari," I hear Sari saying, trying to hand me my letter.

"Oh, sorry, I zoned out for a second."

Zoe cracks up. "You kind of do that a lot."

"I do?"

"Kinda, yeah. It's okay." She smiles. "I still love you."

I look at the stack of envelopes in her hand. "Zo, you get so much mail."

"They're all from my dad. Don't be jealous."

"Mail is mail," I tell her. I go back to my bed, tear open my envelope, and read:

Dear Ari/Arianna/Little Miss Cool Camp Girl/BFFAE:

How's camp? I still can't believe you're gone and it's already been two weeks. I might never get used to it. Literally every morning I go to text you and then I remember you don't have your phone at camp. But at least I can write you letters and you will be home eventually. How does my handwriting look? I'm really trying to be neat and make it beautiful for you.

Soooooo, things here are fine. I've been helping Mrs. Etisof put all her paintings online so she can sell them. She's already sold two so far! Also, she's giving me some art lessons. I'm learning a lot and it's really fun.

I've been hanging out with the lunch table girls a ton. I feel like we're all really bonding. M.W. and Amirah talk so much now. They're not even that shy. Marie really misses you, BTW. And she said she's trying to learn Japanese, so she may not have lunch with us this year? Mega-intense, right?

Oh! And remember Lizzie Lab Partner? She's been at the pool, like, every day, so she's been hanging with us, too.

We all went to this comedy night at the performing arts center. I dragged them there, but we had the best time. Of course Cami hooked us up with a Harvey Deli feast for dinner before. Mega-delish as always.

I've been seeing Jason pretty much every day, but I'm not sure how I feel. I wonder if he's more boy-friend than boyfriend. But don't tell him that, duh. Also I think Ryan has a girlfriend. Remember that girl Maura from the pool who was captain of the swim team and always doing laps? She's over here like all the time all of a sudden. But she's nice.

So far (besides doodling) all I've done on the list is drink water. I've been researching mac and cheese recipes for inspiration. There's one that has this super-fancy cheese, only available in France. Should we try to order it online?

Also the handstand. I've been working on that, too, but whatev. It also needs work.

Oh! One important thing: I'm moving the deadline to finish

11

the list from your birthday to your bat mitzvah since that's like a MAJOR thing about turning 13, for you, ya know? Bat mitzvah = 13. Also, it gives us one extra day! YAHOO! If you have a problem with it, let me know. And the more I think about the list, the more I'm realizing that it is kind of a portal from childhood to adulthood in a way. We are working on big stuff in this list. Like preparing you (and me too, LOL) for womanhood. Ew. That word sounds gross.

BTW—did you get the big P again? I haven't. It's totes normal to get it once and then not again for like a year, right? That's what Cami says, anyway. It happened to both of her sisters.

Write back and tell me what's going on at camp. Oh! I ran into Noah at the movies last weekend. He was there with his dad, and I was there with Jason, and I think he was kinda embarrassed. He said he was leaving for Australia the next day.

Anyway, this letter is really long. I kept remembering stuff I had to tell you!

I miss you more than those sparkly Mary Janes we had in fifth grade.

XOXOXOXOXOXOXO Kaylan

THREE

"SO WHAT'S THE DEAL WITH Golfy?"

I don't know why I've waited so long to ask Alice and the girls about him. I noticed him on the first night of camp and thought he was awesome and cute right away.

It's after curfew, and we're all in our pjs, sitting on the dusty bunk floor, eating snacks that some of the girls snuck in on the first day of camp.

"Golfy?" Hana squeals. "He's been here forever. Like since he was seven."

"For real?" I ask, reaching into the bag for another handful of chips.

"Yeah, his dad went here, and his uncles and his older sisters go here, too," Zoe explains. "They're like a sixth-generation Camp Silver family."

"The camp is only fifty years old," Alice adds. "So . . ."

"You know what I mean," Zoe says. "We both came when we were seven. He's basically my brother at this point. Anyway, why do you ask?"

"I don't know. Just curious." I smile, popping a few chips in my mouth.

Hana changes the subject. "Anyway, can we discuss something mega-important? Are you guys all inviting camp people to your bat mitzvahs? My mom said we have to keep the numbers down, because I already have like a hundred home friends on my list. But I don't know what to do!"

"I definitely am," Alice says.

Zoe adds, "Me too."

I shake my head. "Um, no offense, but I just met you guys, so . . ."

They all crack up.

"But, yeah, whatevs, I'll throw you an invite," I tell them. "People in my town are insane about bar and bat mitzvahs."

"Really?" Alice asks. "In what way?"

I take a cookie out of the sleeve of Oreos. "They just go crazy about the parties—with party planners and themes and photo booths and games and logos for the giveaways." I shake my head. "One girl had Rihanna come! And this boy a year older than me gave out sneakers! Like a brand-new pair for each kid."

"That is insane!" Alice shrieks. "I've literally never heard of that. There aren't tons of Jews in my town, so people are usually like *what's a bat mitzvah?* And I just say it's like a sweet sixteen but at thirteen, for Jews."

"Good description." I pat her knee.

"Bar and bat mitzvahs are crazy in the city, too," Zoe adds, standing up. "But my dad isn't into it. He's like *the service is the important part.* Blah, blah, blah. We're just having a low-key party at the temple."

I jump in. "My parents say that, too, and that they're not throwing an over-the-top party. But then my mom starts talking to her friends, and all of a sudden it's like she starts to fancy it up."

"Wow," Hana says. "In my town, it's like a luncheon and maybe a DJ and that's it. The giveaway is whatever the DJ hands out."

"Oh! I need to ask you guys something else. . . ." I smile. "If I invite Golfy, do you think he'll come?"

"OMG! You love him!" Alice throws a chip at me. "Why didn't you say anything sooner? I mean, I don't see the appeal, but I'll help with the mission."

"Mission? There's a mission now?" I yelp.

"There's always a mission," Hana adds. "For Alice, at least."

"What does that mean?" I squeak, and throw a handful of pretzels in my mouth.

15

"You'll see," Hana says. "Anyway, tomorrow's visiting day so the mission will be delayed a little bit. And you don't have much time. There are only two more weeks of camp."

Alice taps my knee. "And you won't see him tomorrow. Everyone's off on their own on visiting day, and some kids extend it with dinner out, so we won't really see the boys at all."

"Oh," I say, feeling the tiniest bit deflated. I'd wanted to point Golfy out to Kaylan and see what she thinks. Boyfriend material or not—that kind of stuff. I mean, we haven't really talked a ton, but a little bit, and I need Kaylan's stamp of approval.

"It'll be okay, Ari." Hana rests her head on my shoulder. "I mean, he's Golfy. It's not like you have tons of competition or anything."

I scrunch up my face, all offended looking. "What does that mean?"

"It means we've known him forever. He's just, like, there," Zoe chimes in, coming out of the bathroom with a crusty-looking green face mask covering her cheeks and forehead. "So, whatever, we're not into him like *that*."

"Got it," I say.

"Have you had, like, lots of boyfriends?" Zoe asks me, bulging her eyes open and closed, like her face is itchy from the mask but she's trying very hard not to scratch.

I laugh a little. "Why? Do I look like I have?"

"Kinda, yeah," Alice says. "You picked Golfy, and now you're determined, and you seem like you know what you're doing."

"No, I've kissed one boy. This kid Noah from Hebrew School. He was maybe gonna come here this summer, but then at the last minute his dad got an assignment in Australia and New Zealand and his whole family went with him." I pause, sipping my iced tea. We made it with the powder kind and sink water, and I didn't mix it well enough. A glob of powder sticks to my tongue.

"Maybe he'll write you a postcard," Hana suggests. "That'll be romantic."

"Yeah." I shrug. "Maybe."

I realize I haven't really thought of Noah all summer. I guess I haven't really missed him.

We keep talking, and the quiet girls are at the front of the bunk, looking at us, but when I glance over there, they pretend to not be paying attention to us at all.

I wonder how I got so lucky to not be automatically lumped in with the quiet girls, to be included with Alice and her crew. I say a quick silent prayer of thanks to God or whoever helped this along. I like being part of them. I like that they like me. I like that it didn't take a long time for me to fit in here and that I'm friends with the girls who talk to the boys.

But I want to be nice to the quiet girls, too. I don't want to be the kind of girl that other girls hate. I want to be the kind of girl here (and everywhere) who's friendly to everyone.

"I'm really tired, guys," I announce. "I'm gonna go to sleep to be ready for tomorrow. I really, really hope that we'll see each other and that you get to meet Kaylan. You guys will love her. For real."

"Oh, BFF Kaylan," Alice says. "Yes, I def want to meet her."

FOUR

"ARIANNA NODBERG!" I HEAR SOMEONE yell.

I look up from where I'm sitting on the bunk porch, and there's Kaylan, running up the hill as fast as she possibly can.

It feels so funny to see her here, like when you run into your teacher at the grocery store. It's not where they belong, even though you obviously know they don't live in the classroom.

"Kaylan!" I hop up off the chair and run to greet her, and when we meet, we freeze together in an as-tight-as-possible hug.

"This place is amazing," Kaylan says when we finally pull away from the hug. "The pool is awesome, the lake is beautiful, and Adirondack chairs everywhere—I feel like we're at a resort!" She laughs. "Can I convert to Judaism and come here next summer?"

"Um." I giggle. "I think that's kind of an intense thing to decide right now, so can we put it on hold?"

"Def," she says. "Pos for the next list? Just kidding! Come on, I want to see your bunk. Your parents and Gemma got stuck talking to someone from the temple back by the dining hall, but they said they'll be right up. And then someone guided me to the section of camp for your age group, and I figured I'd find you."

"Guess my family really misses me." I roll my eyes as we walk back to my bunk. "Oh well. But anyway, I'm happy to have alone time with you!"

"Me too. Me too." She stops for a second and bends down to tie her shoelace. "You have no idea how much I've missed you at home. It's just not the same without you."

"I can imagine," I say. "But I only have two more weeks here, which is so, so, so, so sad, even though I'll be excited to be home with you."

Kaylan makes a frowny face and then hugs me again. "We'll have fun at home. Honestly, the lunch table girls have been, like, super cool this summer. Plus, we have our list to keep us busy."

"That's true," I say as we walk into the bunk. I don't think I really want to hear about what's been going on at home. When I'm at camp, home doesn't really exist in my mind. I mean, I know it's there, and I miss everyone, but I'm not there, and that's okay. "So . . . . this is bunk nineteen. The counselors' beds are up here. Aren't their areas so awesome?"

Kaylan looks around. "Their areas?"

"Yeah, like their single beds, and their sideways cubbies, and they can put all the stuff on top—like their lotions and picture frames and stuff. It's just so cool."

Kaylan looks at me like I might be slowly losing my mind. "Um, it just looks like an old wooden cubby to me."

"It's a camp thing, I guess. Maybe you have to really be at camp to understand."

"Ouch." She bites her lip. "JK, whatevs."

I crinkle an eyebrow. Did I offend her by that comment? I may have to adjust to being around Kaylan and her intense ways again.

"And my bed's over here." I lead her down the middle aisle of the bunk. "I felt lucky they assigned me the top bunk bed, and the one closest to the bathroom. You know me and needing to pee in the middle of the night."

"Oh, girl, I know."

"Oh my God, is this Kaylan?" we hear someone shriek from the bathroom.

Alice. Of course it's Alice. Her shriek is unmistakable.

"Yes it is," Kaylan sings, and curtsies like she's famous and she knows everyone here has been waiting to meet her, which is kind of true, but I don't want to let it go to her head.

"Hi-i-i-i," Alice sings after drying her hands on a towel hanging from the rafters. "I'm Alice, and can I just say that I've been coming to this camp for four summers and I've loved every second, but then Arianna came, and it's like even better?"

Kaylan nods and smiles. "You can say it. Because it's true! Because Arianna is awesome. My BFFFFFFFFFFF." Kaylan laughs, and then Alice does too.

"You're hilarious," Alice says. "I knew you would be. Of course Arianna would have a hilarious BFF. And also she told me you're really into comedy."

Kaylan rolls her lips together and looks over at me, like she's waiting for me to say something.

"Girls, girls," I start. "I'm awesome. You both know it. I'm a gift."

A second later, Alice's family walks in.

"Alice Judith Kalman," we hear someone say.

And then Alice mouths, "My mom," with a casual eye roll.

Of course my parents have found some random people to talk to and haven't even made it to the bunk yet. I wonder if they'll even make it here before visiting day is over.

When Alice and her family leave the bunk, Kaylan whispers, "I thought this was a Jewish camp?"

"It is. Why?"

Kaylan looks around. "Alice is black, so . . ."

"There can be black Jews," I whisper-explain. "But

anyway, Alice was adopted. She was born in Tennessee, and then her parents went to pick her up when she was, like, a few hours old. She told us all about it; she's really into the story."

"Oh. Interesting." Kaylan thinks about that for a second. "Sooo . . . before your parents get here," she whispers again, "you need to have a talk with them about your bat mitzvah. Like, ASAP."

"What? Why?" My stomach drops. We put the *tell a boy how we really feel* thing on the list, but I think we maybe should've put *tell a BFF how we really feel* because Kaylan's intensity is out of control at the moment. Especially since I'm a bit out of practice dealing with it.

"Can we sit on your bed?" she asks. "I'm super jelly that you're on a top bunk bed."

"Sure." I shrug and start climbing the little ladder on the side. "But tell me what you're talking about, like fast. I feel like my parents will be here any second."

"Okay. They were discussing it in the car," she starts as soon as we're up there. "Your mom has all these plans, and they're cool. But"—she looks toward the door to see if they're coming in—"I'm not sure they're exactly what you want. And it's *your* day."

"It's okay. I can deal with whatever it is." I gently tap her knee. "Just tell me."

"Okay! A band instead of a DJ, super adult-y passed hors d'oeuvres like lettuce wraps, something with caviar, ewwww." She makes a face. "A whole station of carved meats? And she wants hot-pink tablecloths! You don't even like pink! You need to talk to her about that."

"Seriously?" I clench my teeth. All of a sudden, I feel a rush of gratitude for Kaylan—that she's here, and she's telling me all of this so I can put an end to the pink, and possibly the caviar. Maybe her intensity is good in situations like this one.

"Yes. And also, she wants, like, Israeli dancing at the party! How crazy?" she asks me. "You don't want that, do you?"

I laugh a little. "Kinda yeah, to be honest. We do Israeli dancing on Friday nights here, and it's awesome."

Kaylan looks perplexed. "Okay, but you want regular dancing, too, right? Like current songs and stuff, and games, like Ashley Feldman had at hers?"

"I do, yeah." I smile. I have to admit—I'm getting excited thinking about the fabulous party I'm going to have. "Israeli dancing is cool, though. For real."

"Aren't you going to be embarrassed to have Israeli dancing? Like for the kids at school?" Kaylan asks. "I can't imagine the lunch table girls doing Israeli dancing."

"Maybe they'll think it's cool, too?"

"But wait a second—"

"Ariiiiiiiiiii." We hear Gemma singing right then, and I'm grateful for the interruption. I do need to get back to that pink-tablecloth conversation, though. I am most definitely not a pink person.

I hop down from my bed and my feet make the loudest thud against the wooden floor. "Gemmaaaaaa," I sing back, smiling as wide as possible as soon as I see her.

I run over and hug her, and I swear I've never loved her as much as I do right now. I guess they're right (whoever they are) when they say that absence makes the heart grow fonder.

My heart is very, very fond of my little sis right now.

"I've missed you so much," Gemma says. "It's so boring without you. And Mom and Dad keep making flounder for dinner because they think I like it, even though I've told them a billion times I most definitely do not like it!"

"Flounder, guys, really?" I roll my eyes at my parents as soon as they walk into the bunk. "You're torturing your poor daughter with flounder, and I'm not even there to commiserate!"

"Oh, Ari, come here," my mom says. She pulls me into a hug, and the whole world smells like her fruity perfume. It makes me miss her even though she's standing right here. I hadn't really missed her that much, but now that she's near me, I kind of realize that maybe I have.

I never knew emotions could be so tricky and confusing.

We're still in the hug when my mom says, "We have

so much to discuss about your bat mitzvah. We need to discuss our plans with the caterer, the song list for the band. I hope you can decide which logo you want for the hoodies. And obviously, we need to touch base about how much you've been practicing for the service, the cantor called and—"

"Mom. Chill." I look up and pull out of the hug. "It's gonna be fine."

"Hey! My turn!" My dad puts an arm around me and an arm around my mom, and we all group-hug for a minute. Then Gemma pushes her way through and starts dancing in the middle of our hug.

I get this instant sticky guilt feeling that Kaylan's not part of our family group hug and that her family isn't together anymore.

"Come here, Kay, join the hug!"

She runs over and I let her in, and we stay that way for a second but then I feel completely crazy that we're all just standing in the middle of the bunk hugging.

"Come on, guys, can we please go?" I say. "We only have a few hours, and you promised me real food!"

"Real food?" my dad asks. "What does that mean?"

"Anything other than camp food!" I squeal. "Let's go!"

FIVE

"BY THE WAY, LAST NIGHT I got an idea for one thing on the list!" I tell Kaylan after lunch. "I am so happy we can talk about it in person."

We're sitting on the grass, our legs stretched out in front of us, soaking in the sun. I'm so stuffed from pizza and mozzarella cheese garlic bread and cookies-and-cream ice cream that it's a little hard to talk. But I'm not sure we'll be alone together again until I'm home from camp, and I need to get this out.

"What is it?" Kaylan scratches an itch on her forehead and looks at me all suspicious.

I take a deep breath and exhale. "Okay, so you know the thing about finding the perfect man for your mom?" I look at her, butterflies rumbling up my throat. We put this on the list for a reason, but it was one of those things we just added quickly and then never talked about again. Like she wanted it to be there, but she didn't really ever want to acknowledge that it was there.

She nods, looking off into the distance.

"Well, I have someone amazing. My friend Zoe's dad. Her mom died when she was really little, and he never remarried and he's honestly the nicest. He writes her a typed-up, single-spaced, two-page letter every single day. And they live in Manhattan in a fancy apartment and get this—they have a pool on the roof!"

"For real?" Kaylan's eyes go super wide. I knew the pool would be enticing; that's why I saved it for last. "Tell me more!"

"Um, he works on Wall Street but he's really nice, not scary or anything. I met him on the first day of camp, and then she told me about her mom. Everyone else knew already. But she's really open about it." I pause and think of what else to share. "Oh, and they have a beach house out east on Long Island, and sometimes she invites everyone to sleep over."

"Wow," Kaylan says. "But they don't live so close to us. I mean, Brookside is over an hour away from Manhattan."

I nod. "I know. I thought about that. But he drives and stuff, and your mom does, too, and it's not, like, that far. They can also take the train to each other."

Kaylan slow nods like she's thinking about it. "I know that we put it on the list, and I know we have to accomplish everything we put on, but can I be honest?"

"Sure."

"I kind of felt shaky even putting it on in the first place, and then I just kind of wanted to ignore it because it's a super-weird thing to find a man for your mom," she tells me. "I mean, you see that, right? And also why would grown-ups want to be set up by kids?"

"I know. It's all a little weird." I look around at the families spending the day together at camp. They're all smiling and having fun. Kids playing catch with their parents. Other families picnicking on Universal Lawn. My parents walked with Gemma to the bathroom forever ago; I wonder what's taking them so long. "Anyway, it was just an idea."

"But loyal to the list, ya know?" Kaylan adds. "We put it on, and we're making it happen. I just need some time to really process it," she explains. "So if you think Mr. . . . um, what's Zoe's last name?"

"Krieger," I tell her. "His full name is Robert Irwin Krieger. Doesn't that sound so distinguished?"

"Oh, totally." Kaylan laughs. "That reminds me about something I wanted to ask. The lunch table girls and I were discussing it at the pool the other day. Are we TH friends or PF friends?"

"Um, I have no idea what you're talking about." I laugh. "Can you speak in English now?"

"Okay." She readjusts her legs on the grass, and thinks

for a moment. "TH friends are total honesty friends and they tell the other one whatever is on their mind, all of their plans even if the other person isn't included, etc." She looks at me.

"And PF?" I ask.

"Protecting feelings. Like, you don't tell all because you want to make sure the other person doesn't feel bad." She nods, like this should really be making sense to me now. "So what are we?"

"I feel like I need time to think about this!" I yelp. "I guess sometimes TH and sometimes PF. It depends on the situation."

Kaylan shrugs. "I get that, but think about it. Okay?"

"Okay."

"All right, girls, enough of this whisper-whisper stuff," my mom says when they get back from the bathroom. "We're leaving soon, and I'd like to spend some time with you, Arianna."

"Yes, Mother." I try as hard as I can, but it's impossible for me not to roll my eyes.

"Can we do some camp activities together?" she asks. "Boating, maybe? Or can you show us the art shack?"

"Fine, sure. Let's go."

I grab Kaylan's hand and say, "This is actually a good thing. Hopefully we'll pass Golfy and I'll be able to point him out or maybe even introduce you."

"Ooh, Golfyyyy," she says, and cracks up.

"Shh." I laugh.

We keep walking down the main path through camp, and Kaylan launches into this long explanation about the day she and the lunch table girls went to this famous pie place out east with M.W.'s family.

"Are you listening, Ari?" She taps my head with her finger. "Hello! You're on another planet."

"Sorry, my mind was wandering." I smile. "Go on. Something about pies?"

"Yeah, so, they're obsessed," Kaylan explains. "It's called Briermere Farms and they drive for hours to get there. And they make a whole day of it. And M.W. finds it so boring, so she invited us all to come."

"How'd you all fit in the car?" I ask.

"Her dad has his own taxi service, did you know that?" Kaylan asks me. "So he has one of those big Sprinter vans, and we all went."

"Oh," I say. "I guess I don't know so much about M.W."

"She was your friend first," Kaylan reminds me, laughing a little.

I crack up. "I know, but we weren't, like, one-on-one friends, just like group friends. Ya know?"

Kaylan nods. "Anyway, the raspberry cream was amazing, and we had the best time, just, like, singing random songs in the van, like karaoke style, and it was all really funny. We kept cracking up, like, the whole day."

"It sounds fun," I say. "Oh! There's Golfy," I whisper as we walk past the soccer field.

"What? Where?" Kaylan looks around. "I can't get a good look."

I lean over to whisper in her ear, "The one with the red T-shirt and the baseball cap."

"What are you two talking about?" Gemma asks, walking a few steps backward and getting in between us.

"Nothing," I say.

Gemma rolls her eyes. "Yeah, right. Kaylan'll tell me."

"Um," Kaylan starts. "I was filling Ari in on the new stuff at the pool—she's so excited to see the new water-slide."

"Okay, yeah, whatever. It's not that good." Gemma skips back up to join my parents, who are just aimlessly wandering around camp. I was supposed to be showing them around, but they walked in front of us, so I'm not really sure what's happening.

"Just glance over there, but don't make it obvious that you're looking," I whisper to Kaylan. "And quick because my parents just stopped walking."

Kaylan nods and gently glances over to the soccer field and then back at me.

"Okay, so want to see the pottery studio?" I ask my parents because I can't think of anything else to say and I'm not sure it's the right time to introduce Golfy to everyone.

"Sounds delightful," my mom replies.

"Yo! Arianna Nodberg!"

I roll my lips together and eye-bulge at Kaylan, who eye-bulges at me, because we both know who just yelled that. And also because he's coming right over to us.

"So nice that everyone knows your name here," my dad adds.

"Hey," Golfy says, semi out of breath when he catches up to all of us. "Arianna, this is your fam?"

I nod. "Yes, my lovely family. Mom, Dad, Little Sis. And this is my best friend, Kaylan."

"Hi, Best Friend Kaylan," Golfy says, twisting his cap around so the brim is in the back. "Also hi, Mom, Dad, and Little Sis. I'm Jonah. But everyone here calls me Golfy."

"Hello," my dad says, in the most awkward dad tone I've ever heard.

"Nice to meet you, uh, Golfy, you said?" My mom smiles her classic side-tilt smile; it's what she does when she's trying to figure someone out.

"Yup! You guys enjoying visiting day?"

Everyone nods.

"Loving it," Kaylan adds.

"Totally," Golfy says, his hands on his hips, like he's trying to think of something else to say. "Well, I better get back to my game, so have fun and I'll see ya around."

He runs back over to the soccer field, and we all stand there, watching him.

"Well, he was friendly!" my mom says with her eyebrows raised. I can tell she's waiting for me to give some more information about Golfy, but I can't give her that satisfaction. Also, I don't really have any more information.

"Yup," I reply. "Come on. Pottery studio. Move along, move along."

Kaylan nudges my shoulder. "Your cheeks are redder than Golfy's T-shirt right now. Just FYI."

"Shh," I reply. "They're totally normal cheek color. I'm just tan, remember? Be cool, Kaylan."

"I'm cool," she says defensively.

"But isn't he the cutest?" I whisper.

"He's up there on the cute scale, for sure," she replies.

SIX

A FEW NIGHTS LATER, I'M lying in bed thinking about visiting day when I realize I never even discussed my bat mitzvah with my parents. I'll be home soon so I guess it wasn't essential for us to talk about it on visiting day, but still. The pink tablecloths and the super adult-y food—none of it is a big deal, but I need to step in before it all gets out of hand.

"Pssssst, Arianna, are you up?" I hear a whisper from the bed below me.

"Yes, I'm up." I hang my head over the side of the bunk bed and look at Zoe.

"Come down, I want to talk to you."

I throw my legs over the wooden railing and hop down as quietly as possible so I don't wake anyone up. I climb into her bed and flip up my hoodie hood and tuck my feet under Zoe's paisley comforter.

"What's up?" I whisper.

"Alice was supposed to be here for this declaration, but she fell asleep. Like she always does." She pauses, rolling her eyes. "Golfy definitely likes you."

"For real? How do you know?" I ask. "We didn't even start the mission."

"Well, we kind of did. Alice and me. You just didn't know it because we didn't want you to get upset if it didn't work out. And anyway, it was a short mission. . . ."

"Okay. Tell!" I whisper-yell.

"Okay, so he was talking to some people outside the dining hall before evening program, and I totally heard them, but I pretended that I didn't."

"What did he say?" I ask.

"Okay, I'm lying." Zoe bites her lip, laughing a little. "I need to start again. Soooo . . . we just asked him if he liked anyone. And he shrugged. And then we were like, *do you like Arianna?* and he smiled a little, and then nodded and said, *yeah.*"

"Whoa."

"I know." She shakes me a little bit and whispers, "Are you freaking out right now?"

"Um, I'm not sure. I don't think so. I just feel, like, ridiculously excited!"

"I think any other girl would be completely freaking out, but okay." Zoe stretches out her legs. "And camp is almost over. We gotta get on this."

"Totally," I reply. "I'm into it."

"How is this your first summer at camp?" she asks. "You just decided to randomly come when you were twelve not knowing anyone here? It's so weird. I mean, it's good. But also weird."

"I mean, there was always tons to do at home." I shrug. "Kaylan and I love the pool, and we just hang out twenty-four/seven. But then some people from camp came to make a presentation at my temple, and it sounded awesome, so I figured it was worth a shot? And I am soooooooooo glad I came. Obviously."

"Obviously."

"Shh," Sari loud-whispers from her bed. "Girls! Arianna! You shouldn't be out of bed right now."

"Sorry!" I loud-whisper back.

"We'll talk more tomorrow," Zoe adds. "But I just had to tell you . . . about the love of your life, Golfy Malkin."

"Girls, shh," Sari says again. "Go to bed. I don't want to hear you whining that you're tired tomorrow."

I roll my eyes. "I'm going back to bed. Lailah tov."

"Lailah tov," Zoe replies. "Nighty night."

I lie awake for what feels like hours thinking about Golfy, and the fact that he likes me. I just wish we had figured this out earlier in the summer. I wonder why certain things take so long to figure out, to develop and come together. I guess you can't really force situations like this; they just have to happen in their own time.

And anyway, there's always next summer.

"Arianna," Sari whispers, standing next to my bed. "Now that you've woken me up—this got delivered to the wrong bunk. Sorry. And go to sleep. For real." She hands me a letter.

"Okay. Thanks. And sorry," I whisper back. "Good night."

Dear Ari,

I just got home from visiting day, and I miss you already. It was so great to see you and meet your friends and see Golfy. It made me kinda jealous, too, though. I wish I had a place like that, that was my own, where I could be different than I am at school. You see that you're different, right? I mean, you're the same but you're just more in that direction of free-spirit Ari who's just relaxed and calm?

Anyway, I think I'm going to finally tell Jason once and for all that we're better off as friends. It can check off the "tell a boy how we really feel" thing even though it's not a good thing to tell. Did we need it to be a good thing?

Write back and tell me right away.

Are you going to tell Golfy how you feel before camp ends?

I love you! XOXO Kaylan

I consider Kaylan's question as I try to fall asleep, but then I push it away. The thing is, I don't want to think about camp ending. I just want to enjoy every second that I'm here.

I want to stretch it. Make it last, as my Bubbie always says.

SEVEN

AT REST HOUR THE NEXT day, I write back to Kaylan.

Dear Kaylan,

I'm so glad you got to meet everyone on visiting day! You got to experience the magic of Camp Silver for a day. Isn't it the best? It literally feels like the happiest place in the whole world to me. Better than Disney World.

And guess what? Golfy likes me! Zoe and Alice found out. I am soooo excited. I'll keep you posted.

Did I tell you they have this crazy dessert here? It's like pudding, but it's called mung, and even if you turn the whole bowl upside down, the mung stays in the bowl. It doesn't fall out! How insane is that? I don't even know how it works. It's delicious, too.

And guess what? The other day it rained all day so we got to stay in the bunk and just hang out. And then we put on bathing suits and brought out our shampoo and body wash and we showered outside! It was the best. So, so funny. All the girls here shave their legs. I'm so glad we started shaving before the summer. It would have been weird otherwise. Did June's mom let her start shaving yet? She's not super hairy, but still . . .

BTW—haven't gotten the big P again. But I'm prepared.

Anyway, I miss you! Can't wait to show you all of my doodles.

LOVE YOU FOREVER, Ari

After rest hour, I'm in my Mindfulness elective, and I'm completely doing it wrong. I mean, I guess the whole point of Mindfulness is to be able to feel your feelings a little more and accept that you can't control them. Just feel them and let them move along.

I don't really know. I'm still learning.

"We want to let our thoughts have their space in our mind, and then allow them to flutter away, like a little bird," the counselor in charge says to the group. "We need to think about how we relate to our thoughts and then acknowledge when they become distracting to us."

This counselor's real name is Barack, so naturally his camp nickname is *Pres*. He reminds us all the time that he had his name before Barack Obama was president, though. "And we're focusing on our breathing," he reminds us. "Breathe in. Breathe out."

I try this, but my mind still wanders. It wanders to Golfy, and to my bat mitzvah, and to Kaylan and the list, and then the pink tablecloths, and then to wondering what the lunch table girls will think about Israeli dancing at the party.

"Spend a moment thinking about how the floor feels underneath you," Pres says. "Does your body feel heavy against the floor? Really feel the weight of your presence in this space."

I'm able to do every instruction he gives us, and for a moment my mind is on that thing, but then it wanders away again like a toddler at the playground.

We all have so many thoughts going through our minds at the same time; it seems impossible to focus on one thing for more than a few seconds.

"Now think about how it smells in here," Pres instructs. "Really breathe in, take in the aroma of this space, and then release your breath."

I look around the room—none of my friends are in this elective, and at first I was annoyed that I was separated from them and that I got put into an elective I didn't even really want to do.

But right now it feels calm and peaceful to sort of be on my own. And mindfulness is actually more interesting than I thought it would be.

"Now close your eyes for a moment," Pres tells us. "Feel the weight of your eyelids. Open them. Close them."

He pauses. "When we are at camp, so much is happening around us at all times. We love this place. We want to take it all in. We want to make sure we take the time to be mindful here, to notice our beautiful surroundings, to really feel as if we are part of this place."

As he talks, I think about Kaylan's most recent letter and something dawns on me.

Everyone (especially Kaylan) thinks of me as chill, relaxed, free-spirit Ari. And I am, or at least I appear to be. I mean, nothing ever feels like that big of a deal to me—that's true. But that doesn't mean I don't think about stuff. My mind isn't really super chill—it's always wandering off in a million directions. Not necessarily bad directions, but it is moving all over the place.

Maybe if I keep working on this, my mind can be chill, too.

EIGHT

"CAMP IS REALLY OVER TOMORROW?" Golfy asks me. We're sitting on the basketball courts after our evening program, and there's chatter all around us. The air smells sticky and wet like freshly mowed grass after a rainstorm. I look up, and I see there are a million stars in the sky—way more than I'd ever see in Brookside. The crickets are making their metally hissing sound and it sounds louder than it usually does. I think they're sad, too, that camp is ending tomorrow. "How is that even possible?"

"I have no clue, but it is," I reply. "Maybe next summer I can stay for the whole eight weeks, although Kaylan would probably kill me, and I'm not sure I could leave her for that long."

Golfy nods. "Yeah."

I keep looking around for my friends, and I'll spot them

for a second but then they'll disappear, lost in the crowd.

I roll my lips together, wishing I had lip balm in my pocket. "You always stay the whole summer?"

"Always, since I was seven," Golfy replies. "Hey, do you want to go see a really cool place?" He hops up. "You're gonna love it."

"Uh. Sure." I look at him for a second, starting to laugh. "I love really cool places." I don't even really know what I'm saying. When Golfy's around, everything just feels silly and funny and easygoing.

I scan the crowd to find Zoe or Alice or Hana, but I don't see any of them. I sort of overheard them talking about making a memory box for me, but I pretended I didn't hear because I know they want it to be a surprise.

He puts his hands in his pockets. "Okay, so I'm actually going to show you two things because I just remembered another thing I want to show you. Okay?"

"Um, sure," I say, walking along with him. "So no one calls you Golfy at home, right?"

He laughs. "No, of course not. At home, I'm just Jonah."

"Just Jonah sounds like the name of a one-man show that's off-off-off-off-Broadway," I tell him, and he cracks up.

"It totally does!"

He stops walking. "Okay, so here's the first stop, which is actually what I just remembered I had to show you."

We're standing outside of a bunk at the top of the hill,

where the oldest campers live. They're shaped like tents and they're really old and only like six kids can fit in them.

I look at Golfy and wait for him to tell me what I'm supposed to be looking for.

"See that name?" he says.

"Um, there are a million names here," I remind him. Graffiti is something that's not really allowed at camp but still happens anyway.

"Nathan Malkin, 1980," Golfy says. "Did you know my dad went here, too?"

I shrug. "Yeah, I kind of heard that, I think."

"I always think it's cool to find his name around camp, like he was actually a kid once, and a counselor here, and it just feels so funny but cool at the same time, ya know?"

"Yeah, definitely."

For a second, I imagine my parents as kids and teenagers, and I wonder what they were like. I wonder how they would have felt if their parents decided on a tablecloth color without consulting them first. I wonder how people thought of them: Were they anxious Kaylan types? Or were they more go-with-the-flow?

Actually, why am I even considering this? My mom was totally an anxious Kaylan type. She still is. Come to think of it, maybe that's why it feels so easy to be friends with Kaylan.

"Okay, ready for the next stop? It's not too far. I'll have you back at the basketball courts in like four minutes. And then we all have to go to the lake for the final friendship circle." He pauses and looks at me. "Are you ready for everyone to cry?"

"Um, is anyone ever ready for that?"

"Good point."

We walk for a little while, and all of the noise of camp feels so far away. We can still hear it, but it's muffled.

"One more promise. You have to make this one. Okay?" he asks me.

"Okay."

"Promise you're coming back next summer?" Golfy asks.

"Oh, definitely."

There's this thing with Golfy where it kind of feels like I've known him my whole life. Like maybe we were both born in the same hospital, and we don't know it. Or our parents knew each other when they were kids. There's this cosmic connection kind of feeling I get with him, but it feels too soon to tell him that. I know the *tell a boy how we really feel* thing is on this summer's list, but I don't think that's the thing, or this is the time for that anyway.

"Okay, close your eyes," he says. "Just for a second."

My heart pounds, but I don't know why. I trust him, and I feel totally cool in this situation, but it's still a little strange to not know what's about to happen. "Um, okay."

I put my hand over my eyes, and he guides me just the tiniest bit like that.

"Okay, open them," he says.

I look around, and I swear we haven't walked that far but I still have no idea where we are.

We're standing in front of a teeny-tiny waterfall that flows through a tree and down into a little babbling brook. It looks so perfect, like someone made this for a school project or something—constructed it just so and got it to look exactly the way they wanted it to.

"This is my favorite place at camp," Golfy says. "I'll tell you a secret if you promise not to tell anyone else?"

"We're making a lot of promises today, did you realize that?" I giggle.

"You're right," he says. "So does that mean you're promising? Again?"

I crack up. "Yeah."

"Sometimes I come here in the afternoon when we have free time, and I just, like, sit here and stare at the waterfall." He pauses and looks me right in my eyes, and all of a sudden there's a shiver down my back. A good shiver. "Like for a long time. Is that so weird?"

It's not really all that weird, just a little unusual because I've never heard a boy talk like this before. And also they don't usually sit still for long stretches.

"You haven't answered," Golfy says.

"Oh, I got lost in thought," I reply, laughing a little. "No, I don't think it's that weird. I mean, maybe it's a little unique. But it's good to just sit and be with nature sometimes. I think so anyway."

"Thanks for reassuring me I'm not the strangest person in the world." He pauses and looks at me. "Do you want to sit for a second?"

"What about getting me back to the basketball courts in four minutes? We're so getting in trouble, Golfy."

"Okay, you're right."

We stand there staring at the waterfall and then he puts his arm around my shoulder, and we stay like that. I still want to get back to my friends and the basketball court, but I also want to stay in this moment, too. It's strange to be really happy in a moment you're in, but then also kind of want to be somewhere else at the same time. I guess the best option would be the ability to split yourself in half and get to be in both places.

Golfy leans his head on my shoulder, and I have no idea what's about to happen.

"Okay, we're running out of time and I just want to do one more thing but I don't know how to do it, so can I just come out and ask you?" Golfy says, talking more quickly than I've ever heard him talk before.

I nod, and he picks his head up from my shoulder and

moves his arm away, and then he's standing in front of me. The rushing of the waterfall seems to get louder, and then it's the only sound I can hear, like the whole world is this patch of grass and this waterfall and this tree.

"Camp's over tomorrow, and I may not see you for a whole year, but you already promised you'll come back next summer, so I'm not worried about that. But . . ." He stops talking. My heart races and I can't stop biting my lip.

"Golfy! Please just tell me," I blurt out, half laughing.

"Can I please kiss you?" he asks. "I have to tell you I've never kissed a girl before, and I don't know what I'm doing, and please don't tell anyone. But can I?"

I put my hands on his shoulders. I've never done that before, but in this moment it just kind of feels right and okay. "First of all, it's not like I've kissed a million boys. Most people I know haven't kissed anyone." I smile. "I'll just stand here and you can kiss me, and don't worry, you really can't mess it up."

So that last part may have been a little bit of a lie because of what happened with Kaylan and Jason and the redo, but I think that's pretty rare, and I don't want to make Golfy nervous.

"Okay," he says, and rubs his palms on his shorts. "Ready?"

"Ready."

He leans his head in a little, and I lean my head in

a little, and our lips touch. We're standing in front of a waterfall and I'm kissing a boy and it's summer and I'm away from home and when we pull apart we see a shooting star.

None of this feels like real life.

NINE

ON THE BUS RIDE HOME from camp, I read all the letters that Hana, Zoe, and Alice put in the memory box for me.

I can't even believe that camp is over and everyone is going home. That all of the bunks will be empty when they were filled with so much love and so much happiness for so long.

I have to go the full eight weeks next summer. I need to take advantage of the magic and be there for as long as they'll let me.

I don't even feel like the same person I was before I left, but the weird part is that I didn't sense myself changing. I didn't know when it was happening. I just know that I feel different now.

Dear Arianna,

You're the best person ever. I am so glad I met you this summer. Everyone at camp loved you, and you fit right in immediately. That never happens. Thanks for teaching me to sing with my hairbrush, to twirl my spaghetti, and to do the tree pose in yoga without falling over. I miss you soooooo much already.

I love you forever, Zoe

Arianna, love of my life:

Why are you so amazing? I don't even know. From the second I saw you get off the bus in your heart sunglasses, I just knew you were going to be the coolest, chillest girl in the world. You came to camp and didn't know anyone, and it wasn't even a big deal. You have the best hair and the best socks, and we were so tired of being a trio, so thank you for making us a foursome.

XOXOXOXO AlKal (Alice J. Kalman, the fabuloso)

ARIANNA NODBERG! Did you know about this tradition before you came to camp? You can never throw out these letters. You

are obligated to save them forever, and then
on the last night of our last summer, we read
them all to each other. So don't throw this
out! Okay? Thank you for coming to camp. We
all love you and think you're amazing. I will
miss you soooooo much.
LOVE YOU FOREVER!!!!!!!
Hana Elizabeth Bergman

We're only halfway through the bus ride home and I'm sobbing. I've only known these girls for four weeks, but it feels like we're linked together forever. I don't understand how that happens. I've gone to school with girls for years and years and I like them and everything, but it's not like this.

Maybe it's different when you live with people. When you see them in the morning and at night, in towels and in pajamas. When you eat all your meals together and stay up late talking and doing activities. Maybe that's how you go from a friend-friend to a soul-mate-friend.

I want to tell Kaylan all of these things, and share every detail of camp with her, but I'm not sure I'll be able to. I don't want her to get jealous. I don't want her to feel like she's been replaced.

How can you tell your best friend you had the most amazing four weeks of your whole life without her?

I don't think you can.

TEN

ARI: I'M HOME!

I text Kaylan within three minutes of walking into the house, very excited to be reunited with my phone.

Ari: But my rents are insisting on fam din & fam time 2night. Pool tmw tho?

Kaylan: Wahhhhhh.

She writes back less than five seconds later, like she was staring at her phone this whole time waiting for me to text.

Kaylan: I can't wait. so much 2 tell u. BTW—I told Jason I just want 2 be friends. we still have so much 2 do on the list. But fine! TEXT ME LATER. MWAHHHHH-HHHHH.

I pause for a second before I reply.

Ari: 4 real about Jason?

Kaylan: yes but igg now. lunch table girls r coming over.

Ari: C—u r totes fine w/o me @ home. Proud of u, kay-kay! Smoochies.

A few minutes pass before she texts back.

Kaylan: I missed u so much. I am not ok AHHHHHH k bye

I laugh at Kaylan's dramatic ways, and then I spend the next few hours unpacking and going through all of my stuff. As I take everything out of my duffel bag and throw it in the washing machine, I smell it, really breathe it in.

I wonder if it would be okay to leave all of this stuff dirty in my duffel bag forever so I could preserve the delicious camp smell. I could sniff my clothes any time I felt sad.

Probably not.

"Ari! Dinner!" I hear my mom call from downstairs.

I get down to the kitchen and there are balloons all around, colorful plates on the table, and platters of hamburgers, hot dogs, corn on the cob, coleslaw, and potato salad.

"Barbecue night, your favorite, Ar!" my dad says, pulling me into a hug. "We've spent the past week planning what to make for your welcome home dinner, and this is what we decided on. The balloons were Gemma's idea."

"Amazing, right?" Gemma squeals. "I didn't think

they'd let me buy so many, but they did! I guess they really missed you!"

"So sweet, thanks," I say quietly, and sit down in my chair.

The thing is, as awesome as all of this is, I don't really want to be here, eating dinner in my kitchen. I want to be at camp, in the dining hall, with my bunk, complaining about the food and trying to concoct some crazy combination from the salad bar. (Chickpeas in the tuna salad actually turned out to be quite delicious.)

I want to be singing all together, and making up silly dances in the aisles, and stacking the dirty plates, and wondering what the evening program is going to be.

"It was so sad to see your empty seat at the table this whole time," my mom adds, bringing over a pitcher of her famous strawberry lemonade. "But we knew you were having fun, so that made it better."

I force a smile, but my insides feel like they're drooping. All of this delicious food, and the balloons, and Gemma drew me pictures of our family all together.

"And ice cream sundae bar for dessert," my dad adds. "We are going all out!"

All of this amazingness—and yet all I want to do is cry.

"So eat up, guys," my mom says. "Ar, I hope you'll tell us all about camp."

I swallow hard, looking down at my plate. I squeeze

some ketchup onto my hot dog and take a handful of potato chips.

After a bite, I say, "Mmm. Delish."

I don't want to be here, but they've tried so hard. The least I can do is pretend I'm enjoying it. I guess that's one thing I learned in Mindfulness—to really be in the moment. To focus on each bite as you chew, each word you say, every detail of your surroundings.

I want to be at camp with Alice and Hana and Zoe and Golfy.

But I'm here in my kitchen with my parents and Gemma.

And camp is over. And there's no way around that.

I'll make it through this dinner and eat the food, and it'll be fine. But part of me doesn't even want to eat hot dogs and hamburgers. I think I may want to be a vegetarian. I guess I can save that conversation for another time.

"Ari, we are so, so, so happy to have you home," my mom says, leaning on her elbow, staring at me from across the table.

"Was it really that bad without me?" I laugh, scooping some potato salad onto my plate.

"Kind of, yeah," Gemma says, seeming like she's about to launch into something.

"Why?" I laugh, after a sip of strawberry lemonade.

Gemma looks at my parents and then back at me.

"What?" I crinkle my nose.

Everything seemed totally normal and fine on visiting day, and even when they picked me up at the camp bus stop earlier.

"Just busy with bat mitzvah planning." My mom sits up straighter and forces a smile. "Don't forget you have a meeting with the cantor first thing tomorrow morning."

I nod.

"And we're meeting with the caterer later in the week," she adds.

I nod again.

"I just don't know how we will get everything done." She takes a tiny bite of coleslaw—so small I don't think she's actually eating anything. "And are you really studying your Hebrew? I mean, you're going to be so busy this year, Ari. It's really a lot for a seventh grader to take on."

"Mom!" I laugh-yell. "Stop." I reach out and put my hand on hers. "It's going to be fine, and it will all get done, and whatever. It'll be good. Seriously. But chill. Come on." I look over at my dad and Gemma, who look a little zoned out. "I just got home."

My mom nods again and pushes the food around on her plate. I wonder if I should ask why she's not really eating, or maybe I don't want to know.

A few minutes later, the phone rings, and when I look at the caller ID I see that it's Bubbie. I didn't really even need to look—few people call us on our landline. But Bubbie always does.

"Hi, Bub," I answer, and walk back to the table with the cordless phone.

"Arianna, my darling! It's so good to hear your voice." She pauses. "How was camp?"

"Amazing," I reply, jabbing a cucumber with my fork. "The best."

"See! I told you," she replies. "Camp is in our blood. The best times of my life."

"I know. You were right. You're always right." I laugh and chew some more of my hot dog while Bubbie tells me some more of her camp stories, something about a prank involving tarring and feathering. I'm kind of glad that sort of thing didn't happen at Silver.

"You're eating dinner?" she asks. "Go finish. I'll call you tomorrow. Welcome home."

"Okay, sounds good. Love you, Bub."

"Love you more," she replies. I usually fight her on it and claim that I love her more and then she claims she loves me more and on and on. But since we're in the middle of dinner, I let it go this time.

Later that night, we're all in the den sort of watching TV. My parents are staring at their phones and Gemma is doing some make-a-pillow creation thing that Bubbie got her.

"Gem." I nudge her knee with my foot. "Come in the kitchen; I want to show you something."

She looks at me all suspicious.

"Just come," I whisper again.

When I get there, I scan the pantry for some cool snack I can show her, and my eyes land on the boxes of Annie's mac and cheese. My mind jumps to Kaylan and the list. It's a little weird she didn't ask me to come hang with the lunch table girls, but I guess I did tell her it was a family night.

"What are you showing me, Ari?" she asks, a hand on her hip.

"This amazing fruit leather!" I yell, faking excitement. "Did you even know we had this? It's like candy, but healthy and all organic. OMG. Healthy candy!"

She lowers her eyebrows. "We've always had that." She looks me up and down. "Are you okay, Ar? I think you got kind of crazy at camp."

I pull her closer. "I'm fine. I was just making that up about the fruit leather." I pause and guide her over to the table. "Tell me what's going on. I'm getting weird vibes that something went down when I was away at camp."

She shakes her head a little and leans in. "I don't know," she whispers. "It's just strange. Mom and Dad are always whispering about stuff, and talking with the door closed, but I don't know what it is."

"What do you mean you don't know?" I hiss. "Explain."

"I don't know," she repeats. "There's just something going on." She gets up from the table. "Stop harassing me. I'm only nine! Sheesh." She walks out of the kitchen.

I sit there at the table for a few more minutes, perplexed. I feel like she should have a better idea of what's happening. But then again, it's probably not that big of a deal if she doesn't know what it is.

I look at my phone to see if Kaylan texted, and she didn't.

I do have a long string of back-and-forth texts from the camp girls, though.

Hana: I miss u guys so much.

Hana: Why r'nt we in the bunk rn.

Hana: Ugghhhhhggghhhhhhh.

Alice: Wahhhhhhh.

Alice: I miss u beyondddddd.

Zoe: I know. This is legit missing u guys.

Zoe: How many days until camp?

I look up the date of camp for next summer, and quickly calculate.

Ari: Only 317 days until we r back 2gether again, my luvs.

I stare at the text for a few minutes after I send it.

Three hundred and seventeen days really isn't that long at all. Before I know it, we'll all be at Camp Silver again—showering in the rain and eating mung and singing Hebrew songs.

Three hundred and seventeen days isn't that long at all.

ELEVEN

"THE CHEESE ARRIVED," KAYLAN SAYS, gently nudging me awake.

For a second I think that I'm dreaming, but then I realize it's for real. I open my eyes and there's Kaylan sitting on the edge of my bed—the red polka dots of her tankini peeking out from under her navy tank top.

I stare at her. I don't even know what time it is. Or what she's talking about.

"The cheese from France." She glares at me. "Remember? I wrote you about it. I found it online and I ordered it. I think it's going to make all the difference in our mac and cheese."

"What time is it?" I ask, sitting up slowly, rubbing my eyes, and looking out the window.

"Almost nine thirty. And I know you have your cantor

meeting; your mom told me. Duh. But I needed to tell you about the cheeessse." She cracks up. "I can't wait to make this with you!"

"Okay, maybe you're focusing on the mac and cheese part of the list, but you're clearly forgetting the *keep our friendship strong*. I am going to end our friendship right now because you're waking me up so early!" I hit her arm with my pillow and then cover my head with it. "Bye, Kay-Kay."

She snatches it away. "It's a normal time to wake up, Ar. You need to be prepared for school starting in less than two weeks. And also didn't you wake up early at camp?"

"I did, but we basically walked to breakfast half-asleep in our pajamas," I tell her. "So it was different. We weren't really awake. And we definitely didn't talk about cheese this early in the morning."

I start laughing and so does Kaylan, and then I realize I'm actually awake for real now.

"Okay, here's the deal," Kaylan says, looking at her phone. "I want to do the mac and cheese on the list soon because what if cooking is my passion? I want to discover that. I mean, that's why we put it on the list."

I nod. "True."

"I mean, I'm, like, ninety-nine percent sure comedy is my passion, because duh . . . but ya know? I could be wrong."

I nod and listen to her ramble on. I zone out a little, but she's talking so much that I doubt she'll notice.

She continues, "And I want to do the *stay up all night to watch the sun set and rise,* too, because I want to hear aaaalll about camp," she explains. "So maybe we can do both at the same time! Tonight! My house! Okay?"

I deep sigh and exhale. Kaylan's intensity is back in full effect. "Um, okay. I stayed home last night, so it shouldn't be a problem. That sounds good."

"Bring your mac and cheese ideas, too," she instructs. "It can't just be me and my fancy cheese."

I throw my head back and crack up. "I don't know why, but the way you say 'fancy cheese' just sounds so, so funny."

"Fancy cheese," she says again in a fake accent, and we laugh so hard my stomach hurts.

I don't really get how someone can be so mega-intense and controlling and so over-the-top hilarious at the same time.

My mom drives me over to the temple, and I expect her to get out of the car and come in with me to see the cantor, but she drops me off in front of the main doors.

"You're not coming in?" I ask.

"No, it's just a bat mitzvah lesson," she replies. "I need to take care of a few things."

I shrug. "Okay. I thought, like, parents were supposed

to be there or something. You came with me to the ones back in the spring."

"I don't need to be there for every one," she replies. "Come on. Go. You'll be late."

I walk into the temple, and it's so quiet and empty feeling. I'm used to the crowds of kids in the hallways during Hebrew School and the muffled sounds of grown-ups holding cups of coffee and chatting after services.

When I make it back to the cantor's office, her door is closed, so I sit down on one of the cushiony chairs in the hallway.

I text Alice.

Ari: How's ur 1st morning @ home? I'm @ meeting w/ my cantor.

A response comes right away.

Alice: Ooh fun. I'm lounging in pjs. Is ur cantor old or young? Mine is like 100. LOL

Ari: Ha-ha-ha-ha mine is medium. IDK what age. She's like 50 maybe?

Alice: Ooh a lady cantor. Good voice?

Ari: Ha-ha yes. V good. She sings the prayers sooo well. LOL

Alice: LOL. Have fun. Miss u so much, Noddie.

Ari: Miss u more, AlKal.

"Arianna!" Cantor Simon says, coming out of her office. "How was camp?"

"Amazing," I reply. "Best time ever."

"You were at Silver?" she asks, going to sit down behind her desk. I take a seat on one of the leather chairs on the other side.

"Yup."

"Best place in the world. I went there for thirteen summers, as a camper and then as a counselor." She smiles. "Did you know that?"

I shake my head.

She adds, "It's magical. So how's everything going? Torah portion, prayers, fill me in." She folds her hands together.

I look around her office at all the books on the shelves and the framed pictures and the artwork. Part of me can't even believe that I'm sitting here, in Cantor Simon's office, getting ready for my bat mitzvah. It always seemed like something that other people did, something I'd get to do one day but really far in the future.

"Um, it's going." I laugh. "I worked on the prayers a little at camp, and I started my speech but I don't think I've figured it out quite yet. And I'm working on my Torah portion a little every day, and, um, yeah, I'll be ready. Don't worry."

She laughs a little, too. "I'm not worried. It's just my job to check in. Rabbi Oliker and I will be up there with you, but it's your day to lead the service—you're going to be the one behind the podium, singing and chanting and reading in front of everyone." She clenches her teeth, smiling. "Can you believe it?"

"Um." I smile, trying to appear like I have it all under control. "Honestly, I can't believe it."

"So before you show me your skills—let's talk." She folds her hands on the desk.

"Okay." I nod.

"So on a scale of one to ten, how important of a role do you think Judaism plays in your life?" She wobbles her head from side to side.

"Um, well, the thing is, before Camp Silver, I think it was, like, a five maybe. I mean, we lit the candles on Shabbat and went to temple sometimes, and I went to Hebrew School, obviously." I pause. "But then at camp— and this sounds so, so cheesy—it kind of just came alive for me, and so now I think it's like an eight."

Cantor Simon pulls her hair back into one of those tortoise-shell clips. She's like a fully adult person but she seems so young, in a good way. "That's marvelous. I like that."

I laugh for a second. "Me too."

"Do you know what made it come alive?" she asks me.

"I don't really know." I pause to think. "I guess, like, the people, and being all together, sharing in the music and traditions and stuff."

"Interesting." She high-fives me. "I can tell you're thinking about this."

"I am." I smile. "But I still have a ton to figure out."

"That's okay," she assures me.

"So it's normal to not really know how I feel about this whole thing yet? Like not one-hundred-percent know, I mean?" I ask.

"Totally normal." She nods, taking a sip of tea. "Questioning and thinking is a huge part of Judaism. You're totally doing it right."

"Well, phew." I laugh a little.

"Ready to practice? We'll start at the beginning of the service. Opening song will be '*Hineih Ma-Tov*'? Did you sing that at Silver?" She laughs. "I don't know why I'm asking. Of course you did."

"OMG, yes! *Hinei ma tov u'ma nayim*," I start singing, and then Cantor Simon joins in. "*Shevet achim gam yachad*." We sing the rest of the song together, cracking up.

She sits back in her chair. "I have to tell you how much fun this is for me, to share in your Silver experience. I'm getting to relive my youth!"

"As I leave mine behind." I force a few fake sniffles and look down at my lap. "Just kidding."

We practice more of the songs and melodies and prayers together, and she compliments me after each one. "Your pronunciation is very good," she tells me. "And as we get closer to the day we'll practice your Torah portion in the real Torah."

My heartbeat speeds up a little when she says that. "Like the real scroll?"

"Yup. The real deal. The five books of Moses. The

whole shebang of Jewish law and teachings."

"Right." I smile. "But the whole thing about fasting for forty days if you drop the Torah scroll is a myth, right?" I ask her. "Not that I plan to drop it, but ya know, just in case."

"I'll make sure you don't drop it." She smiles at me. "We have to wrap up in a minute, and I'll see you next week, but before we go, and I know you're still figuring things out, but how are you feeling about the whole bat mitzvah thing? Is it meaningful to you? Something you have to do because your parents are making you? Are you more interested in the party? Talk to me. Be honest."

I pause to think about that for a second, leaning my head on my palm. "I think it is meaningful to me. It's kind of a sense of accomplishment thing, too, in a way. I keep working on the prayers and the melodies and the Hebrew and little by little I'm getting better at it. It's like the biggest project of my life. And that feels exciting." I shrug. "I mean, if I can be honest, I was sort of going through the motions up until now. But the more I practice, the more meaningful it becomes."

"First of all, you can always be honest. And you never know, Ari," she says. "Sometimes people discover their passions at a young age—when they least expect it."

"Did you know you wanted to be a cantor when you were twelve, uh, almost thirteen?" I ask, looking at the pictures of her family on the desk.

"Hmm." She rolls her lips together. "Not at thirteen . . . when I was about fifteen or sixteen I did, though."

I nod, debating telling her about the list and that trying to figure out my passion is one of my goals this year, but it feels like too much to explain and we're almost out of time.

"It's been great talking to you," Cantor Simon says. "Looking forward to next week."

I stand up. "Me too."

I walk out of the temple and sit down on the little wooden bench while I wait for my mom to get back and pick me up.

The whole *pursue a passion but first find one* thing makes a lot of sense for someone who's about to turn thirteen. I mean, duh, that's why we put it on the list.

But finding a main passion is kind of tricky. I think I'm passionate about a lot of stuff, and I'm not sure how I'll know what my main passion is, the thing I most want to focus on. And we don't actually have that much time.

My mom is already five minutes late when I feel my phone vibrating. I take it out of my pocket, expecting to get some kind of frantic call from her. But it's Kaylan.

"Yo," she says.

"Yo, yo."

"I'm at the pool. Cami, M.W., June, and the rest of the crew are here," she tells me, but it's kind of hard to hear with all the noise around her.

Crew? Are we a crew?

Kaylan keeps talking. "Marie and Amirah may come by later, too. Are you coming?"

"I'm waiting for my mom to pick me up at the temple."

"What?" she yells.

I repeat it, yelling this time. "I'm waiting for my mom to pick me up at the temple."

"I can't hear you! Come to the pool." She stops talking and bursts out laughing about something that's going on there. "Okay? Bye!"

She hangs up before I have the chance to say anything else. I sit there feeling slumpy on the bench. It's not like I expected Kaylan to roll out the red carpet for me when I got home, and her intensity was a little much on visiting day, but now that I'm here, it almost feels like she doesn't need me to be around. She's totally cool on her own. She even has a crew that I may or may not be a part of.

Maybe that's a good thing. Or maybe it's not.

It's like the opposite of last summer when she was mega-intense Kaylan agita girl.

I wonder if we're still making the mac and cheese and staying up all night tonight. I don't even know.

Alice texts me a few minutes later.

Alice: How was the meeting?

Ari: Fab. Can I ask u a q?

Alice: of course my dearie

Ari: How r u feeling about ur bat mitzvah? Like what does it mean 2 u?

Alice: ummmmmmmmm

Alice: I guess, just like feeling more connected to my community and heritage and stuff, and like playing more of a role in it

Ari: Cool. I agree. Just trying to fig it all out

Alice: ur so thoughtful

Ari: Huh?

Alice: like u think a lot about stuff. it's cool

Ari: Thanks, babe. I miss u sooooooo much.

Alice: I miss uuuuuuuuuuuu tooooooo

Ari: Love youuuuuuuuuuu

Alice: smooches forever

At least I have Alice. Even if Kaylan's busy with *the crew*, I have Alice and Zoe and Hana. And hopefully Golfy, though I haven't heard from him. Which I have to admit is a little odd. What happened to the super-introspective kid by the waterfall?

I wonder if he forgot all about me now that camp is over.

I hope not.

TWELVE

"HOW WAS YOUR LESSON?" MY mom asks me as I get in the car.

I reply, "Good," and buckle my seat belt.

I expect her to ask more questions, but that was it. She stays quiet and doesn't even turn on any music.

"Oh, can you please take me to the pool?" I ask her, flipping through some playlists on my phone.

"You have your suit with you?" She turns to look at me for a second and then stares back at the road in front of her.

"Always do." I smile. "You never know when you'll find yourself in front of a body of water."

"Is that so?" She half smiles. "Sunscreen too?"

I nod.

Something is up with her, but I have no idea what. We

stay quiet for a few minutes until my mom launches into a reading of her to-do list.

"Oh! Ari, I almost forgot. We must finalize address labels, confirm our caterer meeting, order the yarmulkes—did you say you wanted navy blue or we could also do a houndstooth pattern—that would be cool, right?"

"Houndstooth yarmulkes? Um, yeah, could be cool."

"We also need to figure out if we want to do a brunch on Sunday for out-of-town guests," she says, talking to me, but more like talking to the air. "It could be too much, but then again people do need to eat before they leave town."

I rest my head against the window and let her keep talking. I think it calms her to say everything aloud, even if I don't respond.

"All right, well, see you later, Mom," I say when we get to the pool entrance.

"It looks like you're settling just fine into life at home." She seems to be starting a conversation when I'm already halfway out of the car. I never understand why people (mostly moms) do that.

"Yeah, I guess." I shrug. The truth is, I don't know if I am or if I'm just pretending to be. I wish I was still at camp, no doubt about that. But I'm here. And there's stuff to do—like the list, and figuring out what's up with my parents, and studying for my bat mitzvah, and all of that.

Might as well lean in, as people say.

I walk into the pool, write my name in the sign-in book, and scan the area to find Kaylan and the lunch table girls. I also kind of want to see if Jules is here, so we can discuss bat mitzvah lessons and preparing and stuff. I think her bat mitzvah is in December.

"Hey, Arianna," Noah says, catching me completely off guard. "I didn't know you were back from camp."

"Oh, I just got back yesterday," I tell him, startled. "I thought you were, like, in Australia or something?"

"I was," he says. "I just got back a few days ago. And then Jules invited me to the pool today, so yeah, I'm here now."

Jules invited him to the pool? "Cool."

I look away, trying to think of what to say to him. We didn't really keep in touch over the summer.

"Did you have fun at camp?" he asks.

"Yeah, best time ever. I loved it."

"That's cool." He shuffles his feet on the pavement. "Anyway, I better go. Jules ordered us lunch. See ya around, Arianna."

I look away, and then back at Noah. "Um, okay, bye."

"Ari!" I hear someone scream and look around. I'm pretty sure that it's Kaylan, but I can't seem to find her. "Ari! . . . Here! . . . By the diving board!"

I nod and walk over to where Kaylan's sitting. She's not in our usual spot, and I never would have expected I'd find her sitting over there. She's with Cami, June, M.W.,

Amirah, Kira, Sydney, and Marie. She really did mean the whole crew.

When school started last year, we were definitely two separate groups—me with Sydney, Kira, M.W., and Marie, and Kaylan with June and Cami. I don't really remember where Amirah fit in, but it doesn't really matter. Little by little, we all became fused together into one big group.

That girl Lizzie's here, too, Kaylan's lab partner from last year. I wonder if she'll sit with us at lunch now.

"Hi, guys," I say, plopping down on an empty lounge.

"Arianna's back, and she's better than ever," Cami sings. "Hey-la, Arianna's back." She gets up and starts doing a little shimmy, and I gotta admit—it's a little much.

If I had to describe Cami in one phrase, that would be it. *A little much.*

"Nice to see you missed me." I smile at the group. "So what's up? Tell all. Spill it. Fill me in. What did I miss in Brookside?"

They all look at one another, silent for what feels like three centuries, and then they stare back at me.

"What?" My cheeks feel hot.

"Um, your boobs got really big over the summer," Marie whispers, but loud enough for the whole group to hear. "Did you have to get new bras?"

I crack up. "Wait, what? For real?" I fold my arms across my chest.

"It's true," Kaylan adds.

"Guys, first of all, shh." I move closer to the group. "Awkward to talk about boobs at the pool, first of all. And second of all, I'm still wearing the same sports bras I was wearing last spring, so I don't know what you're talking about."

June shrugs. "Okay, well, maybe the sports bras stretch or whatever. You have, like, serious big boobs now, Arianna."

"They're really big," Kira and Sydney say at the same time, and then stop to do their jinx ritual.

"Stop!" I laugh. "I don't want big boobs. How come I don't get a say in my boobage size?"

They all start cracking up.

"But seriously, what did I miss when I was away at camp?" I grab my sunscreen out of my pool bag and start dabbing it all over my legs.

"See what I mean." Kaylan rolls her eyes at the others. She whispers, "She's obsessed with this place."

I ignore her comment and roll my eyes right back at her. I didn't even say anything obsessive.

M.W. clears her throat. "Well, there was that incident with the slimy noodle."

"OMG, slimy noodle." June cracks up, falling back onto her lounge and almost onto the pavement. "Slimy noooooooodle."

"The slimiest," Kaylan adds.

"No one would believe noodles could be *that* slimy," Lizzie says in a spooky voice.

Marie is laughing so hard she's not able to get any words out, and finally she just shakes her hands and admits defeat in that area.

Amirah raises her eyebrows. "Obvs."

"Okaaay." I scrunch my face tight. "I guess I'll just have to accept the fact that I missed the slimy noodle incident."

They all start laughing again, but no one explains it. It's not like I really care to understand it, since it seems like one of those "you had to be there" moments. But it's still a little awkward.

Cami announces, "We're going to swim," and all the others follow her.

Kaylan stays behind, lying back on the lounge, reading something on her phone.

"I didn't know you and Lizzie were still hanging out," I whisper, making sure no one can hear.

"Oh yeah, well, she's been at the pool all summer, so she just started hanging with us." Kaylan looks up at me. "It's just been, like, whoever's here kind of hangs out."

I nod. "That's cool."

Kaylan goes back to looking at her phone, so I tap her knee and announce, "Jules invited Noah to the pool today."

"That's a little strange. I haven't seen them hang out all summer, really. But who knows." She shrugs. "So this mac and cheese is going to be literally life changing. I've been prepping. I have all the ingredients ready at my house. So when we're done with the pool, we'll both go home, shower, get into comfy clothes, and get started." She claps. "Okay?"

I nod. "Sure. Sounds good."

"Ari, you need to be more pumped up," she insists. "Please. Come on. Show me some camp-level enthusiasm here."

"I'm pumped, I'm pumped." I fist-bump the air. "But should I tell Noah I'm not really into him anymore?" I ask Kaylan. "Can that be my *tell a boy how I really feel* thing?"

She considers it for a minute. "Nah, doesn't seem big enough. Plus I don't think you need to—you didn't really hang out much last spring, either."

I stare at the sky. "True."

"Okay, come on, handstand time," Kaylan says. "Lounging here isn't accomplishing anything on the list, though that would have been a good list item."

I crinkle my eyebrows. "What? Perfecting the art of lounging. We've already mastered that."

"Yeah, true." She grabs my hand. "Come on, let's go to the grassy area by the basketball courts and practice handstands."

As we walk over, I think back to last summer and

realize that pre–middle school Kaylan would never have suggested this. Handstands in public? With kids we know from school here? No way. But now she's all about it.

Maybe she's more go-with-the-flow than she thought.

The more time I spend with her, the more I realize that Kaylan's changed. I didn't think it was possible to change so much in four short weeks. I guess it is.

"Okay, I'll go first," Kaylan says. "You judge me, give me pointers, stuff like that. And then I'll do the same for you. K?"

"K." I plop down on the grass and rub my eyes under my sunglasses. I don't think I've fully recovered from camp fatigue yet.

Kaylan kicks off her flip-flops, stretches, and stands up straight with her feet apart, one in front of the other. Then she tips her body forward and keeps her arms perfectly straight. She ends up in the most perfect handstand. Legs toward the sky, arms secure. It looks like she could stay in that position for the next three hours and be totally fine.

She comes down and stands normally with her hands on her hips. "So?"

"Perfect. That was definitely a ten. You mastered it." I lean back on my arms.

"I did," she says, sounding disappointed. "I kind of wanted to keep working on it. Maybe because all the other stuff on the list is super hard."

"Maybe. I mean, you can keep working on it, but it's pretty perfect," I say as I stand up. "Okay, my turn."

"Make sure you kick with your dominant leg," Kaylan instructs. "I think that's the key part of it."

I try to follow exactly what Kaylan did, but I can barely do it. When I'm up there, my palms are flat on the grass, and I try as hard as I can to keep my legs straight, but I know they're crooked, lopsided, like a pair of scissors, and when I try to straighten them, I fall forward.

Kaylan stands back, assessing the situation, a finger on her lip. "Yeah, so it needs work, Ar. But you'll get there. Let's hold off on the JHH, though."

I nod. "Yeah, I'm too tired to jump in the air. I could high-five or hug, though. . . ." I sigh. "I am not a gymnast. Remind me again why we put this on the list?"

"Because we used to be good at handstands and we used to love to do them, and we're trying to keep a little of our old selves alive as we grow up," Kaylan explains. "It can't all be new and exciting. Ya know?"

"Right."

I plop back down on the grass, lie back, and stare at the sky the way we used to do in between activities at camp. When I did this at camp, it almost seemed like I could feel the earth moving very, very slowly.

But here, not really. It's just too noisy and chaotic.

"I'm gonna do another one," Kaylan says. "Watch my form."

"Okay."

"Pay attention!" Kaylan snaps, and I sit up.

Right as she's curling up into a handstand I see Jason walk by. He stops and looks at us and then almost walks away, but then he stops again. I wonder if I should warn Kaylan or not, but I don't think I can without making it too obvious.

My stomach sinks as he walks over to us.

It's one of those moments where you see yourself in the situation and you really think you should be doing more to intervene, but you actually don't know what you're supposed to do. So you just watch it all unfold.

"Nice handstand," he says while Kaylan's still in position. "I think you can check that off the new list."

Kaylan showed him the new list? I'm flooded with icky embarrassed feelings, like someone just walked in on me changing into a bathing suit. But I mean, it's just Jason. He knew about our other list, so I guess he can know about this one, too.

She finally comes down from the handstand and her cheeks are bright red—could be from all the blood rushing to her face since she was upside down for so long, could also be because Jason, the boy she just broke up with, is standing right in front of her.

"Hi, Jason," I say, confused about why he didn't even say hi to me. "How was your summer?"

He raises his eyebrows at me. "Um, I'd say it was a mix

of good and then terrible." He turns to face Kaylan and glares at her.

I don't think I know what's happening here.

"Now you should ask her how camp was," Kaylan instructs. My heart pounds, and I feel a sudden urge to run away and leave this awkward interaction.

"I can decide what I should ask," Jason replies. He sits down next to me on the grass with his back to Kaylan.

"How was camp?" he whispers, and I see a little crinkle of a smile form in the corner of his mouth.

"Amazing. Better than anything ever in the whole entire world," I tell him. "I wish I could live at camp forever."

"Wow." He jerks his head back.

I sit up and look at him. "How are you doing, Jason?"

"Craptastic," he says. "Your BFF is grrrrrrr."

I giggle because I can't really tell if he's trying to be funny, but it's good to laugh either way.

"Don't laugh," he says. "I thought things were good between us, and then she, like, just decides she's done with us being an us." He goes on and on, while I pretend to listen but mostly try to figure out how Kaylan can do all of these crazy gymnastics moves.

She's doing handstands all over the grass, and cartwheels and back handsprings and roundoffs. It was totally not fair for her to put the handstand on the list.

She's super advanced at gymnastics, and I'm like a negative beginner.

"So what should I do?" he asks me.

I quickly scan my brain, trying to remember anything he just said. "Well, maybe she'll change her mind again," I suggest. "She kind of does that a lot."

He shrugs. "It's so awkward now, though. And why is she flipping all over the place in front of me? It's weird."

"No offense, Jason," I start. "But she'd be doing this whether you were here or not. She likes to show off sometimes."

"Why did I even like her in the first place?" he asks me like I should know the answer.

"Because she's the best girl ever," I remind him. "And you guys had good times together. But sometimes that stops. The good news is it can start again. You just need to wait and see."

"I don't like waiting and seeing," Jason says. "I'm bored. I want to hang out with you guys."

"Well, no one said you couldn't hang out with us," I tell him. "I'm cool with it. And you're obviously still going to be friends. Plus school starts in, like, two weeks, soooo . . ."

We stand up and walk over to Kaylan, who's talking to Jules and Noah by the snack bar. "I did some competitive gymnastics when I was in elementary school," she tells them. "But then I stopped. It's good exercise, though."

"What did you order?" I ask her.

"Water, for the list," she whispers. "I left my water bottle at the lounges. And also mozzarella sticks."

"How's your water drinking going?" Jason asks me.

"Doesn't my complexion look fabulous?" I ask him.

He shrugs. "I don't know what that even means, really."

"Water drinking is going well." I glare at him. "I feel like you're trying to do the list with us. Are you?"

"Not anymore." He sulks.

I'm starting to wonder if putting *tell a boy how we really feel* on the list was such a good idea.

THIRTEEN

WHEN I GET HOME FROM the pool, Gemma is watching TV in the den, still in her paint-splotched shorts and T-shirt from her last day of day camp.

"Where's Mom?" I ask her. On the walk home, I realized I hadn't told my mom that I was sleeping at Kaylan's tonight, and I need to finesse this in just the right way so she doesn't get all agitated and flustered that she wasn't aware of my plans.

"Upstairs in the office with Dad. I've knocked three times so far asking if we can order pizza tonight, but they keep telling me they're discussing something important and I need to watch more TV." She stretches her legs out on the ottoman. "Can't complain about that, though!"

I hang up my wet towel on the back of the laundry room door and then head up to my room to shower and change for Kaylan's. On the way, I make a quick pit stop outside the office to do a casual eavesdrop and see what's going on.

"Well, they've been alluding to this for months now, Marc," my mom says. "It's hard to live in this uncertain state."

Who's they? And what are they alluding to?

My dad mutters something back, but I can't hear what it is.

My mom adds, "I just didn't think we'd be in this position."

And another mutter from my dad.

Then silence.

As much as I want to stand outside the office door for the rest of the night and figure out what's going on, it actually ends up being pretty boring, and I do want to get to Kaylan's for our big night ahead. I can't wait to tell her all about camp and make the mac and cheese and see the sunset and the sunrise.

Whatever is going on with my parents is clearly a grown-up thing, and there's no way I could do anything to help with it anyway. Might as well move on.

I hop in the shower and then take the time to really lather the shampoo, extra condition, and feel the warm water rushing down my back.

Ten minutes later, as I'm walking out of the bathroom

with a towel on my head and another towel tight around my body, my mom stops me.

"Oh, you're home," she says.

"Not for long. Going to Kaylan's and sleeping over." I go back into my room, and she follows me. "Sorry."

After a deep sigh, she says, "Okay, Ari, but please remember there is a lot to do before school starts. We haven't even discussed the change in your classes for this year. Are you excited to be on the honors track? Stressed?"

"I haven't really thought about it yet. It's still summer." I tilt my head, wondering how it's possible to go from a super-relaxing shower instantly into a stressful line of Mom questioning. "Mother, I'm fine. Don't stress. Seriously. I can handle it." I do a little dance in my towel. "Do I seem stressed to you?"

She giggles. "Not really. No."

"We're good then." I look in my closet for something to wear. "Okay, let me get dressed. Byeee," I sing.

"I guess you're at that age where you need privacy now, huh?" she asks, leaning against my doorframe.

"Ew, Mom. Don't be weird." I try to gently close the door. "Please."

She walks away, and there's a tiny speck of guilt on my brain that I was mean to her, but I wasn't really. It's awkward to talk about changing bodies and privacy with your mother. Moms should know that daughters don't want to discuss it with them. It's an unspoken rule to just ignore it until things feel normal again.

I take a final peek in the mirror, dab on some of my strawberry lip gloss, and head down the stairs.

"Bye!" I yell out to the house. "Going to Kaylan's. Be back tomorrow!"

No one responds.

"Okay, bye for real!"

Finally, Gemma comes up from the basement. "Wait, you're leaving me alone with them? Again?"

"Um, I guess so. Yeah."

"Ari, something weird is happening." Gemma looks at me all confused and frowny.

"Gem." I pull her into a tight hug. "It's not a big deal. Honestly. Grown-up drama. Who cares?"

"Whatever you say, Ari . . ." She turns around and goes back down to the basement.

I'm halfway out the door when the landline rings and no one seems to be answering it. It's Bubbie's number so I put down my overnight bag and pick up.

"Hi, Bub," I say.

"Hi, doll. How are you?"

I lean against the pantry. "Good, going to Kaylan's for a sleepover. How are you?"

"Good, good, but missing you. I'm sorry Zeyda and I aren't coming for our end-of-the-summer visit, but with your bat mitzvah in November, it just felt like too much travel." She sighs. "I'm an old lady."

I laugh. "You're not old at all, Bub. Don't say that."

"Okay. I won't." She pauses. "Okay, tell Dad to call me."

"I will."

"Bye, doll."

I hang up the phone and yell out, "Daaad, call Bubbie back!"

On the walk over to Kaylan's, I think about how everyone in my house seems to be mildly freaking out, and how it's kind of a startling way to zap back into life at home.

It's summer—we should be experiencing the highest level of peace and tranquility.

I'm about to go down the walkway to Kaylan's front door when my phone dings.

An email from Zoe!

Dearest Arianna,

My dad is into the set-up idea. I can't even believe it! Maybe he's just doing it to be nice, but he said he'll meet Kaylan's mom. We actually have plans to visit cousins kinda near you at the end of September. Will you guys be around? Write me back and tell me, and we'll make a plan.

I miss you soooooooooo much. Can't wait for next summer!
LOVE YOU FOREVER! Zoe

P.S. Have you heard from Golfy? ☺ ☺ ☺

I pause a second before I go into Kaylan's house, slightly deflated that I haven't heard from Golfy. What is he even doing? I don't get it. I have no clue how boys spend their time, really.

I open the front door and run up the stairs to Kaylan's room.

"Oh my G, look at this." I shove my phone in Kaylan's face. She's on her bed, reading an issue of *Seventeen*.

"Oh my GGGGG." Kaylan clenches her teeth. "I haven't told my mom anything about this yet."

"Um, okay." I stare at the ceiling fan going around and around and try to think. "We can figure this out."

She adds, "Also, this is still mildly awk, ya know. I'm into it, and it's on the list, but still—red-alert-level awkwardness."

I consider that for a moment. "I mean, not really. It's like awkward in a way, but not totally. They're just meeting, not like going on some romantic vacation to the Cayman Islands or something."

Kaylan cracks up. "Ew, ew. Stop. Parents and romance, major ew."

"We did put this on the list, Kay," I remind her, hopping up to lie next to her on the bed.

"I know. Give me time." She pauses for a minute, pushing the magazine away. "Your parents have to throw one of their famous barbecues. We can do it at the end of September and it can be like a celebration for the fact that we survived a month of school. They'll invite my fam, and Zoe and her dad since they're passing by or whatever, and then we'll make sure they talk to each other."

"Um, you just said you needed time and now you've planned it out." I laugh. "But okay. Let's backburner this list item since we're doing two tonight anyway, and we have so much to talk about."

"Right, okay. So mac and cheese." She sits up and folds her hands on her lap. "My mom took me to the store, and I got all the ingredients for what I think would be in a super-secret, best-in-the-world mac and cheese. Plus the fancy cheese from France. Obviously."

"Obviously."

"I think we can master this tonight. Right?" She looks to me for support. "I mean, I've done a little cooking before, so I feel like it'll be easy."

"Sure. I mean, I've never cooked before. But you seem to know what you're doing—so I don't see why not! And we know what we like in a good mac and cheese. I mean, duh."

"I love your confidence, Ari." She makes a smoochy

face. "Love it. Oh! And once we've mastered it, we can make it for the barbecue!"

"Genius! So when do we start?" I ask her.

Kaylan replies, "When my mom goes out with her book club for dinner." She looks at her phone. "So, in like a half hour. I don't want her bugging us. But she knows we're staying up all night, and she's good with it. I told her I'm totally fine using the stove, and she didn't really argue."

"Nice." I lean back against her pillows and think about the last line of Zoe's email.

Have you heard from Golfy? It's nagging me.

I'm staring at the glow-in-the-dark stars on Kaylan's ceiling, debating about telling Kaylan about Golfy's mysterious disappearance, when she yelps, "OMG. They're totally right."

"Who? What are you talking about?"

"Your boobs! The girls are totally right. I just got a good look, and they're huge, Ar."

I pull my hoodie tight across my chest. "Stop, Kay. This is weird."

"It's not weird. It's a totally normal thing to happen." She juts her head forward for emphasis. "It just happened really, really fast for you. That's it. Did it hurt?"

"No, it didn't hurt. I'm fine. Okay?" I smile. "Can we talk about something other than my boobs?"

"Big P?" Kaylan asks. "Did you get it again?"

I shake my head. "No. You?"

"Nope. And most of the lunch table girls have gotten it more than once already. Except for Kira and June, who still haven't gotten it. They're freaking out a little," she explains.

"My camp friends are all super chill about it. Some haven't gotten it yet. No one really seems too concerned." I pause. "I feel like the lunch table girls are a little obsessed with periods and boobs. Remember when Cami started bringing it up every day last spring? They've been obsessed ever since."

"No they're not." Kaylan recoils. "It's normal to talk about this stuff, Ari."

"I know that," I say defensively. "I'm just saying they talk about it a ton, and not everyone does."

Kaylan hesitates for a second and then says, "I know you like Alice and the camp girls better than the lunch table girls. It's so obvious. Just admit it."

"That's not true," I lie just a tad. "I love you, duh. And Marie is a good friend. And M.W. and Amirah are cool."

"Well, it's clear that you don't love them as a group."

We're quiet after that, and Kaylan goes back to her magazine and I take my phone out to write back to Zoe and quickly text Alice to see how her reentry to home life is going.

Ari: How's life @ home? Miss u, AlKal.

She doesn't write back right away, so I go back to staring at Kaylan's glow-in-the-dark stars.

When Kaylan and I first came up with the new list, I really didn't think keeping our friendship strong was going to be very hard. We'd already been through some rocky waters last year, with adjusting to a new school and figuring ourselves out, and the whole debacle when I asked Marie to do the list.

I figured all the difficult stuff was behind us.

But maybe we do still need to work on it? Maybe all sets of friends are working on keeping their friendships strong.

Just because I have my camp friends now, and Kaylan seems to have totally bonded with the lunch table girls while I was away, doesn't mean that Kaylan and I aren't still BFFs.

My phone dings, zapping me out of my thoughts.

Alice: life @ home is eh. gg now but I miss u soooo much

"Who's texting you?" Kaylan leans over to read over my shoulder. "Alice! Again! Ari, be honest. Do you tell Alice more stuff than you tell me?"

"What?" I gasp. "Noooo."

"For real?"

"For real. And also, it's not a competition. Chill, Kay. Chill."

"Your bad habit is telling me to chill," Kaylan declares. "Sometimes people can't chill."

"Okay." I laugh a little even though I don't think she

was trying to be funny. "But I think I need to come up with my own bad habit, just like you need to come up with yours."

"Fine."

"Did you come up with yours yet?" I ask her.

"Yes, it's freaking out all the time." She bursts out laughing. "I'm trying to break that."

I laugh, too, and rest my head on her shoulder. "Good plan."

"We're keeping our friendship strong by talking all of this out, ya know?" Kaylan says softly. "That's what got us into trouble last year. We didn't talk stuff out. This time we are. And it's very important."

"I know. For sure."

"There's another bad habit you may want to consider." Kaylan changes the topic. "I know you have to think of it on your own, but I'm not sure you realize you're even doing this. . . ."

I roll my eyes. "Okay, what is it? Just tell me."

"Now don't sound so annoyed, Ar." She pauses. "I don't think you tell people how you really feel. You're all chill and relaxed and whatever is happening is fine, but you never actually say what's on your mind."

"Uh-huh."

"See! Even now, you're not really saying anything."

"Uh-huh." I crack up and so does Kaylan, and she hits me with one of her pillow shams.

"Kaylan," her mom calls up the stairs. "I'm going out now. I have my phone if you need me. Is Ari here yet?"

"Yes, I am! Hi, Mrs. Terrel," I yell out.

"Hi, Ari. Behave, girls. See you later."

"Bye, Mom." Kaylan adds, tapping my knee, "Oh! I forgot to tell you."

"What?"

"My dad is taking Ryan and me on a surprise trip next week! Any guesses?"

I stop and think for a second. "Um . . . California? I don't know." I hesitate and then say, "Are you excited about this? You haven't talked much about the dad sitch lately."

"Well, you and I haven't talked much lately. Duh. You weren't here, and letters don't cut it!" She smiles. "Kidding. Um, I think I'm okay with the dad sitch. I dunno. He's been making an effort, I think. And he says we're staying in a fancy hotel, and you know me and hotels . . ."

"You do love fancy hotels, true." I sniffle. "Well, that's great. I'm excited to hear all about it. You better text with updates while you're away."

I kind of can't believe Kaylan is so cool with this—going away with her dad, especially the week before school starts. It all feels so anti-Kaylan.

I start to wonder what I'll do at home without her. Finish my summer reading, I guess. Or maybe Alice will want to come sleep over! I'd text her now and ask but I don't want to Kaylan to get jealous—I'll wait until she goes to the bathroom.

I wonder when Kaylan heard about this mystery trip; if she's known for a while or if she just found out.

Kind of seems like a big deal.

I thought we'd have a little time together at home before school starts, but I guess not. I mean, I'll survive without her, but it's a strange feeling to have something you're kind of expecting just snatched away at the last minute.

I look over at her, wondering if I should tell her how I'm feeling, after the whole discussion we just had about telling people how we really feel. Is this a time for TH or PF? I think PF since I wouldn't want her to feel guilty for leaving.

It's not fair make her feel bad about something she had no control over.

FOURTEEN

"OKAY, SO HERE'S THE THING," Kaylan says, talking with her hands when we get down to the kitchen. "I got enough ingredients that we can make two batches. So we each need to do our own version, and then we can compare, and that's what will really help us master this."

I nod, staring at the array of ingredients on the counter. It really seems like Kaylan spent a ton of time mapping this out, and I feel a pinch of guilt that I didn't do any work for it.

"We're not following a recipe, though." She stares at me, waiting for a nod in agreement. "It has to be our own."

"I got it. I'm ready to rock this," I announce, although that kind of feels like a lie. I'm still feeling all weird about how she's leaving for a week right before school starts, and the bizarre stuff at home feels a little unsettling too.

And where is Golfy? I don't even know. I mean, none of this stuff is huge, but each little thing feels like a wiggly worm on my brain. "After we compare our two batches, we'll take the best of each and combine them."

"Okay, so you work over here." She guides me to the kitchen island and then walks back over to the counter by the stove. "And I'll work over here."

"Okay."

"And let's not try and look at what the other one is doing, so we can really make this our own, and then compare, and then we can take the best parts of yours and the best parts of mine. Sound good?"

"Yes, sounds good."

Kaylan puts on some music, her famous Summer Jams playlist. Our favorite song comes on and I change the lyrics.

I sing into one of the mixing spoons, *"Mac and cheese ooh na na."* I spin around and put the spoon under Kaylan's mouth like I'm passing her the mic. She sings, *"Half of my heart is in mac and cheese."* I join in, *"Mac and cheese. Ooh na na."*

We crack up, singing the rest of the song. "I'm going to put this in the dishwasher and take a new spoon," I announce. "I mean, since we were just singing into it."

Kaylan's still laughing, but soon she catches her breath. "Okay, good idea."

We keep singing quietly and get to work. We both

know to boil the water first for the pasta, but after that I'm completely lost. In front of me, I have bags of shredded cheese, and half of the fancy cheese Kaylan ordered from France. I also have breadcrumbs and milk, a hunk of Velveeta, and Cheez-Its.

I'm tempted to turn around and see what Kaylan's doing, but I know I can't. But then I remember—this is mac and cheese. There's really no way to ruin it. Even the worst mac and cheese (school cafeteria, camp, the rehab where my grandfather was after he broke his hip) was edible. It's cheese and pasta—how could it even be bad?

After the pasta is boiled, I drain it in a colander, then I pour it into a bowl, then I start shaking in the shredded cheese and pulling off globs of the mozzarella and the fancy cheese. I mix it all together. Then I dump in a handful of bread crumbs and a handful of Cheez-Its. I add a bunch of mini Velveeta cubes on the top, in the shape of a heart, just to make it look prettier.

I arrange it all in a glass casserole dish Kaylan left out for me.

I stare at it for a few minutes. Looks pretty beautiful, I think.

"Done! Can I turn around?"

"You're done?" Kaylan asks. "How is that possible?"

"Um." I crack up. "I'm a fast cook?"

I finally turn around and notice Kaylan arranging hers artfully in another glass casserole dish and checking to see the oven temperature.

She stares at my dish, and then at me, and then back at my dish, trying not to laugh. "You didn't bake it."

Then she does fully start laughing, and I can't help but laugh, too. Through my chuckles I say, "I know. Does it need to be baked? Not all mac and cheese is baked." I catch my breath and shrug. "And the cheese is all melting together anyway from the hot pasta."

She puts a finger over her lips, deep in thought, still laughing a little. "Well, I guess not. But I'm baking mine. Should we taste yours after mine goes in the oven?"

"Yeah, of course." I grab two forks from the drawer right next to the oven and hand one to Kaylan. "I kind of wanted to present it nicely on plates or something, but I guess we don't need to."

"Yeah, I feel like you're not the fancy presentation type of gal, ya know?" she says, digging in with a fork. "This mac and cheese is so you—just throw everything in and go with it, and hope for the best."

At first I think that's a compliment, but then I wonder. Maybe some things should have a fancy presentation. Maybe some things do need to be really thought out in advance, and not just figured out as we go along. Maybe go-with-the-flow isn't always good.

We both take a bite at the same time, and then stare at each other.

"Wow," Kaylan says, looking into the dish and then

back at me. "Wow, wow."

After my bite, I'm not sure if she means wow good or wow bad. People have different taste buds, so it's hard to say for sure what she's thinking.

I dig in for another bite. I can't say it's the worst.

She puts her fork down. "So, want some pointers?" She takes a seat on the stool at the kitchen island and checks the timer on her phone.

I nod and sit down on the stool next to her, still eating from the casserole dish. I honestly don't think it's so terrible. Sometimes I do get a bite with an entire soggy Cheez-It, which is less than ideal. But still edible.

"The Cheez-Its were really meant to be a topping," Kaylan tells me. "And the Velveeta needed to be melted more. No one wants to eat a big hunk of Velveeta. And then of course, I'd recommend you bake it in the oven. But other than that, really good first try."

"Thanks." I stand up and take a bow. "I'm pleased with it."

"Also, maybe a little less milk next time. It was a little soggy."

"Got it."

Kaylan takes another bite. "But the cheeses are all really well mixed together. That part is amazing."

I bow again. "Thank you, darling."

The timer goes off, telling us it's time to take Kaylan's mac and cheese out of the oven. She then resets it for the amount of time it needs to cool.

The casserole dish rests on the counter, and we wait for it to cool down. It looks like ooey-gooey cheesy perfection. Even without taking a bite, I can tell that hers will be better than mine.

"By the way, we're saving all the camp talk for when we're staying up waiting for the sunrise, okay? I feel like there's so much you haven't told me, and I need to know all the details."

"I'll tell you anything and everything." I readjust myself on the stool. As I say that, I realize I'm lying again, just the tiniest bit, because I don't want to tell her about the weirdness at home. Not that there's really anything to tell yet, though. "Camp is my favorite thing to talk about."

"Okay, it's cool now." Kaylan looks into her beautiful casserole dish. "Let's eat."

After we've both taken a few bites, I tell her, "I think you can JHH now. This is mastered."

"You mean it? For real?" she asks, but I know she's just fishing for compliments. This is good. Like restaurant-quality good. Like she literally became a chef overnight and didn't tell me good.

"For real. You basically did everything differently than I did, and it turned out so much better." I dip my fork in for another bite.

Kaylan sits back on the stool and thinks for a second.

"That's so funny that you say that, because I think we pretty much do everything in life different, and that's why we're BFFs. We balance each other out, and we have different ideas and processes and stuff. And we can see that our own method isn't always the best." She pauses. "Ya know?"

I reply, "Yeah, totally. But we're always changing the way we do stuff. Like after today, I probably won't just throw a bunch of cheese into a bowl with cooked pasta and expect it to be mac and cheese."

"Good point." She wipes her mouth with a napkin. "Learn from mistakes. It's the only way."

"I agree."

We eat as much as we possibly can and then we're so stuffed that we have to unbutton our jeans and go lie down on the couch.

"I've never been so full in my whole life," I mumble to Kaylan with my eyes closed.

"Me neither. But the weird part is—I still want to eat more mac and cheese."

"Not me. I can't think about food." I groan. "For at least another hour. Maybe forty-five minutes."

After that, we sink deep into our food coma. And I'm not sure when it happens, but we end up falling asleep.

"Ari! Wake up!" I feel Kaylan shaking me. I glance at the clock above the fireplace and realize almost two hours have passed. "Come on! Now! We're going to miss the sunset."

I hop up from the couch. We slip on our flip-flops and run outside to Kaylan's front porch.

"You have to admit I have an amazing view of the sunset." We're sitting side by side on Adirondack chairs, watching the sky turn a pinky purple. "I mean, this is literally the best view. Why do I not watch the sunset every night?"

"You should, Kay." I smile and lean back. "But not all sunsets are this good. I mean, this one just happens to be perfect and magical. Look at those colors!"

"I know. When the sky turns pink, it honestly feels like a miracle. Like God is up there painting on a canvas for us." She pauses, trying to take a picture with her phone. "Sunsets never look as good in pictures. Our eyes can do so much better than a camera."

"We had amazing sunsets at camp. We called them sky appreciation moments, and we'd just stop doing whatever we were doing, put our arms around each other, and stare at the sky," I tell her, moving to sit on the edge of the chair. When I talk about camp, my heart starts to beat faster, and I get all excited, and this happy, warm, blankety feeling washes over me, like I can't get the words out fast enough. "And this is so funny—Alice was so obsessed with the sky and the sunsets at Silver that she would joke she was going to name her kid after it."

"Name her kid after the camp?" Kaylan looks at me funny.

"No, after the sunsets. Like she'd name her kid Silver Sky whatever last name of the guy she married. She's in love with this boy Danny Minkler from home, so she'd say her son would be Silver Sky Minkler. And then we'd all crack up." I look at Kaylan, waiting to see Kaylan's reaction, but all I see is confusion.

"That's such a crazy name." Kaylan shakes her head. "She wouldn't really name a kid that. Right?"

"It was just a funny thing. I can't explain it." I look back toward the sunset.

"I feel like you have so many camp things you can't explain," Kaylan says, trying again to take a picture. "It's like this other world that only makes sense to people who go there or something."

"I guess. But, I mean, you came to visit, so you sort of, kind of get it, right?"

"Only the teensiest bit."

We're quiet for a little bit after that, just staring at the sunset, and I try to figure out if Kaylan's response to camp stuff is weird or if I'm just imagining it. Maybe she's right. Maybe it really doesn't make sense unless you're there.

When the sun is almost totally set, Kaylan turns to me and says, "Okay, now I'm freaking out."

"About what?" I ask.

"I didn't think about all the little details of being alone with my dad and Ryan in a hotel room. Changing. What if I get the big P while I'm away?" She stares at me, eyes bulged.

I clench my teeth and try to think. "Well, you can change in the bathroom. And bring big P supplies, and then you'll be ready just in case." I look back at the sky and then at Kaylan. "It'll be fine. You were just feeling so calm about this. What happened?"

"I thought about the big P and now I'm not fine. Ari, you have to help me." She scooches her chair close to mine and leans her head on my shoulder. "Please."

"Okay, okay, we'll map it all out. Deep breaths." I look into her eyes. "Honestly, we'll figure out a plan. You know these things are never as bad as you imagine them to be."

"Yeah. I guess, but the imagining part still freaks me out."

Well, it seems like the Kaylan I know and love is back.

I'm not sure if that's good or bad, but we have a long night in front of us, and at least it's something I know how to handle.

FIFTEEN

AFTER OUR FIRST MOVIE OF the night (*Grease*—Kaylan's choice) we're back out on Kaylan's front porch, covered in afghans her grandma knit years ago. Her mom is home and going up to bed, and we're snacking on a big bag of popcorn she picked up at the movie theater for us.

The air still smells like summer—like citronella candles and wet mud. It's hard to believe that school is starting so soon, that the next time we have a summer I'll have already had my bat mitzvah, and we'll be going into eighth grade.

"So Camp Silver . . . ," Kaylan starts. "People just go back summer after summer? Does it get boring or anything?"

"No, it's the best. People just love being together, and being there, and they wouldn't want to be any other place in the summer. It's like they all savor every second." I stand up, tuck my legs underneath me, and cover myself with the blanket. "I'm mad I didn't start when I was younger like all of my other friends. I missed out on so much."

Kaylan's mouth drops. "Ari! That's so rude. You're saying the summers we spent together didn't mean anything to you!"

I hesitate a second, and my heartbeat speeds up, like I need to defend myself. "No, that's not what I'm saying at all. I love being with you in Brookside. Obvs. It's just that camp is awesome, too, and I didn't even realize how great it was."

"Uh-huh." Kaylan rolls her eyes. "You wish you could live at camp! If you had a choice between being here with me or being at camp—what would you choose?"

I shake my head. "Not a fair question."

"So is a fair question. You just don't want to answer."

I laugh. "Kay-Kay. Chill."

"If I had a dollar for every time you told me that, I could buy my own camp!" She stands up and stretches her legs.

"All right. Not a bad plan." We crack up for a few minutes.

"Let's go back inside for the next movie." I stand up and grab her hand. "I need to warm up a little."

Back in the house, we make some hot chocolate and

cozy up for our second movie of the night (*Wet Hot American Summer*—my choice). I picked this one because I think (or hope) that it will give Kaylan more of an understanding of the summer camp experience. It's true this movie is supposed to take place in the 1980s, though, and it's not so much like my time at Camp Silver. But close enough. Also, it's hilarious.

"I just don't get why people pay money to live in dirty wooden cabins, all crammed in together, and eat bad food and then do activities they're forced to do, even if they don't want to," Kaylan says after the movie is over. "Like why is any of that fun?"

I sit up straight on the couch, tucking my feet underneath my legs. "Because you're with amazing people, and you're outside, and it's basically only kids there, no parents, and you get to stay up late, and you really learn more about yourself, and at Camp Silver, you get to, like, do Jewish stuff but it's actually fun and kind of comes alive there."

Kaylan crinkles her eyebrows like she's trying to figure out what I'm saying. "I'm hearing you, and I'm so glad you love it, but I still don't get it." She tilts her head to the side. "Why would you want to have to wait for your turn to shower? And then scrape all the food waste into a big bin? Gross."

"It's okay if you don't get it, Kay." I stretch my arms above my head and rub my eyes. It's almost three in the morning, and we still have four more hours to wait until the sun rises. "Honestly, I'm okay with you not getting it. I just like telling you about it."

"Sure?" she asks. "I can keep trying to get it."

"It's okay. For real."

I wonder if our friendship can still be as strong as it was if I don't share all of this with her. Will it be like there's this huge divide between us? Like I'm on one side of a river and she's on another side? Eventually the river will keep getting wider and wider and will we really be able to reach other again?

I don't know for sure.

Somehow we make it to the sunrise, but I must admit—it's harder than I thought it was going to be. The movies and the snacks helped us stay awake. And a few more dance parties to Kaylan's Summer Jams mix.

"I'm so tired," Kaylan whines when we're back outside but facing the other direction. "Why did we put this on the list again?"

"Because we got so much great talking in, didn't we? And we had to bond and reconnect after we were apart for so long. And it's magical to see the sunset and sunrise. All of this goes on without anyone even telling it to. There's no person pulling the strings. Or some computer. Or a timer. Or anyone having to work to make it happen. It just does. The sun rises in the morning and sets at night, and no matter what's going on in the world, or in anyone's personal life, it still happens." I pause and swallow hard, feeling a lump in my throat. I didn't expect to get choked up by the sunrise. "Doesn't it make you feel super calm knowing that the sun will always rise and always set? Like, no matter what."

"Um." Kaylan stares at me and bursts out laughing. "Not really. Also, don't take this the wrong way, but I think you may have gotten a little cheesier since you got home from camp."

"Okay." I lean back against the chair and cozy up under the afghan. "I won't take it the wrong way, but that may be the only way to take it."

"Maybe that's why you're calm, though. You spend time thinking about the sun rising and setting." Our eyes meet and then she looks away. "But also, you don't have so much to be stressed about."

Her last comment startles me. "What does that mean?"

"Just that your life is pretty chill. So you're chill."

"I'm too tired to debate this with you," I tell her, closing my eyes. "Can we go to sleep after the sun rises?"

"Duh. Of course."

We stay quiet for a little bit after that, and I think about her comment. I guess my life is pretty chill. But Kaylan also freaks out about nothing so much of the time. She went crazy when people were watching us too closely during freeze dance last summer, and then the whole

Tyler thing at first—she was obsessed. And she freaked out when she tore her black stockings on Halloween in fifth grade and said her costume was ruined. I mean, no one was even going to notice the tear.

There has to be a balance somewhere.

We finally see the sun rising and the sky turning orangey pink, and it's like the whole world is waking up all at once. Everything felt sleepy and dark just a minute ago, and now it's vibrant and bright and energized.

"I think we should do this more often, Kay," I tell her as we stumble up the stairs to crawl into her bed. "It's really a miracle that this happens every day."

"Uh-huh," Kaylan says, pulling up her comforter. "Now we sleep. And when we wake up, we JHH."

"Okay." I lie there for a little while, thinking about Kaylan and all of her plans—preparing to make mac and cheese, then actually making the mac and cheese, staying up all night, sleeping, even JHHing.

I think when we plan too much, we kind of miss the moment. And then we freak out when things don't go exactly the way we planned them. Because there's literally no way for anything to ever go exactly as we plan it. It's just not possible.

But I'm too tired to get any of these words out of my mouth right now. And Kaylan's sleeping anyway.

I kind of thought staying up all night with Kaylan right after I got home from camp would make us feel closer, bonded the way we were before I left. But now I'm not so sure that happened.

It's not like we're farther apart, really.

We're just a little uneven.

SIXTEEN

MY PHONE BUZZES FROM ACROSS the room on Kaylan's desk, where I left it the night before, or actually not the night—it was this morning.

I will it to stop buzzing because I've only been asleep for a few hours and I want to sleep more. My eyes are heavy, and my mind feels all cloudy, like the time we drove home from Pennsylvania in the craziest fog I'd ever seen. It literally felt like we were driving through a cloud.

The phone doesn't stop buzzing, though. Eventually, I pull myself out of bed and shuffle over to get it.

"Hello?" I mumble.

"Ari! I forgot to remind you we have the meeting with the caterer this morning! He had to move it up a few days. Dad and I are picking you up at ten thirty, okay?"

"Um, wait. Say that again."

"Just be ready at ten thirty."

I crawl back into Kaylan's bed. She's in a deep sleep. I look at the clock. 9:03. Okay. I can sleep for another hour and set the alarm on my phone and still be up and ready when my parents get here.

"What's going on?" Kaylan mumbles. "What time is it?"

"Only nine. Go back to sleep," I tell her, rolling over onto my stomach and praying I fall back asleep right away.

Thankfully, we both do, so much so that when my phone alarm screeches an hour later, we both startle, jolting up in bed like there's been an explosion.

"What's going on?" Kaylan asks again.

I squeeze my eyes tight, open them, and then squeeze them closed tight again. There's a physical pain that creeps over you after you've stayed up all night. It's like every single cell in your body hurts at the same time, and you're not sure you'll ever feel completely put together again.

Everyone is Humpty Dumpty after they stay up all night. It's a fact.

"I have to go with my parents to meet with the caterer for my bat mitzvah," I tell her. "My mom forgot to remind me, and I forgot. Anyway, sorry to rush out like this after sunset/sunrise night." I stand up and go over to the corner of the room to find my overnight bag.

"Oh! And we have to JHH!" Kaylan screeches, hopping

out of bed and running over to hug me from behind. "And also, OMG, I'm leaving tomorrow for the trip with my dad! For real! This can't be good-bye!"

"Kay." I laugh, wiggling into my jean shorts. "It's obviously not good-bye. It's a week. I'll see you at school. We'll text, talk, Insta, whatever while you're on vacation anyway."

She sits back down on her bed, holding her head in her hands. "No. Please. It can't end this way."

I fully crack up. "Dude, nothing is ending. I think you're just exhausted. Go back to sleep."

She lies back down, and I go to the bathroom to wash my face and brush my teeth and generally try to make myself look presentable. But I still feel like Humpty Dumpty.

When I get back to Kaylan's room, she's all dressed in her favorite jean cutoff shorts and a pink cold-shoulder top. Her dirty-blond hair is in a high ponytail and it looks as if she definitely got the full eight hours of sleep, maybe even nine or ten.

How is it possible for someone to look this good on so little sleep?

"I'm coming with you to the meeting," she declares. "We need this extra time together, and I've never been to a caterer meeting, and this whole bat mitzvah thing feels so exciting." She pauses, clasping her hands together like she's praying. "Please can I come? Please, please."

"Um." I look around her room, thinking of what to say. I don't actually know if she can come or not, but I don't see why it would be a problem. And I can always make the case that she's leaving for a week, and I just got home, and all of that.

She makes her bed, and grabs her phone, and then says, "Come on, let's go grab something for breakfast. Oh, but first! JHH!"

"Yes!"

We clear some stuff off her bedroom floor so we have room to do the moves, and then we jump in the air, high-five, and hug.

"Amazing," I say. "We're so good at JHHing now."

"Well, we've had a lot of practice," Kaylan says as we head downstairs.

"Ooh. Do you have any of your mom's banana nut muffins for breakfast? Those are my fave."

"I think we do!"

When we get to the kitchen, we find a note on the table that Kaylan's mom and Ryan have gone for a run and they'll be back soon.

"They run now?" I ask, tearing off a piece of muffin.

"Yeah, it's, like, their new thing. My mom joined a running club in the neighborhood with some other moms, but sometimes she just goes with Ryan." Kaylan sips some orange juice. "They like it. Mother-son bonding or whatever."

"Yeah, that's cool." I pour myself some orange juice, right as I hear a honk coming from outside. "Oh, my parents are here. You ready?"

Kaylan jumps up and puts the orange juice back in the fridge.

"Oh, uh, hi, Kaylan," my mom says as we get into the car.

"Hi." Kaylan smiles, buckling her seat belt. "I am so excited to join this meeting. This whole bat mitzvah experience is so fascinating for a Catholic girl like me. I just want to soak it in. Ya know?"

"Well, we didn't know you were coming." My dad looks at my mom, waiting for her to say something. "But, uh, okay."

I feel my mom tensing up from the backseat. She doesn't like sudden changes in plans, and for some strange reason, anything bat mitzvah related seems to bring out even more of the control freak in her.

"This isn't a joke, though, girls," she adds. "It's a serious meeting."

When someone tells you something isn't a joke, it can make you crack up. There's not a real explanation for why; it just is.

My mom repeats, "I just said this isn't a joke," in the middle of our laughing.

"We know. We know." I try to calm her down. "Mom, it's all gonna be great. Honestly. Just chill."

Kaylan leans over and whispers, "Sounds like you're talking to me," and then bursts out laughing again.

"Shh." I slap her knee. "Stop. For real."

The rest of the ride is quiet except for my parents muttering things to each other in the front seat, but it's impossible to hear what they're saying.

Kaylan whispers, "Are you going to have a sushi station? Remember Ashley Feldman's was amazing."

I nod. "No clue. We'll see, I guess."

"Oh! And remember how we had, like, seven Shirley Temples?"

I giggle. "Yeah, what were we thinking?"

"Well, we were only nine, so it kinda makes sense . . . I still can't believe we were even invited!"

"You were invited because Colleen and I were in a book club with Eleanor at that time," my mom chimes in from the front seat.

"Okay, Mom. Thanks for the explanation." I roll my eyes in Kaylan's direction.

She whispers, "Anyway, we gotta tell Gemma to go easy on the Shirley Temples at yours."

We get to the golf club and park in the member parking lot, and as we walk in, I think about how nice it feels to be a member of something. My parents are members here, and we're members of the temple, but I think we take it for granted. To be a member of something is to really be a part of it, a built-in community.

I hope at some point in everyone's life they get to be a member of something—even if it's something they started themselves, a made-up club or whatever.

"Hello there." Caterer Man meets us at the door. He shakes my parents' hands.

"And you must be the bat mitzvah girl?" He looks at me but then hesitates a second and looks at Kaylan.

"I am." I smile. "This is my BFF."

"Nice to meet you, BFF." He shakes her hand.

"Nice to meet you, too. You can also call me Kaylan."

"Got it. So, please follow me back to my office, and we'll start discussing the plans for your big day!" He claps. "We are going to make it phenomenal."

Kaylan and I crack up. There's just something about the way he says everything that makes it all sound like it's out of a movie or something.

"Ari. Stop." My mom shakes her head, all furious. "Now."

We walk on, following Caterer Man, who never told us his name.

We get to his office, and we all sit down around a round table. There are bottles of Pellegrino for each of us, and a vegetable platter with some fancy-looking dip.

"Ooh." Kaylan opens the Pellegrino and takes a sip. "Lovely."

"So." Catering Man looks down at his notes and then back up at us.

"I'm so sorry, but I don't know your name," I say. "Did I miss it?"

"Ari!" my mom says again forcefully.

I don't get what I did wrong this time. Seriously, what is her deal?

"Oh, no trouble. I'm Ken. Ken Wainscott."

"Nice to meet you, Ken," Kaylan and I say at the same time, and then we jinx, and my mom shoots daggers at us from her eyes.

"Mr. Wainscott," my mom hisses.

"As I was saying," he continues. "For the cocktail hour, we're thinking a tuna tartare appetizer. An extensive crudités spread. A sushi station. A noodle bar. A carving station. The caviar as we discussed." He pauses. "Does that sound about right? Anything we're missing?"

My parents look at each other, and back at him, and then at me.

"Um, yes," Kaylan shrieks. "Mini hot dogs. Am I right?" She laughs and then pulls back a little. "I mean, if you all agree, but the thing is, everyone loves mini—"

"You are definitely right," I chime in. "That's literally the first thing people look for at a cocktail hour. The first thing."

"Okay, let's get back to Mr. Wainscott's menu, girls," my mom says, still shooting daggers. "We only have the sitter for Gemma for a short time, and we need to get this done."

She clenches her teeth in my dad's direction.

"This isn't up for debate," I tell them. "Mini hot dogs are a requirement for me."

My dad closes his eyes and then opens them again. "Excuse me, I don't like the way you're talking, Ari. This party is not something you're entitled to. You need to be more respectful when speaking with us, and Mr. Wainscott."

"I'm sorry, Mr. Wainscott." I look over at him and fold my hands on the table in front of me. "But wouldn't you agree that many partygoers enjoy mini hot dogs?"

He does a little head wobble while he considers the question. "I think many do, yes. I wasn't envisioning it for your event, but we can certainly work it in if they're a priority for you."

Kaylan leans forward. "Hot dogs are always a priority for us." She elbows me. "Right, Ar?"

All of a sudden, I can't help it. I completely crack up, falling over onto the table and resting my head on my arms.

"Arianna, please," my mom says. "This is madness. Your behavior is completely unacceptable. This is beyond silly."

The way she says silly makes me crack up even more.

"We're in the silly season now," I loud-whisper to Kaylan.

We both burst out laughing again, and we can't stop.

"Girls!" my mom yells. "I am furious! Enough!"

We roll our lips together to stop the laughter and look down at the table. I really want to take a piece of cucumber with some of this fancy dip, but I sense this may not be the time.

My mom looks at Mr. Wainscott. "Okay, so what else should we discuss? This process is unraveling at a rapid pace, much to my chagrin. I am so deeply sorry."

"No trouble," he says, looking down at his notes. "I think we're covered on the cocktail hour. We have three options for your main course: salmon, chicken with a sesame demi-glace."

The way he says that makes Kaylan and me completely lose it again, but he ignores us.

"And a veggie risotto." He raises his eyebrows, trying to stay calm. "And we'll have the usual fare for the kids."

"Usual fare?" Kaylan asks, drumming her fingers on her cheek. "What does the usual fare consist of?"

I kick her under the table. Does she not see how angry my parents are?

"Well, I'm glad you asked." He sits back in his chair and smiles. "We have chicken nuggets, hamburgers, and a pasta option."

"Sounds about right." Kaylan looks at me. "Arianna? You approve?"

I nod. "Yup."

My parents are going to kill me when I get home. They

won't even need a caterer because I won't be having a bat mitzvah.

Because I'll be dead.

I don't feel totally bad about it, though. It was actually a super-fun time with Kaylan that has tons of private-joke potential.

We really needed a silly experience together after the mega-super-serious intensity of our stay-up-all-night sleepover.

SEVENTEEN

MY PARENTS TAKE KAYLAN HOME and I run into the house with her because I forgot my overnight bag.

"Come home right away," my mom says as we get out of the car. "Immediately. I don't care that Kaylan's going out of town. You are in trouble. This is not hangout time, Arianna."

I nod. "Okay."

We run inside and upstairs and I grab my bag. "Well, have so much fun. I can't wait to hear all the details."

"I'll keep you informed." Kaylan laughs. "And while I'm away, feel free to keep working on your mac and cheese, and your handstand, and pursue your passion, break your bad habit. Ya know. Just because I'm away doesn't mean you can't work on the list."

"Kaylan." I stare deep into her eyes. "I know. Calm down. I'll work on it all."

"Freaking out, Ari."

"Calming down, Kay." I smile. "Breaths. Deep breaths. Focus on your breathing."

"Here's another copy of the list. In case you lost yours." Kaylan hands it to me.

"Uh, okay." I take the list and look it over. "Just have fun. Try to be in the moment. Mindfulness. We learned about it at camp. . . ."

1. Keep our friendship strong.
2. Drink enough water (for a glowing complexion).
3. Make our mark.
4. Master the art of mac and cheese (from scratch!).
5. Perfect our handstand.
6. Help someone else shine.
7. Stay up long enough to watch the sun set and rise.
8. Find the perfect man for Kaylan's mom.
9. Draw a doodle a day.
10. Tell a boy how we really feel.
11. Pursue a passion (first find one).
12. Break a bad habit.

"Camp, camp, camp." She rolls her eyes.

"It's good advice," I remind her.

"I'll try." Kaylan reaches out and gives me a hug. "You can hang with the lunch table girls while I'm away, ya know."

"I know. Bye, Kay." I run down the stairs, my overnight bag slung over my shoulder.

"Really hope you're not in too much trouble!" she yells to me.

"Me too!"

"Oh, and let me know if you hear from Golfy!"

On the walk home, my heart starts to feel a little droopy. Still no text or call from him. And a week without Kaylan, right before school starts—not exactly how I envisioned the end of summer. She's leaving me right at crunch time.

Maybe I *will* call the lunch table girls.

I sit down on my front steps and scan my phone for their numbers, planning out a group text, but when I walk in the door, my mom snatches it out of my hands.

"Phone privileges revoked. Arianna, that was completely unacceptable. Come in here now." I follow her into the den, and she keeps talking. "It was distracting and not nice to the caterer and frankly, you came off as very spoiled. I'm disappointed in you."

"I'm sorry." I sit down on the edge of the couch.

"That doesn't sound convincing," my dad chimes

in from the recliner. "This event is about becoming a woman, and you're acting like a child. I don't know what's gotten into you. We send you to camp and since you've been back, you're like a different person."

"Well, to be honest, I kind of am a different person," I admit, as respectfully as possible. "I am so glad you finally noticed."

My parents make eyes at each other.

"Ohh-kay," my dad says, and hesitates for a second. "Can you be this different person while also staying respectful to adults?"

"I don't know what got into me." I sigh. "Kaylan and I stayed up all night to watch the sun set and then rise, kind of a spiritual thing before my bat mitzvah, and I think the lack of sleep really got to us."

"I see," my mom says. "At least there's an explanation. Now please go look over the honors track packet that arrived when you were away at camp. Make sure you know what is ahead of you. And this would be a perfect time to practice your prayers and your Torah portion."

"I've got this, Mom." I roll my head back against the couch. "You don't believe me, but I have everything under control."

"I wish I could say the same thing for the two of us," my mom mutters to my dad.

"What?" I ask.

"Never mind, Arianna." My dad closes his eyes,

exasperated. "Go do whatever you're going to do."

I traipse up to my room, about to text the camp girls and check in, but within a few seconds I realize my phone is still in my mom's possession.

Email will have to do.

I turn on my laptop and sign into my email.

I jump when I see it. An email from Golfy!

Arianna Nodberg!

I lost your phone number and they haven't sent the roster out yet! But then I remembered when you gave me your email and I realized I could email you! I hope you get this. How's life @ home? What's new? All is well here. We're going to Maine for a few days, and we all have to go screen-free the whole time (my mom's rule). So if I don't write back, don't think I'm ignoring you. I'm not!

Peace!
Golfy

I read his email over three times and then decide to write back later. He sent this yesterday and he said he was going away, so I doubt he'd see my reply anyway.

I copy and paste it into an email to the camp girls:

OMG, you guys!!!! Golfy emailed me. Soooooo happy. Things @ home are a little crazy. Kaylan is away this week w/ her dad and bro. My parents are mad @ me because we were rude at a meeting with the caterer for my bat mitzvah. And I can't totally tell if I'm feeling my home friends or not. I just miss u guys soooo much. Maybe u can all come 4 a sleepover this week??? I just thought of the idea! Wb & lmk what u think. I would rather be texting u guys, but my phone is confiscated at the moment.
XOXOOXOXOXOXOX ILYSM! Ari

I wait a few minutes to see if anyone writes back, but so far, nothing. I don't even really know all the lunch table girls' email addresses, so I guess that will have to wait until I get my phone back.

I think the best way to get it back quickly is to basically do the right thing—clean my room, practice my bat mitzvah stuff, maybe set the table later.

There's no point in begging for it now. If I do the right things, then my parents will see that I'm really sorry, and I've done everything I needed to do, and they'll give it back to me. And then I can ask them if the camp girls can sleep over this week.

Easy-peasy lemon squeezy, as my preschool teacher, Jamie, used to say.

I think I can use this week at home with Kaylan away to really focus on the list, especially *pursue my passion* and *make my mark*. I need to figure out what those things are, what I want them to be.

And as I sit here practicing my bat mitzvah prayers and my Torah portion, I think back to all of the people who have come before me and said these exact same prayers, and how we're all linked to one another. Connected. We're all part of something.

I start to jot down some ideas for my speech but end up doodling my daily doodle instead.

But I do have a mini epiphany! My Torah portion. The Life of Sarah. I haven't really spent much time thinking about Sarah beyond this portion. I mean, who was she? I know she was the wife of Abraham and the mother of Isaac and she's one of the matriarchs of the Jewish people.

Maybe there's wisdom to be found in her life, stuff I can apply to my struggles.

As I research, I discover that Sarah actually had a ton of struggles. She had to leave home, with Abraham. She wasn't able to have a child for many, many years. And when she did, her husband almost sacrificed him for God. I mean, that is crazy stuff.

In comparison, my life does seem like a day at the beach. But my main question is, how did Sarah get through it? What was her secret? And how does this apply to me and the bat mitzvah experience?

I don't have a clue.

I don't think I know any of those answers yet. I hope I'll be able to figure them out, but it may take some time. I feel kind of lucky that my bat mitzvah date had such a meaningful, thought-provoking Torah portion.

One of the best things I learned at camp this summer was that it's okay to not know and it's okay to ask questions.

EIGHTEEN

I'M THREE DAYS INTO THE week at home without Kaylan and less than a week away from school starting, and I haven't seen a single friend.

The camp girls and I have been emailing, but it doesn't seem like a Camp Silver reunion sleepover will happen. Everyone's busy with little trips and family visits and stuff. I keep thinking about getting the lunch table girls' email addresses from Kaylan, but then I don't really feel like it.

"I'm so glad you've been home so much," Gemma says, buttering her bagel at the kitchen table. "It's been really fun."

"I know. Want to play Twister again later?" I ask her, pouring myself some orange juice.

"Of course!" She smiles. "And I can't wait for you to

show Kaylan your new and improved handstand. It's amazing. I'm so glad you finally get that it's all about your core."

I crack up. I don't think most nine-year-olds talk like this. "Thanks, Gem."

She high-fives me.

I JHHed that one last night after Gemma watched me do three perfect handstands in a row.

And I'm planning on making the mac and cheese for dinner tonight.

"Girls." My mom walks into the kitchen, rubbing her eyes, still in her nightgown. "Dad and I have to talk to you."

Gemma and I make eyes at each other and wait for her to continue.

A minute later, my dad comes in wearing his plaid pajama pants and his blue terry-cloth bathrobe. We call this his "sick robe" since he only wears it when he's sick.

Uh-oh. Does he have cancer? Is that what they've been hush-talking about?

"What is it?" Gemma asks. "You're both so weird. Just tell us. Come on!"

"Gem, chill." I put a hand on her hand. "It's okay."

They sit down at the table with us, look at each other, sort of like they're waiting to see who will talk first. The clock above the sink sounds louder than it usually does. *Tick. Tick. Tick.* Whose idea was it to make clocks tick and make them tick so loud? No one wants to hear the seconds of their life literally ticking by.

My dad clears his throat, neatening up the napkins in the napkin holder. "Um, this is hard to say, and I don't want you guys to worry." He looks up at the ceiling. "But I lost my job yesterday."

We stare at him and then glance toward my mom, who's holding her head in her hands. Ironic that he says we shouldn't worry when my mom is literally the human embodiment of worry, especially right now.

"So sorry, Dad." I look down at my bagel. "What happened?"

He hesitates and then says, "Well, they had to downsize. And I was the one hired most recently, and it's really nobody's fault. I'll find something else. I just wanted you guys to know. So you weren't confused about why I was home all the time all of a sudden."

We nod, and Gemma takes a bite out of her bagel. I scan my brain for something to say to make this whole situation feel a little bit better.

"Well, we can spend more time together until you find another job!" I smile, hoping to add some positivity to this conversation. "So that's good, right?"

A corner of my dad's lips turns up, but it's not a real smile.

"Does Bubbie know?" I ask.

My parents look at each other, conversing with their

eyeballs as they often do. And then my mom says, "Not yet. And please don't tell her. We don't want to worry them."

I nod. When someone tells you not to tell someone something, you almost feel like you're definitely going to tell them, even though you don't want to.

"Gem, go have your bagel in the den, okay?" my mom says, all soft and exhausted sounding.

"I thought you don't want us eating in there," she replies.

"Just go. Thank you."

"Why am I always being kicked out?" Gemma's chair screeches against the floor, and she huffs out of the room. "The injustice!"

It's always so funny to me that they kick Gemma out of these "adult" conversations, but I get to stay. I mean, I'm only three years older than she is.

My mom sniffles. "Ari, I am so sorry to do this, but I think we're going to need to make some adjustments to your bat mitzvah."

"What kind of adjustments?" I force myself not to laugh when the Mr. Wainscott meeting pops into my head.

My parents look at each other again and then down at the table.

"Hello?" I ask, when it feels like three centuries have passed.

"We can't do the big party at the golf club," my dad

says. "It just wouldn't be wise. Money will be tight until I find a new job, and we need to conserve."

"Okay . . ." My voice trails off. I look away for a second. Their faces are so sad that I almost feel little tears forming in the corners of my eyes.

It feels like I've been sitting in the freezing cold, covered by one of those superpowered thermal camping blankets, feeling cozy and protected but then the thermal blanket was just yanked off of me, and now I'm frigid.

"I'm disappointed, too," my mom says. "We had all the plans. And I made all the arrangements and it was going to be so beautiful." She starts crying, resting her head on her arms.

"Uh, it'll be okay, Mom," I say, forcing out the words. Shouldn't it be her comforting me? I mean, we're all disappointed here. But I'm trying to hold it together so I don't make my dad feel worse about the whole thing.

She sits up finally, nodding fast. "It'll be okay. It'll be okay. We'll still have a small luncheon at the synagogue."

It occurs to me that they never even really asked me what I wanted at my bat mitzvah party. If they had, I would've said a beach theme with super-plush personalized turquoise towels as the giveaway. We'd have mini hot dogs, of course, but also all of my other favorite foods—french fries with mozzarella cheese, a make-your-own omelet station, spicy tuna rolls, and brownie sundaes for dessert.

I wish they had asked me, and it never occurred to me to really make a request. I mean, except for the mini hot dogs because duh—they're a requirement.

I stay at the table with them for a couple more minutes, but then after a few minutes of my ideal bat mitzvah daydreaming, I feel an overwhelming need to leave the room. I walk upstairs and find my phone sitting on my bed.

Well, at least I have my phone back.

I debate who to text first—Kaylan and tell her what happened, but she's away with her dad and dealing with her own stress. The camp girls? Well, we've been emailing and they're all busy this week, so no. I have to tell Alice, though. She'll know what to do. And I think we're at a closeness level that makes it okay for us to interrupt family time.

Ari: AlKal, u free? Need 2 talk 2 u.

She writes back less than a minute later

Alice: out w/ fam now. Can we have a phone date 2night? R u ok? Ilysm

Ari: 2night is ok. ILY2

I want to text Golfy, too, but I know he's away and I know he's screen-free this week. So there's no point to texting him.

I decide to group text the lunch table girls since they're all here, and I kind of do want to get out of the house and away from this drama for a little bit.

Ari: Hi. Any1 around to hang 2day?

I wait for a response.

M.W.: Hiiii, Ari. I'm going back 2 school shopping w/ my mom 2day. Maybe tomw or l8r?

June: I'm at my grandparents' house in MA, back 2night.

Cami: I may b free 2 night 2.

Marie: Same. We r going to that new water park out east 2day with my cousins.

Amirah: my cousins r visiting 2day 2 E

Kira: So sorry I got this text so late. Can't hang 2day.

Sydney: Me neither. ☹

Even though they all have good reasons, it still stings a little that no one is free to hang out. I charge my phone across the room and lie back on my bed.

I try to fall back asleep, but my mind is racing. I practice the mindfulness stuff I learned at camp, but it's not working. I pick up my bat mitzvah stuff again, but I'm too distracted to focus on it. I finally decide to look through the honors track packet that arrived over the summer, but my heart starts pounding on the first page.

School stress, bat mitzvah stress, home stress; Kaylan away, friends are busy.

My heart pounds, and I feel sweat beads forming on the top of my forehead. The more I lie here, the more stressed I feel.

I decide to call the one person who always makes me feel better, no matter what is happening.

"Hi, Bub," I say as soon as she answers. *Don't say anything about Dad. Don't say anything about Dad,* I repeat in my head over and over again.

"Hello, my darling!" Whenever I call, she greets me on the phone like I'm the Queen of England. "How are you, my girl?"

"Good," I say. "Well, kind of bored. Kaylan's away this week."

"Oh. With who?"

"Her dad. And brother."

"That's nice that she's getting along with her dad again," Bubbie replies.

"Yeah. That's true."

"You okay, Ar?" she asks, her voice quieter now. "Getting ready for the big day?"

I sigh. "Yeah, I guess. I dunno. It's kind of a lot to do."

"My money's on you," Bubbie tells me. She says this every time I doubt myself, no matter what. And when she says it, I kind of believe her—that I can do whatever I need to do and make it happen.

"Thanks, Bub." I pause, feeling tears crinkling in the corners of my eyes. I better get off the phone before I slip about anything I shouldn't slip about. "Gem wants to play Twister so I better go."

"Okay; you're such a good sister."

"Thanks, Bub. Love you."

"Love you more." She laughs.

I hang up the phone and walk over to my window to see if Jason's outside. He's not. Then I walk back to my closet and scan the hangers for a first-day outfit. Nothing looks good, and I can't even ask my mom to go shopping.

I focus on my breathing. In. And out. In. And out.

It's okay. I can handle all of this.

Nothing in the world feels easy right now, but that doesn't mean I need to freak out.

I can stay calm.

It's totally possible.

NINETEEN

MY DAD'S NOT HOME FOR dinner, so I decide I'll make the mac and cheese tomorrow night instead. He tells us he's going to meet with his friend Bruce, who may have some leads for him on new jobs. So it's just Mom, Gemma, and me at the table, and no one's talking at all.

My mom made spaghetti and meatballs, but it doesn't taste as good as it usually does. The meatballs are dry, and the sauce is watery. I think she forgot to add garlic. Nothing tastes right.

Gemma reads a book at the table, while my mom looks through a file of bank statements.

Lovely dinner company.

When I can't handle staring at them anymore, I take out my cell phone and scroll through my email and my texts, and when I see nothing new there, I check Instagram to see if Kaylan has posted any new photos from the trip.

A strip of "people you may know" accounts pops up, and I see that while I was away Cami and June have both joined Instagram. Amirah too.

I click on Cami's profile, and instantly my body feels like it's been scorched.

Right there in front of me is a picture of Cami, June, Sydney, Amirah, M.W., Kira, and Marie, posted eleven minutes ago.

They're all at the Ice Cream Shop, eating the super-mega cones—the ones with the Rice Krispies treats on the outside, and the sprinkles and the Oreo crumbles.

I just texted them earlier! They said they were maybe going to meet up tonight. And then they didn't even text me or invite me. Or ask me to come.

I put the phone screen-down on the table and go back to my plate.

Just put it out of your mind, I tell myself.

Stop thinking about it.

Is it really even a big deal?

You don't like them anyway.

Who cares?

None of that works because I do care. Because it is a big deal. Because they're clearly a crew, and I'm not part of it, and maybe they don't even want me to hang out with them anymore.

I never knew a happy picture of some girls eating

ice cream could make me feel so isolated and terrible and left out. Sometimes you know you're not a part of something, and it stings. But to see it right in front of your face—it's the ickiest, slimiest feeling. Like there's something majorly wrong with you, and you might never figure out what it is.

Gemma and I go into the den to watch TV after that, but I don't pay attention to a single thing I see on the screen. My head is in a million different places. And I wonder if I should text the lunch table girls and find out why they didn't invite me. Should I call them out on it?

But that will only make me seem even more pathetic.

I can't.

Thankfully, a few minutes later my phone buzzes on the coffee table.

I see that it's Alice and pick it up right away and run up the stairs to my room.

"Hi," I say, sounding gloomy.

"Um, you sound like your puppy ran away. I know you don't have a puppy, though." She pauses. "What's up?"

I sniffle, holding back tears. "Well, where to start? So my dad lost his job. My bat mitzvah party isn't happening really, and all of the girls I sort of hang with at school got together without me tonight!"

"Ari, my love!" Alice exclaims. "That's completely terrible. All on the same day?"

I sigh. "Pretty much, yeah."

"You need to reach out to Hana and Zoe, too. Tell them what's up. Okay?"

"Um, I was planning to tell them. But why right now?" I slump back against my pillows, grateful to hear Alice's voice on the other end of the phone.

"It sounds cheesy but that's what friends are for. Duh. You need to lean on people in hard times, Ar." Alice sighs. "We're here for you."

"Thanks, AlKal. I love you tons."

"Ditto, Noddie."

I change into my pajamas and get into bed early, reading over the honors track packet and trying to strategize. Eventually, I aim to fall asleep, but I can't.

I remember what Alice said about leaning on people, so I decide to email the camp girls since they all have a "no texting after ten p.m." rule.

Hi, Lovies:

The craziest stuff is happening here. My dad lost his job and now there are going to be some adjustments to my bat mitzvah party. I don't even really know what that means. Also, the girls I was friends with last year went out for ice cream tonight and didn't invite me and then posted a photo on Instagram! I mean, how could they do that? If you're going to go out and not invite someone, the least you can do is not post about it. Am I right?

Ugh. I miss you guys so much. You're the only ones who get me.

My mom is crazy stressed. And those girls are always telling me my boobs are so big all of a sudden. WAHHHH. Did I have big boobs all summer and not realize it?

Why can't we still be at camp?

I love you all.
Ari

After that, I still can't fall asleep. I know people say not to use screens in bed, that it only leads to insomnia, but I have so much on my mind, I need to get it out somehow.

I type and erase and type and erase at least ten texts to Kaylan, but finally I decide to send it.

Maybe she'll have some explanation for the lunch table girls.

Ari: Yo. U asleep?

Kaylan: no, my bro & my dad r both snoring. Grrrr

Ari: having fun tho?

Kaylan: kinda yeah. IDK. Hard 2 explain.

Kaylan: how r u?

Ari: lunch table girls insta'd 2 night & didn't invite me even tho I texted earlier

Kaylan: hmm

Ari: ??

Kaylan: they prob 4got b/c u were away 4 so long

Ari: IDK seems weird

Kaylan: want me 2 text them?

Ari: noooooooo

Kaylan: k. what else is up?

I debate texting her about my dad, but it's too much to type.

Ari: not much sleepy

Kaylan: k nighty night

Kaylan: oh! We went 2 a comedy club here! So amaze. Def my passion! Going to pursue.

Ari: duh.

Kaylan: just reconfirmed it

Ari: k bye

I cry myself to sleep that night, not because I'm sad, really. I don't actually know why I'm crying. It just feels like things are shifting in this very slow way. Like every day I'm farther and farther away from the person I used to be. I don't know this new person—the girl who feels overwhelmed, like things are slightly out of control. The girl who apparently has big boobs all of a sudden.

I didn't get a say in any of this.

As soon as Kaylan gets home, I'm going to tell her that none of her planning makes a difference or makes any sense at all.

Things just happen, without us knowing when or how or even why.

They just happen.

TWENTY

Ari,

We love you so much. We are always here for you. And we'd never leave you out and never Insta without you. We think you're the best. Of course we get you. The four of us are soul mates. Don't worry about your bat mitzvah party. We'll rock whatever it is, whenever it is, and make sure it's amazing.

We love you!

Alice

———————————

Dearest Ari,

I just asked my dad if I could take the train by myself so I could visit you and give you a hug.

He said no, but we will be near your town in a few weeks and we are definitely hanging. You're amazing. Don't ever forget it! XOXO Zoe

---

Ari, Zoe and Alice have said all I wanted to say. So I will just add that those girls are totally sucky. You don't need home friends when you have amazing camp friends like us. You rock! MWAH! Hana

We go back and forth emailing all week, and we Face-Time, too, and it almost feels like we're back together again. Almost.

I spend the rest of the time practicing for my bat mitz-vah and considering what my passion might be so I can eventually pursue it and mostly trying to calm my mom down.

I write a rough draft of my speech but then delete the whole thing because it's not what I want to say. I don't know what I want to say. I don't really know what Juda-ism or my bat mitzvah mean to me, and I don't know how it relates to the Life of Sarah.

Sometimes I'll get a twinkle of an inkling of what I want to say, but then it doesn't feel completely right and sort of just fades away.

TWENTY-ONE

EVENTUALLY KAYLAN GETS HOME, THE afternoon before school starts, and we FaceTime first-day outfits.

"I love that plaid dress," Kaylan says. "And it's so lucky it's going to be a chilly first day of school so you can wear it."

I nod. "Yeah, I feel good about it."

"You think the overalls are too much?" Kaylan asks me. "Like trying too hard for first day or cute and funky?"

I pause. "Cute and funky, I think. Especially with the stripes."

"Promise?"

"Promise!"

"Okay, we're good to go then." Kaylan sits back on her bed. "Cami and June were also into the overalls. But

Amirah and M.W. weren't sure, so thanks for confirming."

"You FaceTimed all of them to discuss first-day outfits?" I feel that sting again, the left-out sting I felt when I saw the ice cream photos.

"Yeah, they're all super obsessed with group Face-Timing," Kaylan explains. "They haven't tried it with you?"

I shake my head. "No, but I've been busy this week, practicing for my bat mitzvah and stuff."

Kaylan nods. "Okay, well, it's cool." She looks away for a second and then back at the screen. "How come you and Marie aren't close anymore?"

I shrug. "Not sure, really. We didn't keep in touch when I was away, and when I got back, she was all BFF with the other girls."

"Well, it'll even out at school," Kaylan says. "So much to catch you up on from the trip with my dad. Can't believe I got back today! How insane?"

"Insane," I repeat. "Okay, I gotta go to make the mac and cheese for my parents. I really think I've mastered it! Crushing up the Cheez-Its makes all the difference. See you at the bus. Oh! Remind me to tell you about my bad habit tomorrow!"

"Ooh! Okay."

I go down to the kitchen and find my mom at the table

looking through a pile of papers. "You sure you want to make dinner, Ari? Night before the first day of school and everything?"

"I do! I need to!"

"Huh? Why?"

"Oh, I don't know. I mean, I don't need to. I just want to." I laugh, forgetting my mom doesn't really know about the list. "Anyway, you're all under so much stress. I figured this would be a nice treat."

"Thank you." She goes back to her papers.

I turn on the water to boil the pasta and then I mix all the cheese together. I don't have any of Kaylan's fancy cheese from France, but the thing is, I don't think I need it. And my version of perfect mac and cheese doesn't need to be the same as hers. We can both master it, using our own methods.

It's not like everyone in the world makes mac and cheese the same exact way. How boring would that be?

I do bake it this time, though. And I mush up the Cheez-Its as a topping this time instead of just throwing them in whole.

When it's in the oven, my mom finally gets up from the table and helps me put out plates and forks and napkins and glasses of ice water.

"Dinner, everyone!" I call.

Gemma bolts down the stairs ready to dig in, and my

dad comes in a second later. I sigh with relief when I notice he's changed out of his sick robe and into jeans and a T-shirt.

"Smells delicious," he says, but there's no feeling in his tone, no emotion in his voice. He's basically robot dad, programmed to say what he's supposed to say.

"I'll serve everyone." I scoop perfect portions onto plates, careful not to mess up the topping.

"Wow, this is amazing, Ari!" Gemma squeals. "This is literally the best thing I've ever eaten."

"Really?" I take a bite.

"It is good," my dad chimes in. "I'm not just saying that because I have to."

We all crack up.

Even my mom is eating, and I'm not sure I've seen her consume more than a few bites at any meal since I've been home from camp.

"It's delicious," my mom says, putting her hand on mine. "Who knew we had a chef in our midst?"

"I didn't, that's for sure." My dad smiles.

"Me neither!" Gemma yelps.

We all crack up and eat our mac and cheese, and I think this may actually be a happy, fun family moment. I don't want to think too hard about it because I don't want to jinx it. But we're all smiling. We're all eating. No one is crying right now.

We're all good.

My parents clean up dinner and I go up to my room to JHH the mac and cheese. I've mastered the recipe, sure. But I also mastered taking the stress off, even for a little while. That counts in a big way, too.

I look over the list as I fall asleep that night.

1. Keep our friendship strong.
2. Drink enough water (for a glowing complexion). ✓
3. Make our mark.
4. Master the art of mac and cheese (from scratch!). ✓
5. Perfect our handstand. ✓
6. Help someone else shine.
7. Stay up long enough to watch the sun set and rise. ✓
8. Find the perfect man for Kaylan's mom.
9. A doodle a day. ✓
10. Tell a boy how we really feel.
11. Pursue a passion (first find one).
12. Break a bad habit.

There's still a lot to do, but I'm definitely on my way.

Maybe my passion will be cheering people up and calming them down when they're stressed. It reminds me of that program we had at camp when I got called up to explain my definition of a good leader. Cheering people up is definitely a part of leadership, and to be honest, I think I'm good at it. Maybe better than good. Great, even.

I think that may be my best skill.

Or maybe that's how I make my mark.

I still have time to figure it out.

TWENTY-TWO

BUBBIE AND ZEYDA CALL GEMMA and me to wish us good luck on the first day of school.

We all talk on speakerphone and the chaos of no one being able to hear anyone else that well cracks me up.

"Good luck, my darlings," Bubbie says. "We hope it's a wonderful year."

"We do too," Gemma says, laughing.

We talk for a few more minutes, say our *I love yous*, and Zeyda says "bye now" the way he always does.

I get to the bus stop five minutes before Kaylan—all set to tell her about my week of self-discovery. Yes, some terrible things happened (my dad losing his job, the ice cream photo incident), but I also had a lot of time for soul searching. And I JHHed the handstand and the mac and cheese. Big stuff.

"Hiiiii," she says, running up to me. "Do I have food in my teeth?" She opens her mouth for me to inspect.

"No. All clear."

"K, thanks." She looks me up and down. "BBA, you look fab!"

"BBA?" I laugh.

She whispers, "Big Boob Ari."

"Shh. Stop." I roll my eyes. "You look great, too." I smile at her, but she's looking all over the place. "What's going on?"

"Oh, Cami and the girls were maybe going to get a ride over here so they could take the bus with us, but I don't see them." She takes her phone out of her bag. "Oh, she texted. They're just going to meet us at the main doors."

"Uh, okay."

"I didn't think they'd be ready in time, but they suggested it, so . . ."

I nod. "Got it."

We're quiet for the beginning of the bus ride, and then Kaylan turns to me and says, "Oh! You were going to tell me about your bad habit and what you did on the list and stuff. Let's discuss now before we see the other girls. Because they don't really get it, and it's weird and stuff."

I don't really feel like talking about it now, it feels almost like an obligation or something, but I force the words out.

"I'm so tired, so I'm going to just give you an abbreviated version and we'll have the longer discussion later, okay?"

She shrugs. "Fine."

"Bad habit: always letting my mind wander. It makes it hard to get work done and really be in the moment. You know how you always tell me I zone out?"

She nods. "Continue."

"Yeah, so, I want to be better at being present, focusing."

"Okay." Kaylan considers it. "I can get on board with that. And your passion?"

I take a deep breath. "So my passion is tricky. I think I have a bunch."

She raises her eyebrows, waiting for me to go on.

"Well, first of all, cheering people up. I really love it. Like, nothing makes me happier, and I think that's part of being a good leader too." I pause. "Also, as I've been working on my bat mitzvah stuff, I'm kind of feeling passionate about religion, and Judaism. There's so much to learn."

"Interesting," she says. "You did get all soul-searchy while I was away."

I laugh. "I guess I did." I try to remember what else I wanted to tell her. "I JHHed the handstand. Ask Gemma when you see her—it's perfect. And I made the mac and

162

cheese for my fam, and they loved it. So I JHHed that too."

She claps quietly. "Sounds pretty good. Want to hear mine?"

"Of course!"

She giggles. "Okay. Bad habit: freaking out all the time, obviously. Passion: comedy. I want to start a youth comedy troupe at school, see who else is into it. Um, no clue on making my mark, though. No clue on helping someone else shine." She sits back in the seat and closes her eyes. "I'm about to do my bad habit. About to freak out. Feeling overwhelmed."

She stops talking and takes out her phone and texts something to Cami.

I pretend I don't see it because I don't need anything else to bother me before the first day of school.

I take my phone out and text the camp girls, wishing them all good luck on their first days of school.

I text Golfy, too.

And then I quickly scan through my email.

From: Cantor Simon
To: Arianna Nodberg
Subject: something to ponder
Hi, Arianna,
Before our next lesson, I'd like you to be thinking
about what it means when we say "an adult in

the eyes of our people." We touched on this last week, but we didn't really get into it. Give it some thought. Also, I need an update on where you are with your speech.

Thanks. See you soon.
Cantor Simon

Kaylan reads over my shoulder.

"What does that mean?" she asks. "'An adult in the eyes of our people'? And how come Judaism expects so much of people who are only thirteen? Does any other religion do that?"

I laugh. "I'm not sure."

"It feels like a lot." She shrugs. "I guess that's why you get that big party. You've really earned it."

I consider what to say, if I should tell her about my dad's job or the fact that I'm not really having a big party anymore. But we're almost at school, and this doesn't feel like the right time.

"Your mind is wandering again! Earth to Ari! Bad habit alert!" Kaylan cracks up as we turn into the school parking lot.

I laugh. "Okay, well, see, I'm still working on it."

The bus rolls through the parking lot and stops in front of the main doors by the gym.

I have a few baby fireflies rumbling in my stomach,

but for the most part I feel peaceful and confident about the year ahead. I take Kaylan's hand as we get off the bus. "Come on, let's crush seventh grade."

She smiles. "Well, duh."

TWENTY-THREE

ALL OF MY MORNING CLASSES are in the honors block, and I don't really know anyone in them. Except for math, which Kaylan and I have together, thank God.

I don't understand how I was the only one of the lunch table girls who tested into the whole block. They're all smart. I wonder if there's been some kind of glitch and if I can switch back. Maybe I'm not even supposed to be in these classes.

I have a third-period study hall so I'm allowed to use the computer and check email since we don't have any homework yet.

And it may only be ten thirty in the morning, but today already has a highlight.

An email from Golfy:

Ari Nodberg!

**So sorry I didn't write back sooner. We just got
back from Maine, and school starts tomorrow. You
start tomorrow, too? GOOD LUCK. You will crush
seventh grade. Text me or call me or email or do
that thing where you connect a can to a string and
talk into it—whatever it takes. Tell me about the
first day! I want to hear all about it. Tell Kaylan I
say hey.**

Peace!
Golfy

I smile through the rest of my morning classes, only
half paying attention because I'm daydreaming about
Golfy. I'm not doing so great at breaking my bad habit,
but I don't even care right now.

It's fun to daydream about Golfy and what he's like in
school. Imagining him in his classroom, taking notes. Is
his hair sticking up in all directions like it did at camp?
Or did he comb it down or use gel or something and make
it look neat and perfect before the first day? Is he wearing his mesh shorts and a faded tee? Or did he try to look
good—a polo maybe? Nice jeans?

When I get to lunch, the girls are at our same lunch

table, and I'm glad that even with our different sched-
ules, we get to eat together.

"Where's Marie?" I ask. Now that we're back in school
and it's kinda too late, I realize that I could've put more
effort into our friendship over the summer, writing to her
or making plans for when I got home. I'll do better now.

"She's taking Japanese at lunch," Kaylan says. "I told
you. Remember?"

"Oh, um, right." I have no memory of her telling me,
but I don't want to admit that.

I sit down at the table and take my chicken salad sandwich out of my lunch bag. I also have cut up cucumbers,
a bag of chips, and one of those mini bags of fruit snacks.

"Ugh, first day and I already have so much homework,"
June says, sipping her iced tea. "Ridiculous, right?"

"Well, at least we're off next Monday and Tuesday,"
Sydney replies. "So we don't have a full week for a while."

M.W. says, "Yeah, but we'll be in temple." She rolls her
eyes in my direction.

"Oh, sad times." Kira frowns. "I think we were all going
to go to that new arcade down near the beach. Right?"

Everyone nods.

Cami jumps in. "Not all of us. I'm Jewish, too. I mean,
half. But I still have to go to temple." She pauses. "So don't
have too much fun without me."

They all laugh.

June is about to say something else about the arcade, I think, but Cami interrupts her. "Wait, Kaylan, you never finished telling us what happened. I don't even understand how you weren't so completely mortified."

I crinkle my eyebrows and look at Kaylan, no clue what's going on.

"It wasn't that bad. I just changed my shorts and stuffed the gross ones at the bottom of my bag, and then I went to the little convenience store in the hotel and bought pads and stuff," she explains. "I was just scared Ryan would see, and my dad, and ew."

"Super crazy, though," Amirah adds.

"That's why I'm so glad to have older sisters," Cami announces. "It's honestly a lifesaver."

"Was it weird to get it at camp?" June asks me, unwrapping her sandwich.

I don't understand how they're not totally grossed out discussing this while eating.

"Um, I didn't get it at camp, actually," I say. "But it would've been fine. My mom sent me to camp with supplies and stuff." I pause. "Can we discuss this later, though? When we're not eating?"

"It's a totally normal thing," Cami defends the discussion. "You don't need to be weird about it, Ari. We're all friends here."

"I'm not being weird about it." My head feels like it's on

169

fire because Kaylan clearly told everyone else what happened on her week away with her dad and brother. But she didn't tell me. "Also, if we're all friends, why didn't you invite me to ice cream last week?"

They freeze and stare at one another, and Kaylan nudges me with her knee.

"What? It's just a question."

"Ari," she says, like she's warning me about something.

"You didn't respond to our text," M.W. says. "We all said we were free that night, but not during the day, and then you didn't respond."

"So? I thought it was a given that if you were all doing something you'd invite me. I was the one who suggested all getting together in the first place."

Cami exhales in a really over-the-top sort of way. "Sorry, Arianna. You're really worked up. I've never seen you this way."

"I'm fine!" I put all my lunch stuff back in the bag and stand up. I think I'll go eat on the bench by the main office and hope no one sees me. If anyone asks, I'll say I need to be picked up early for a doctor's appointment. "I need to go talk to a teacher, though. See you guys later."

I walk out of the cafeteria more slowly than I normally would because I'm totally expecting Kaylan to run after me.

She doesn't, though.

As I wander through the halls, the whole *keep our friendship strong* thing keeps flashing across my brain like a neon sign above a pizza place.

I kind of thought keeping our friendship strong would be the easiest thing on the list this time.

But it seems to be getting harder and harder the closer we get to the deadline.

TWENTY-FOUR

I DON'T SEE ANY OF the lunch table girls for the rest of the day because of my stupid honors track schedule. I'm kind of grateful for that, though, because I don't feel like dealing with any of the fallout from what happened in the cafeteria earlier today.

Cami's one of those girls who brings the drama wherever she goes, and that has seeped into the rest of the girls. Even Kaylan. And Kaylan Terrel is a girl who has enough drama to last the rest of her life—she doesn't need any help with that.

I plan to discuss this with her on the ride home, but she's not on the bus line. I take my phone out of my backpack to check for a text from her, but nothing.

So this is how it's going to be, I guess.

Fine.

We'll work through it.

I get off the bus and walk home, and I find a note on the kitchen table.

Ari, Dad and I have an appointment this afternoon. Grandma's picking Gemma up at school, and then they'll be home. Grab a snack and start HW, and then practice for your bat mitzvah. I love you. Mom

I shake my head. It's amazing that she finds a way to be this intense and naggy even in a kitchen table note! Do moms automatically become that way the minute they have a baby? Or is it something that's always been there, lying beneath the surface, waiting to pounce?

My grandma's not really like that, at least not to me. And Bubbie isn't either. Maybe it's just full-on intense when you're a new mom and then it evaporates when you become a grandmother.

I open the fridge to take an apple out of the crisper drawer, but it's stuck. I pull and pull, yanking it open, until the whole drawer falls out, and all of the fruits and vegetables scatter all over the floor.

"Oh my God!" I scream out loud, even though no one is home to hear me.

I grab an apple and put it on the counter and then

spend the next twenty minutes trying to get the drawer back in. Finally, I give up and put the whole thing on the kitchen table.

Someone will have to deal with that later.

I wash the apple and take it upstairs to my room to start homework, but I decide to text Alice first.

Ari: AlKal! How was ur day? Mine sucked. Drama w/ lunch table grls. Drawer broken in fridge. Mom will freak. So much hw. Uggghhhh. XOXO Noddie

She writes me back right away.

Alice: I was just thinking abt u! miss u so, so much. My day = ok. My grandma fell tho—in the hosp. worried. ☹ love u

Ari: Sooooooo sorry 2 hear that. Keep me updated. Ilysm

I'm halfway through my science lab when our landline rings. I don't answer it because the calls are never for me.

But then it rings again.

And then my cell phone rings.

My mom.

"Hello?"

"Ari! I totally forgot to tell you that the cantor called earlier and she had to change your bat mitzvah lesson. It's today at five. Please be ready, and I'll swing by and get you."

"Um. Okay." I wonder if she realizes how often she forgets to tell me things.

"Make sure you practice before."

I roll my eyes, feeling grateful she can't see me right now. "I will, Mom."

I sit back in my desk chair and close my eyes. I guess I'll have to do this mountain of homework after my lesson, but probably not until way later because I'll have to deal with a lecture from my mom about how I broke the drawer in the fridge.

At four forty-five, I hear the honk, grab my bat mitzvah notebook, and head outside.

"Have a good lesson, Ar," my dad says as he gets out of the front seat and I get in.

"Quick. Buckle your seat belt. We're going to be late," my mom tells me.

"We still have fifteen minutes," I remind her.

"But there's always a slowdown at the light on Sullivan and East Fields Road this time of day." Her hands are so tight around the steering wheel that I bet she could crack the whole thing in half if she tried.

"The drawer in the fridge is broken," I announce. "I tried to put it back, but I couldn't."

"Again?" she shrieks. "Seriously, how many times have I told you and Gemma not to be so rough with it?"

I laugh. "Mom, it's a refrigerator drawer. It's not like a delicate piece of Grandma's china."

"This isn't funny."

"Okay. Sorry."

I stare straight ahead and pray there's no slowdown because I'm not sure how long I can stand being in the car with my mother.

"How was your day at school?" she asks five minutes later.

I debate telling her about the lunch table situation, but it would probably just stress her out too much. "Fine. Classes are hard. But I'm managing."

"Of course they're hard!" she half-yells. "You're in honors and that's amazing, but it's going to take some extra work on your part."

"I know, Mom." I exhale. "I have it under control."

We pull into the temple parking lot, and my mom says, "I'm going to make some calls from the car. So just come out when you're done."

I nod and go inside and find the cantor typing on her laptop. I knock gently.

"Come in, Arianna. Please. Have a seat." She smiles. "Sorry to change your lesson so last minute. Glad you could make it."

"No problem."

"So, tell me. How's everything going?"

"Good." I shrug. "I've been practicing everything. But my speech is still a work in progress."

"Well, that's okay. Let's start to go through the service the way we will on the big day, and then we discuss the speech."

We go over the prayers at the beginning of the service. They're mostly in Hebrew and involve me saying a part and the congregation reading aloud responsively. Cantor Simon corrects a few of my mistakes, but I'm proud to say there are really only a few.

"I think you're in great shape," she says. "A little under two months to go. Can you believe it?"

I shake my head. "No, definitely not. To answer your email, I don't think I can see myself as an adult in the eyes of my people. At all."

She laughs a little. "Well, you start slow. You can't ever really see yourself doing anything until you do it."

I play with the fraying threads around the hole in my jeans. "I guess, yeah."

She nods. "What does it mean to you, though? Being an adult in the eyes of your people?"

I think for a second. "I guess it means putting our own needs aside sometimes and focusing on others."

That leadership program from camp pops into my head. It just seemed like an average thing, and it's surprising that it keeps coming back to me again and again. "And also working harder on the commandments. Being a more active participant in services and stuff."

"All excellent things." Cantor Simon smiles. "I can tell you're putting a great deal of thought into this process, and I love it. It's a journey. Not something you'll have all figured out right away."

"Yeah." I smile back.

She stays quiet for a few seconds and says, "Anything else on your mind? Anything else you would like to discuss today?"

I consider telling her about the situation with my dad, but it feels too personal. And I certainly can't launch into the lunch table drama situation. I kind of want to, though, because she has these soft, sensitive green eyes. They make me feel like she can understand anything and offer advice.

"Well, one thing . . ." I sit back in the chair.

She nods for me to continue.

"This kind of relates to my speech actually—how do you stay so focused? I feel like my mind always wanders. Like, ever since I was a little kid. Teachers would tell my parents I was always daydreaming in class, and I do well in school, but . . ."

She clears her throat. "I'm not always focused. My mind wanders, too. I think it's okay to daydream a little bit. There's a whole Torah portion about Jacob and his dream. That's next week's, by the way." She laughs. "So accept that you daydream, let yourself daydream a little, and then try to regain focus. We're all works in progress, Ari."

"That makes sense, I think." I put all the prayer sheets back in my bat mitzvah folder.

"Do you want to discuss your speech? What you've been thinking about in terms of what you want to say?" She sits back in her chair and takes a sip of her tea. "Here's a bit of trivia for you . . . Chaiyei Sarah is the only portion of the Torah named after a matriarch. Cool, right?"

"That is cool. The thing is, it's hard to tie it all together. And I guess I'm still figuring out how I feel, so . . ." My voice trails off, and so do my thoughts. "Like Sarah had it so much harder than I do, and, um, I don't know." I laugh because I realize I'm not making any sense.

"I see." She smiles. "Well, think about what the story of Sarah's life is trying to teach us. There's not really a right or wrong answer." She pauses. "And everything you've told me about community and responsibility— that all ties in very well. I think you just need to connect the dots a little."

I nod, still feeling confused.

"Am I making sense?" She laughs a little.

"I think so, but it's a lot to take in. My head starts to spin a little when I try to really formulate my thoughts, so I keep starting and stopping and starting again. . . ." I look up at the clock and realize it's almost time to go and I should probably stop blabbering on. "So next week, this time? Or back to our original time?"

"Good question." She looks at her calendar. "Back to the original time. Have a great week, Ari."

"Bye. Thank you."

I walk back out to the car and find my mom crying in the front seat. But when I get in, she wipes her eyes and pretends that she wasn't.

"Are you okay?"

"Allergies. You know how I get this time of year." She sniffles.

"Um, not really. It's September. You usually have bad allergies in May and June."

She starts driving. "It changes every year. How was your lesson?"

"Fine. I'm in good shape."

"That's great to hear," she says. "I still can't believe you're old enough to have a bat mitzvah. In my mind you're still the little baby crawling all over the floor."

"Mom." I roll my eyes.

"You'll understand one day," she tells me. "When you have kids you'll understand."

"Check back with me then, okay?" I laugh, trying to break up the tension.

All she does is shake her head and stare at the road in front of us.

After dinner, I'm back at my desk doing homework when I get a text from Kaylan.

Kaylan: r u not talking 2 me?

Ari: um I could ask u the same thing.

Kaylan: ft'ing u

A second later, I see the FaceTime call coming in and I swipe across to answer it.

"What's going on?" Kaylan asks, scratching an itch above her eyebrow.

"I don't know. You tell me."

"Stop." She stares at me through the screen.

"I didn't do anything."

She puts the phone down so all I can see is the ceiling, and when she comes back to the call, her hair is up in a bun.

"Why did you storm away from lunch?" she asks.

"I just didn't feel super comfy there. It wasn't a big deal."

"You left the cafeteria!"

"So?" I laugh. "It's okay to want a change of scenery."

"Ari."

"Kaylan.

"Those girls are just weird. I don't get why they didn't invite me to hang that night when you were away. And I don't get why you didn't tell me about the big P happening on your dad trip." I shrug. "None of this is a big deal. It's just super weird. So I figured I'd take myself out of the drama."

Kaylan lowers her eyes. "Ari. For real? You hate talking

about the big P! So obvs I wasn't going to tell you."

"I don't hate talking about it. I just don't like discussing it with everyone at the lunch table. But you're my BFF. It's way different."

"Okay. Well, I'm sorry. But please don't storm off again."

"I wasn't storming! I just got up!" I shake my head. "I thought you were all about being TH friends or whatever. So I'm being TH and telling you I don't like discussing personal stuff at the lunch table." I pause. "But you were not TH at all the way you didn't tell me about what happened on your trip!"

"Fine. This is getting confusing." She rolls her eyes, as if I can't see her right in the screen.

We're quiet for a second, just as my mom yells, "Ari! Off the phone! Now! You have tons of homework to do!"

"You heard the woman," I whisper, laughing. "I gotta go, Kay."

"Just be normal tomorrow, okay?" she says. "Like you were before you went to camp!"

"Ew, that's rude, Kay. I am normal. I'm the same as I was before, whatever that is. Who knows. They're the weird ones. I'll be however I'm gonna be, thankyouverymuch."

"TH friends. All I'm saying." She shakes her head. "Whatever, Ari."

"Whatever, Kay," I mock.

I try to go back to homework after that, but I keep replaying the conversation in my head. *Just be normal tomorrow?*

That doesn't even really sound like Kaylan. I could be saying the same exact thing to her.

TWENTY-FIVE

AFTER A FEW DAYS, I get into a habit of starting my homework on the bus ride home because there's so much to do and not that much time to do it.

"We need to figure out if we're doing that barbecue," Kaylan says, interrupting my math problem. "If Zoe is definitely coming in with her dad, we should do it soon while the weather is still warm enough."

"Oh! Her visit is coming up soon, actually."

"So let's plan it." Kaylan smiles. "We can make our mac and cheese."

"Ooh! Good idea." I go back to my math, putting the barbecue plans out of my head for a second.

"Talk to your parents tonight and make sure they're okay with it," Kaylan instructs.

I close my math stuff. "You're sure you're okay with

the set-up, though? And your mom is, too?"

"I think so." She smiles. "Can we invite the lunch table girls, though?"

I raise my eyebrows. "Sure. I guess."

"I mean, you're gonna have Zoe and the other camp girls there, so it's only fair. . . ."

I shrug. "True." I hesitate a second and then turn to Kaylan and say, "Kay, I need to talk to you, actually. Something happened while you were away, and I haven't been able to really tell you yet."

"Big P related?"

"No. Not everything is big P related." I roll my eyes. "Do you want to come over for a little after school?"

"Okay. I told Cami I'd go to her house later for a pizza study date, though, for our history test." She shakes her head. "I didn't invite you since *you're in honors*," she sings.

"Stop."

"Just tell me as we walk," Kaylan says as we get off the bus. "You know I can't handle waiting."

"Fine. Let's just talk here." We stop at a bench outside the little playground in our neighborhood and sit down.

"What is it? I'm freaking out."

I laugh for a second. "I thought you were breaking that bad habit?"

"You can help me! Now spill it!"

I hesitate and then blurt out, "My dad lost his job. I don't exactly know what's going on. But my fancy ooh-la-la bat mitzvah isn't happening. That whole golf club caterer meeting was for nothing." I sigh. "So this barbecue may be a little weird. Like, my parents may not be in a party mood. I need to talk to my mom about it."

"Oh. Um. Wow." Kaylan's eyebrows crinkle. "That's not what I was expecting you to say."

"What were you expecting?" I giggle.

She laughs a little, too. "Not sure, actually."

We sit there quietly for a minute, and she says, "I can't believe you waited so long to tell me. Did you tell Alice and everyone?"

I nod. "Yeah. But you were away, and I didn't want to stress you out, and then school started, and the lunch table thing . . ."

"You should still be able to tell me stuff." She looks at me. "I mean, come on."

"I know."

"Keeping our friendship strong, Ari."

"It is. We are."

"Does your dad want to work at an allergy office?" She shrugs. "Maybe my mom can get him a job there."

"Um . . . I don't think he has the skills. But thanks!" I wait for Kaylan to say anything else, offer any words of wisdom, but we just sit there quietly until I say, "I should go and start homework. I probably have a bat mitzvah lesson. I seem to have them every day, I think."

"Lot of work to become a woman." Kaylan cracks up.

"Ew. Don't say it that way."

"Call me later, Ar," Kaylan says as we part ways to go to our houses.

"Okay."

In my head, I practice what to say when I talk to my parents about the barbecue. If all goes according to plan, I'll invite everyone.

It'll be something fun to look forward to.

TWENTY-SIX

MY PARENTS SEEM TO BE in bad moods for the rest of the week. I can never find a light moment to ask them about the barbecue. So I decide to put it on hold until after Rosh Hashanah. Maybe the New Year will cheer them up.

I sit in temple, and I think about all the stuff that happened this past year and all that will happen in the coming year. It's the Jewish New Year, but it's not a rah-rah, throw-a-party kind of new year. We don't have noise makers or wear sparkly dresses.

It's soul-searchy and introspective and thoughtful. We think about mistakes we made in the past year and how we can make them right, fix broken relationships with people, apologize for things we've done wrong. And we think about how we can be better in the new year. The kind of people we want to be.

It kind of reminds me of the 12 Before 13 list, actually.

It was the completely right decision to make our lists in the summer. Every first day of school is basically like the New Year. We want to be the best we can be.

And this year, Rosh Hashanah feels like an even bigger deal, since I've spent so much time working on my bat mitzvah stuff, really thinking about the role Judaism plays in my life. It's always been kind of an obligation to come and sit in temple and stay quiet and pray and listen to the sermons.

For the first time ever, it doesn't feel like an obligation. It still is, I mean, I'm forced to be here by my parents. But I actually want to be here, too.

And when next Rosh Hashanah rolls around, I will be on the other side—no longer a kid, truly a woman in the eyes of my people. One hundred percent.

Maybe I should include all of that in my speech? God, why is writing this speech so hard? I mean, I thought the Hebrew stuff would be the hard part. But it's the writing in English that's tripping me up.

I leave the service for a minute to go to the bathroom, and when I walk in I find Jules, Cami, and M.W. sitting on the countertops in the bathroom lounge area outside the stalls, making little flowers out of toilet paper.

"Oh, hey," I say, a little startled to find them there.

"Hey," they grumble, not really paying attention.

"Services are so boring," M.W. says, looking up at me. "I can't sit through all of it."

"Me neither. Duh." Jules rolls her eyes at nothing in particular.

I shrug. "Oh. Um. Yeah."

"Have you been in there the whole time?" Jules asks. "Have you seen Noah?"

I grab a tissue from the box. "I've been in there, but I haven't seen him."

"I hope it's okay that we're, like, together now," she says. "I mean, I know you and Noah were, like, a thing."

I laugh. "Not really. It's totally okay."

Cami jumps in. "Yeah, and Ari has a boyfriend now. From caaamp."

"Stop." I smile and walk toward the stalls. "It's totally fine, though, Jules."

While I'm in the stall, I keep an ear out because I think there's a good chance they may be talking about me. I can't say for sure, though, but maybe.

"You're going back to the service already?" M.W. asks after I've washed my hands and I'm leaving the bathroom.

I feel a little flattered that she wants me to stay.

"Yeah, I kind of like it. It's, like, a peaceful, quiet

time to think and figure stuff out." I laugh. "I know, I'm weird."

"Um, yeah." They laugh, but not in a mean way. Not a hundred percent mean anyway.

"Have fun praying," Cami says, giggling. "Would it be okay if your nickname was Rabbi? It could work, I think."

I laugh along with her, because it's better than showing how embarrassed I feel. "Whatever you want, Cami. We can see if it sticks."

I leave the bathroom with my head held high, because it's the only way to be. A *fake it till you make it* kind of thing. Even though I'm almost positive they'll be talking about me now.

But today isn't about focusing on things like that. It's about figuring out how to be better. How to make changes for the new year.

I spend the rest of the service trying to brainstorm my speech in my head. I'd jot down notes, but it wouldn't be right.

I get home from temple, not feeling confident that I've come up with anything good.

I text Kaylan to check in.

Ari: How was the arcade?

Kaylan: Was soooo fabbbbbbb @ June's house now. So fun.

Ari: Cool ☺

Kaylan: Heard u saw cami & mw @ temple.

Ari: Yup.

Ari: What else is going on w/ u?

Kaylan: nm but I gg xo

Ari: xoxo

I've heard of some people who take a technology break from cell phones and texting on Rosh Hashanah and Yom Kippur, and right now I'm kind of wishing that I'd done that, too.

I don't want to think about that awkward text exchange with Kaylan.

It would have been better to stay in the warm-and-glowy-feelings space of looking inward and figuring out what all of this Judaism stuff means to me.

And how to be the best Arianna Simone Nodberg I can be.

TWENTY-SEVEN

"SO," MY MOM STARTS WHEN we're all at the kitchen table for dinner a few nights later. "It's not what we had originally planned, but it's still going to be nice. We'll have bagels and cream cheese and cookies and stuff after the service in the temple social hall, and we can get some balloons. And Dad's friend Jerry offered to play guitar."

After I finish my bite of chicken I say, "Mom, I can just make a playlist on my iPhone and hook up the temple speakers. Jerry doesn't need to play guitar."

"He's very talented," my dad chimes in. "He's in a Billy Joel cover band."

"Nice, but no thanks." I smile. "We'll just do a playlist."

My mom moves the chicken and asparagus around on her plate. "I know it's not what we had envisioned, but . . ."

"Mom, it's not what you envisioned. You were the one who wanted a big party. I mean, I did, too. But you were the one obsessed with it."

She looks at me, stunned.

"What? It's true." I wait for my dad and Gemma to back me up, but they stay quiet. "You never asked me what I wanted, by the way."

"I thought we were all on the same page." My mom sips her seltzer. "I'm just so disappointed now."

"I am too. I mean, we all are. Obviously. But actually, here's something to undisappoint you." I crack up. "I know that's not a word. Can we have a barbecue here next weekend? My friend Zoe will be in town with her dad, and we kind of want to set him up with Kaylan's mom."

"What?" my dad squawks. "Do they know about this?"

"Yes, they do," I say defensively.

"Set up by kids!" Gemma slams her hand on the table and bursts into laughter.

"Stop, Gem." I look around. "Also, I'm almost a woman. In the eyes of my people! Not going to be a kid for much longer . . ."

"Right." Gemma shakes her head, still laughing.

"Well, I'm not really sure setting people up is first on the list of becoming a Jewish adult, plus we're not really in a barbecue mood," my mom starts. "And it's the end of September. Could be chilly."

I put down my fork. "Already checked the forecast. Gonna be in the low seventies. Also, we need a barbecue to put us in a good mood. I know Dad's not working, but we can't mope forever. Plus, did you know if you set up three couples you automatically go to heaven? That's what Bubbie says."

My parents make eyes at each other.

"It's true. So a barbecue? Yes?"

"Okay, but let's keep it on the small side," my dad offers.

"We will." I take a bite of my mashed potatoes. "We'll get all the food at Costco. And everyone is gonna bring a side dish or dessert to keep the cost down."

"I guess she has this figured out," my dad says to no one in particular.

"Ooh-la-la, can't wait to see the lovebirds in action!" Gemma makes kissy faces.

"Gem." I bulge my eyes at her.

After dinner, I go up to my room to email and invite everyone.

From: Ari
To: Zoe, Alice, Hana
Subject: BBQ!!!!!!!!!!!!!!!!!!!!!!!

We are on for the BBQ at my house next Saturday!

Zoe and her dad are coming. AlKal and Hana, can you come too? Puh-lease?

Yay or nay to inviting Golfy?

WB! XOXOXOXO Ari

PS: AlKal, how's ur grandma?

_____

Um, yes to Golfy. Will ask my mom if I can come. Luv Hana

_____

Grandma is ok. In rehab now. I think 2 far 2 come for one night. But yes to golfy. & FaceTime me when ur all 2gether. ILYSM AlKal

_____

YAYYYYYYYYYYY! Will miss u, Al. LOVE U ALL TONS, Zoe

_____

Golfy is slow with email, so I decide to text him instead.

Hi, I'm having a bbq at my house next Saturday. Zoe and hana r coming & some school peeps. Want 2 come?

I stay awake forever after that, waiting for him to respond. But he doesn't.

Boys are so bad with phones.

I toss and turn all night imagining Golfy in my house. He will be in my room. He will go from the camp part of my life to the home part of my life.

I picture him chatting with my parents, being funny and charming with Gemma. I picture him and Kaylan joking around, Kaylan telling him funny old stories about us.

It feels so teenagery in a way—bringing a boy over to a family party. A boy who's more than a friend, way more than a friend.

Even though it feels big and new and a little scary, it feels good, too.

Maybe a key part of the puzzle of feeling okay at home, better than okay even, is to merge my camp life with my home life, mixing it all together like some thick, chunky soup.

I'm imagining a broccoli cheddar level of perfection.

TWENTY-EIGHT

GOLFY WRITES BACK A FEW days later. My heart pounds through my crewneck sweatshirt when I see the text.

Golfy: So sorry. I lost my phone. Just found it! Will be @ ur bbq

I don't understand how boys can honestly be this bad with phones. I would have been freaking out if I'd lost my phone, and he's all calm about it, like it was nothing.

Does he have any idea how hard it is to be chill when someone you love just disappears and you have no idea if you'll ever hear from him again?

"Golfy's coming to the barbecue!" I nudge Kaylan on the ride to school.

"You didn't even tell me you invited him!"

"I know, because then what if he couldn't come? He

hadn't even written back, so I figured he wasn't into me anymore, and . . ."

"You keep secrets!"

"So do you!"

"I invited the lunch table girls, by the way," Kaylan tells me, resting her knees against the seat in front of us. "That was the plan, right?"

I nod. "Yeah, totally. But we're almost at school, and I need to ask you something, so . . . changing topic for a sec," I whisper. "Do you think Mr. Gavinder is weird?"

"All teachers are weird," Kaylan says matter-of-factly.

"No, but I mean, like, he never calls on the girls," I say. "Have you noticed that?"

Kaylan shakes her head. "No, but that's because I'm so completely lost in that class. I can't understand a single thing that's going on. My mom is going to call and see if I can switch back to regular math."

"Please don't switch," I say. "And see if you notice anything in class this morning."

Halfway through math class, Kaylan whispers, "You're so right. He hasn't called on a single girl this period! And Isabela raises her hand for every question."

"She's a genius," I whisper back.

"Arianna and Kaylan. Stop talking." Mr. Gavinder says, facing the board with his back to us.

"He notices we're here, at least." Kaylan giggles.

"If I hear you two talking again, you will go straight to the office."

We sit up straight in our seats, covering our mouths to stop ourselves from laughing.

At lunch, everyone's talking about the barbecue.

"It's kind of late in the season for a barbecue, though," Cami says, pulling apart her turkey avocado wrap. "You're lucky it's going to be so unseasonably warm."

"Global warming," Amirah explains.

"Probably," June adds.

"Is your camp boyfriend coming?" M.W. asks.

"I think so." I smile. I love how that sounds. *Camp boyfriend.* So happy. And summery. I picture flip-flops and splashing swimming pool water and sitting on the grass and a counselor playing guitar.

"Hello! Earth to Ari!" Cami taps me from across the table. "OMG. I am so excited to meet him."

"Yay." I go back to my daydream.

Cami turns to Kaylan. "What about you? Are you on again or off or in the middle again with Jason?"

She peels off a piece of her string cheese. I can't even remember the last time we talked about Jason, or the last time I saw Jason. And he lives across the street from me!

"Who knows." Kaylan rolls her eyes. "Boys! Who needs 'em?"

The whole table cracks up.

"She is honestly the funniest person in the world," Cami declares. "How's it going with that comedy troupe, Kay?"

"I'm gonna suggest it when they ask for club ideas," she tells everyone. "I feel like that should be soon, no?"

"I think so," I chime in. "Ms. Bixhorn was talking about it the other day during homeroom."

There's a lull in the conversation, so I turn to Kaylan and tell her I won't be on the bus later because of my bat mitzvah lesson.

"Oh, okay."

"Your bat mitzvah is so soon, right?" Cami barges into the conversation yet again.

"Yup. November third."

"Insane." Cami puts all of her lunch garbage into the brown paper bag. "Are you so excited?"

I nod. "Yeah, I am. I really like the learning part of it, actually. This is so weird to say, but the more I think about it, the more I feel like Torah portion applies to my life. I am just trying to figure out how, exactly."

"I've literally never heard anyone say that before," M.W. says. "I am so not into the actual prayer part of it."

"Well, you still have a while, don't you?"

"Yeah, true. Mine is in May, so I haven't really started, but I don't think I'll be into it . . . I find it all really boring."

Everyone stares at me after that, like I have to defend my position or something.

"Well, different strokes, different folks, ya know." I laugh.

"But you're not having a big party anymore, right?" M.W. says, not meanly or anything, but it still feels like she just threw some kind of toxic chemical all over the table.

"Um, well—"

"My mom ran into your mom at the grocery store," she interrupts.

Cami interjects, "Wait, what's going on?" and then M.W. starts to explain, but the lunch gong dings and it's time to leave the cafeteria.

Thank God for that gong.

I feel like I've been through some kind of professional-level game of tennis, but I'm the ball.

Wasn't it M.W. who barely talked last year? Now she's like a Cami in training.

I don't know what Kaylan could've done, but she just sort of sat there silently, picking at her string cheese.

I don't think I can handle all of these intense, personal-discussion lunch periods every day.

Maybe I'll have to switch into Marie's Japanese class, just to stay sane.

TWENTY-NINE

SOMEHOW I MAKE IT THROUGH a few more crazy days of school. Between the honors track classes and our intense lunch table conversations, seventh grade is way harder than sixth.

But texting Alice every day totally helps and knowing that I'm going to see Golfy this weekend keeps me sane.

The day of the barbecue arrives, and I'm excited for Kaylan's mom to meet Zoe's dad, and it'll be nice to JHH another list item.

But if I'm being honest, I kind of want the whole thing to be over already.

It feels like a lot of people, going through a lot of different things, all in the same place will make for a chaotic situation.

Maybe if Kaylan and I were at our strongest, I'd feel

more confident about it. We're working on keeping our friendship strong, but I kind of don't even know what that means anymore.

We're, like, on different football teams, and occasionally we meet in the middle of the field for a handshake. But I don't feel like we're really playing together.

"Hiiiii," Kaylan sings, running through the gate to the backyard and snapping me out of my friendship analysis. "Barbecue day is here!" She fist-bumps me. "My mom is coming later, but I wanted to come early to set up."

"Nice." I smile, trying to make sure my parents aren't arguing about something in the kitchen.

When my dad comes out, carrying a platter of uncooked burgers, Kaylan walks over to him and says, "We can take control of the grill, Mr. Nodberg." Her hands are on her hips. "I've grilled before."

"Okay, Kaylan." He turns to face her, eyebrows raised. "First of all, you should know by now that Mr. Nodberg is my dad. My name is Marc." He pauses for a second. (This is their private joke. It's silly that my BFF and my dad would even have a private joke, but it's comforting, too.) He goes on, "Second of all, why don't you girls just enjoy yourselves and leave the grilling to me?"

"Can I just see all the meat?" Kaylan asks.

He sighs. "Knock yourself out."

My dad wipes his sweaty forehead on the sleeve of his T-shirt, and I look away, pretending not to notice.

The lightness in his tone that was always there has dissipated—it's not that he comes across as angry or anything, just tense and not in the mood to deal. Even the private joke comes out as some kind of obligation, like he has to say it, not because he finds it all that funny.

"Looks good." Kaylan shrugs and nudges her head toward the drink table, alerting me that I should follow her over there.

"Does he seem super stressed?" I whisper.

"Kinda yeah, to be honest. He doesn't have his usual chill dad vibe going on right now."

"That's what worries me."

"I know." She puts a hand on my shoulder. "You can't be the only chill one in your family. But let's put that on hold for a tiny sec and game plan this my-mom-meeting-Zoe's-dad thing."

I nod. "Um, okay, when Zoe gets here, you, me, and your mom go over to where they're sitting, and we just start to chat with Zoe and hope that the grown-ups get that they should chat, too."

"Will they get that?" Kaylan asks me.

"I think so, I mean, they are adults who have been in the world a long time, right?" I pour myself a glass of Sprite. "Want some?"

"Sure."

We go to sit on the hammock with our Sprites and keep game planning. For the first time in a while, there's a lightness to everything. There's a small breeze, but it's still pretty warm. The air still has the faintest summer smell. And when it's just Kaylan and me without the lunch table girls, I feel like things can maybe be okay. Strong, even. Like we can still be us, the way we were before camp.

My mom's book club friends start coming in, and it feels nice that she invited some people, too. And then the husbands of the book club ladies traipse in carrying fruit salad platters and stuff.

I'm finishing the last sips of my Sprite when I see Golfy walking through the fence gateway that leads to my backyard.

"Hi, Mrs. Nodberg. I'm Jonah. We met on visiting day, I think," he says, reaching out awkwardly to shake my mom's hand. Seriously, who is this person? Who is Jonah? And also who shakes hands right when they walk into a place like they're a campaigning politician or something?

"Golfy," I yell out, loud enough for him to hear me, but not so loud that my parents and the few other early birds hear me, too.

"Oh, hi!" He waves and then mutters something to my mom, ducking his head a little bit.

"Hello!" he says, all joyful and cheerful sounding, and pulls me into a hug. "Your backyard is super cool."

"It is?" I ask, releasing myself from the hug and looking around. We have an old wooden swing set, a patio with standard outdoor furniture, and a grill.

"It has a very peaceful thing going on," he explains. "I like it."

"Thanks."

Kaylan looks at me crooked, but I just shrug and ask Golfy if he wants any soda.

"I'd love some of that Black Cherry Seltzer," he says. "My favorite."

Kaylan and I both crack up at the same time.

"I am who I am," he says.

We stand around talking about nothing really—where his parents are going for dinner while he's at the barbecue (Gari Sushi), how long he's been going to camp (six years), where is older sister is away at college (Vassar).

Part of me wishes that all of these people could leave so I could be alone with Golfy and we could talk about all the stuff that's been going on. I feel like he'd have interesting perspectives on everything, stuff I haven't thought of.

"Oh, there's Zoe," Golfy says, dipping a pita chip into the hummus.

"We gotta go," I say to him. "Be back soon."

"Uh, okay."

"This wasn't the plan. We weren't supposed to storm over to them," Kaylan whispers to me as we walk over. "We discussed this."

"Oh yeah. I completely zoned out."

"Bad habit alert!" Kaylan taps me on the forehead. "Keep working on it. Anyway, we're walking over now, so we'll just greet them and then we'll go sit and try to get my mom to come over," Kaylan instructs, looking around, probably to locate her mom.

"Zoe, love of my life." I run the last few steps to meet her and wrap my arms around her neck, pulling her in for the tightest hug possible.

"Hey, thanks so much." Kaylan feigns some anger.

"You're the love of my life, too." I reach an arm over her shoulder and pull her in, too, and soon we're in a group hug even though Zoe and Kaylan don't really know each other.

Life is weird like that. Sometimes you end up in group hugs you didn't expect to be in. Sometimes you throw a barbecue to set up your first best friend's mom with your new friend's dad just to complete something on a list you and first best friend made up and are continuing because that's just the kind of people you are.

"Where's your dad?" I ask Zoe, suddenly panicked that he had to go somewhere else and he just dropped her off.

"You're never going to believe this," she starts.

Uh-oh.

"He's already talking to Kaylan's mom. She was out front getting something from the car and then he was trying to park behind her but he's a terrible parker and he ended up having me get out of the car to see if he was too far from the curb and then Kaylan's mom started to weigh in, but in a totally normal, funny way, and then they just kept talking."

"OMG, that sounds insane." Kaylan laughs. "My mom always talks to people she doesn't know. I'm not sure what that's all about."

"It really wasn't insane," Zoe says, now laughing, too. "It sounds like it, but it wasn't."

"Is it weird that it doesn't sound that insane to me?" I push up my cheeks. "Just normal parking on the street kind of stuff." I turn to Zoe. "Sorry our driveway was full."

"That's okay," she replies. "Sorry we were late."

She looks at me, eyebrows raised. "So Golfy is here. . . ."

"OMG. This is happening," Kaylan says.

Zoe nods. "In all of the years I've known him, I have never seen him like this. He's, like, in looove with her."

"Guys, stop. He's right over there." I roll my eyes. "Can we please go see when my dad is starting the grill? At this rate, people will be sleeping over."

While my dad and I are discussing what meats to grill first, I see the lunch table girls walk in.

Of course they all come together and then all sit at the little table by the swing set, plopping their bags on the grass.

Kaylan goes right over to them.

"Go back and have fun with your friends," my dad

instructs. "It was your idea to have this barbecue, right? Might as well enjoy it."

"You can enjoy it, too," I offer. "It won't cost extra."

I wait for him to laugh, but he doesn't. Maybe now isn't the time for money jokes.

I walk back over to Zoe, Golfy, and Hana.

"So sad AlKal couldn't come," Hana says. "I brought a picture of her so we can feel like she's here. And we will FaceTime her later."

"Fab." I sit down on Zoe's lap since there aren't any extra chairs.

"Those are your school friends?" She looks over to where they're sitting.

"Well, I'm not sure *friends* is the right word." I lift my eyebrows. "We sit together at lunch. And I was good friends with part of the group last year, but it feels like they all really bonded when I was away. And now—who knows."

Hana slow-nods. "Totally get it."

"Make new friends, but keep the old, one is silver"— Golfy pauses in his singing and we all yell out *Silver!* like we do at camp—"and the other's gold."

Everyone turns to look at us like we're crazy, but I don't mind. We crack up and start singing other camp songs. For a few minutes, I completely forget anyone else is even here. It's like Hana, Zoe, Golfy, and I (plus the photo of Alice) are the only people in the world.

Out of the corner of my eye, I see the lunch table girls walking over to us.

"We came to meet your camp friends," Cami says, grabbing a cookie from the platter on the way over. "Hiii, everyone. I'm Cami."

I go around and introduce everyone, and then, much to my surprise, the lunch table girls sit on the grass around us.

"Guys, anyone want to play *Two Truths and a Lie?*" I ask. It was the first thing that popped into my head, and it seems like the kind of game the lunch table girls and the Camp Silver crew would really enjoy. Maybe it's a way to bring everyone together, lighten the mood, merge my two worlds.

A little ding goes off in my head—passion alert? Is bringing people together a passion? Maybe.

"Oh yes! I love that game," Kira says.

"Okay, let's all sit in a circle over here." We walk over to the little corner of the yard that's empty for the moment, and I side-eye Gemma that she shouldn't come over here and bug me. She rolls her eyes, but I think she gets what I'm saying.

"I'll start," Golfy says once we're all seated, stretching his legs out in front of him on the grass. "I once threw up on someone at a baseball game, I once needed my grandfather to bring me a new pair of pants when I was stuck in a bathroom at a basketball game and had a stomach incident, and I once peed myself on the New York City subway."

Everyone cracks up, and I glare at him. "Okay, first of all—ew. That was disgusting." I shake my head. Disgusting and adorable all at the same time. "I'm gonna say the basketball game thing was the lie?" I tilt my head, still questioning my choice.

"Nope! Throw up at a baseball game. But good guess!" He stands up and takes a bow. "Okay, now Ari goes."

I fold my hands together and try to think of something good. "Okay, soooo I once fell asleep at a drum performance, I once rode a camel, and I can touch my tongue to the tip of my nose!"

June stands up and does a little shimmy while she says her answer, "You never fell asleep at a drum performance!"

"Ding-ding-ding! You got it, June!" I smile and stand up to hug her. I've never felt this cuddly with June in my life, but the fact that she figured that out about me really means something—I feel like she knows me.

We keep playing, and I sit there as the lunch table girls and the Camp Silver crew really bond.

We FaceTime Alice in to play, and she says to Cami, "You've never eaten one of those mega-spicy chips. Totally believe that you've gone backstage for every Broadway show you've seen and that you knew how to do a cartwheel when you were two!"

"OMG, I feel like you totally get me, Alice!" Cami squeals, making kissy faces through the phone. "And you're not even here!"

We keep playing until Cami tells us that her mom's on her way to pick them all up. "This has been so much fun, but we have to go—everyone is sleeping over tonight."

"Yeah, thanks for coming." I smile, ignoring the sting of the *everyone*. I mean, we all just had so much fun together. There's no sting. I won't allow myself to feel a sting.

"Best barbecue ever," Kira and June say at the same time.

"Seriously, loved it," M.W. adds. "Smooches to all of you. Yay, Camp Silver!"

We all crack up and wave as the lunch table girls walk out of the backyard.

"I'm going to get more soda," Zoe announces. "Anyone want any?"

We all shake our heads.

"Um, love connection," I lean in to whisper to Kaylan when I notice her mom and Zoe's dad across the backyard. And then I get an instant pang of *maybe I shouldn't have said that*. "Is this weird for you?"

She raises her left cheek like she's considering it. "Kinda but also not really." She shrugs. "Does that make sense?"

"Yeah, I think so." I put my arm around her. "But they

213

haven't stopped talking all night!"

When Zoe gets back with her soda she says, "They are, like, seriously hitting it off!" She high-fives me and then Kaylan. "Right?"

"Totally," we say at the same time.

The rest of the crowd stays for another hour and then slowly trickles out. We all pick at what's left of the mac and cheese.

"This really came out amazing," Zoe tells us. "It's like professional mac and cheese."

"It is," Golfy confirms. "No doubt about it."

"Fosh," Hana adds, and we all crack up.

"We are culinary geniuses," I add. "Right, Kaylan?"

"Oh, totally!"

"Are you going to JJH or, uh, HHJ or . . . ," Zoe asks, confused.

"You told her about the JHH!" Kaylan squeals.

"It's not a secret," I remind her. "But, anyway, we both JHHed this one already . . ."

Finally Robert Irwin Krieger decides it's time to go, which makes sense since he and Zoe are the last ones here, except for Golfy and his parents.

"This is the weirdest day ever," I whisper to Zoe. "I never would have predicted that my parents and Golfy's parents would be sitting at my backyard table, eating ice cream cake together."

"That was a nice touch," she says.

"We always have ice cream cake at our barbecues. It's, like, a thing. I don't know why."

"It's good."

"How are you feeling about your dad and Kaylan's mom?"

"Um, it's strange, but he seems really happy. I've never seen him sit and talk with people for so long before."

"Really?" I look over at them again.

"Yeah, he usually gets bored after a little while."

I laugh. "Interesting."

"So what about you and Golfy?" she asks me, as we observe him chatting with some of my neighbors.

"He's the greatest, cutest, best boy in the world," I declare like it's a fact and there's no way anyone can debate it.

She rolls her eyes. "Whatever you say."

"What does that even mean, Zoe Krieger? Tell me now."

"He's funny, but he's Golfy. I've told you this before." She raises her eyebrows. "He's a good boy, though. Definitely."

Finally, after a hundred hugs, everyone leaves, and Kaylan and I are in the backyard helping to clean up. There's a gloomy sadness when I realize I don't know when I'll see the camp crew next. It's always better to have a plan in place; it helps take away the slimy missing-someone feeling.

I glance over at my parents scrubbing the grill and spraying the table, and they're actually smiling. The barbecue took their mind off things. It was like a break from the trouble, just for a few hours.

"JHH time," Kaylan yelps, tying the garbage bag. "For Zoe's dad and my mom. And the mac and cheese again, since we didn't JHH that one together."

"For real. I agree."

Jump in the air. High-five. Hug.

"We're crushing this," Kaylan says. "Like, even more than last summer."

"I think so, too," I say.

And after tonight, I feel even more sure about one of my passions—bringing people together. That concept of leadership really makes sense to me. And cheering people up—that's part of it, too.

For sure.

THIRTY

ON MONDAY MORNING, I WAKE up to arguing.

That has to be the absolute worst way to wake up.

"We need to start telling people," my mom says, loud enough for me to overhear from their bedroom to mine. "It's really getting close. Invitations are printed. We need to make new ones and send them out. I mean, this is nuts, Marc."

"I'm doing the best I can, okay?" He stops talking and then I hear their bedroom door close forcefully. Great—now I have to get up and put an ear against the wall to hear this. Although I'm not sure I really want to hear this.

After that it's muffled until I do get out of bed and put my ear against the inner wall of my closet.

"I know you are doing all you can do, and I am grateful. But we need to think big picture here. About our future," my mom says. "You're always very much wait-and-see, and that just isn't working this time."

"I can't deal with this right now. I need to get ready for my interview. I'm running late," my dad says, intensity in his voice. "Please. Just try and relax."

The door opens, and I hear my dad walk down the stairs. I'm not sure what my mom is doing but she doesn't seem to be leaving the bedroom.

"Daddy!" I hear Gemma yelp from downstairs, one of the kitchen chairs screeching against the floor. "Daddy, can you drive me to school today? Please, please."

"Gem, I have a meeting. I'm sorry."

"Daddy!" she whines again, and then the front door closes.

I get dressed and walk downstairs for breakfast, only to find Gemma pouting at the kitchen table.

"Daddy wouldn't drive me to school today."

"Gem, he had to be somewhere. Mom will drive you. Chill out, okay?"

My mom walks into the kitchen and hands me a hard-boiled egg and a piece of toast. "You gotta go, Ar. You're gonna miss the bus."

I'm almost at the bus stop when I get a text from Kaylan.

Kaylan: Getting a ride w/ cami 2day. See u @ skool.

Cami doesn't even live in our section of the neighborhood, so I have no idea why she's getting a ride with her.

So far this day is off to a terrible start—wake up to arguing, listen to little sister whining, eat hard-boiled egg on the way to the bus, ride bus alone.

No thank you, Monday.

I'm covered in negative, gloomy thoughts; a storm cloud is resting on my head. So I think back to camp and Pres and Mindfulness elective.

I try to focus on each step, feel the ground beneath my sneakers. I smell the air—crisp and a little damp.

I feel the soft cotton of my chunky red sweater against my skin.

I'm not so sure this is working, but it's not making me feel any worse.

I get to school and walk to my locker, and Ms. Bix-horn makes an announcement over the loudspeaker that they're interested in adding new clubs this year, and she asks if anyone has any ideas.

"Students should feel free to submit a suggestion, and then the faculty will pick the ones that seem to be the best fit. We only have room for five to seven new clubs this year, but we will reevaluate in January and see which ones have been the most successful. We are looking forward to an engaged and enthusiastic student body!"

I sit down in front of my locker and work on my doodle of the day. Kaylan and Cami walk in together, but I pretend I don't see them. I'm not mad or anything. I just kind of want them to say hi to me first.

I keep doodling and then three hundred light bulbs go off in my brain at the same time.

It feels so bright behind my eyes that I have to blink to get my head to feel normal again.

This is it. The real chance to make my mark.

We could have a Mindfulness Club and help others who experience the same wandering thoughts that I do. I feel like it's on the tip of everyone's tongues, and now's my chance to make it happen.

Can it be my *broken bad habit* and my *make my mark* at the same time?

I guess I can't really decide if I'm making my mark yet anyway. I don't even know if my club will be picked or if anyone will sign up.

Too soon for that one.

Kaylan plops down on the floor and stares at me, like she knows I'm thinking of something, and she waits for me to tell her what it is. But I don't. I can't, not yet, anyway. I need to keep it locked away in my mind until I figure out exactly how I want to approach it. And I mean, what if it doesn't pan out? And then I've told her and everything? It'll be an embarrassing failure.

"OMG! Comedy club!" Kaylan announces. "It's gonna be great. We can perform at school events and assemblies, and then maybe even travel around to nursing homes and stuff, and make people laugh. I've been thinking about this all summer."

"I love it, Kay-Kay!" I hoist myself up off the floor and readjust my backpack straps, about to walk to first period. "But you may be the only funny one in our school. Can anyone else even tell a joke?"

"Other people are funny," June says. "What do you call a group of disorganized cats?"

I shrug. "No idea."

"A cat-astrophe!" She slaps her leg. "See! Funny."

I force a smile. "Good one."

The rest of the girls all have first-period classes in the B wing, so they stay behind to wait for Amirah.

I start walking to the A wing, and then I hear whispering behind my back. But when I turn around to see what's going on, they all stop talking.

It's probably about nothing, but it still feels like something. Like my dress is halfway sticking into my tights, and I didn't realize.

But I'm not even wearing a dress.

I start to feel a little guilty that I didn't tell Kaylan my idea. But the thing is, it's not fully formed yet. It literally just came to me. Kaylan's been thinking about this comedy thing for a really long time.

When I see Ms. Bixhorn on the way to lunch, I pull her aside and tell her I have a really good idea for a club.

"Okay, wonderful, Arianna. Please fill out a sheet in the main office. I will review all of them and then get back to you if it seems to be a good fit." She nods like there's nothing more to say and she has to get going.

"I will, but I really think it's a good idea, and I really think it will add so much to our school, and I really hope you will pick it!" I scrunch up my body tight, like that will make my case stronger. I regret saying *really* that many times.

"Wonderful. Thanks, Ari." She walks away, a math textbook tucked under her right arm and her eyeglasses on the top of her head.

I gotta be honest here—I wanted a more enthusiastic response.

When I get to lunch, all the girls at the table are talking about their ideas. I'm not sure why I thought Kaylan and I were going to be the only ones passionate enough to create a club.

"Oh, I definitely want to do the coloring thing," M.W. says. "I got so into coloring this summer. I bought every book in the bookstore. I even went to the bookstore owner about starting a coloring club, but it never got off the ground."

Then Kaylan starts going on about the comedy troupe and everyone tells her how great it sounds.

"Advice club," Cami says, rubbing her lips together. "I want to have a club where people can come for advice. Like an advice column, but in person, ya know?" She does a slow head nod, like she's überproud of herself for this one.

"Not to burst your bubble, Cam," June starts, picking the crust off of her egg salad sandwich. "But, like, advice columns work because they're anonymous. So an advice club would be super awk, because it'd be face-to-face. Ya know?"

Cami ponders this for a second. "Maybe. But maybe not. Maybe the person giving the advice would be behind a curtain? Kind of like a priest sort of thing."

"Cami, you're Jewish. What do you know from priests?" Amirah laughs her deep laugh and then takes a sip of water.

"Well, I'm half-Jewish." Cami shakes her head. "I'm just saying." She looks down at her brown lunch bag and starts unpacking everything. "You guys, give me time to figure this out. You're so quick to shoot down my ideas."

"Well, we need to figure it all out before you tell Ms. Bixhorn. You want to give it the greatest chance of success," Sydney adds, peeling an orange. "If it seems like it's only half thought out, they may not even put it into the hat. We're looking out for you, Cameron."

The whole table laughs. Sydney is the only one who calls her Cameron, and for some reason it always sounds funny.

"Ari, you're super quiet," Kira remarks. "What's your deal?"

I shrug. "I don't have a deal. Just eating lunch. La-di-da."

They all laugh again. Kaylan side-eyes me like she knows something is up because she always knows when something is up and there's nothing I can do about it.

We all finish eating and discussing clubs and as I'm leaving the cafeteria after lunch, I bump into Marie as she's leaving her Japanese class in the library. "I never see you anymore. I have a bunch of free guest passes for my yoga place," she says. "Wanna come one day? You could try it again."

I consider giving yoga another chance. "Maybe. I'll let you know."

"You're so quiet, Arianna," Marie says. "Are you off in dreamland again, thinking about your camp or whatever?"

I roll my eyes. "Nooo." I elbow her, again reminded about how much I need to work on this mindfulness thing. "You're so critical, Marie Mundlay Burns."

"I hate my middle name! And you know that!" She elbows me now.

"Why? It's your mom's maiden name, and it's cute," I tell her. "You should be more proud of it."

"Who's proud of their middle name?" she gawks. "You're so weird, Arianna Nodberg."

I laugh. "My middle name is Simone, FYI. And I'm proud of it!"

"Noted."

Marie and I walk for a little while, arms linked,

laughing about middle names and who knows what else.

When we pass the gym, I tell her that I need to go to the bathroom. But it's a lie. I really go to the main office and fill out a club idea sheet.

Name: Arianna Nodberg
Grade: 7th
Idea: Mindfulness Club
Purpose: To help the students at Brookside Middle focus on all the magic that's right in front of all of us. To encourage the students to stay present and in the moment in our ever-changing world.

After that, I feel lighter somehow. More in control.

It's really true—taking steps to do something, to make a change, to improve yourself or a situation *does* feel so much better than not really doing anything and just kind of letting it sit there.

I guess Kaylan and I knew that when we came up with the idea for the lists and stuff, but it's always good to have a reminder.

THIRTY-ONE

ON FRIDAY, KAYLAN AND I get to math a little early and look over the list before class starts. Somehow the week has flown by and we've barely discussed it at all. Plus we only have a little over a month to go. Full-on crunch time.

1. Keep our friendship strong.
2. Drink enough water (for a glowing complexion). ✓
3. Make our mark.
4. Master the art of mac and cheese (from scratch!). ✓
5. Perfect our handstand. ✓
6. Help someone else shine.
7. Stay up long enough to watch the sun set and rise. ✓
8. Find the perfect man for Kaylan's mom. ✓

9.   A doodle a day. ✓
10. Tell a boy how we really feel.
11. Pursue a passion (first find one).
12. Break a bad habit. ✓

"We should make a plan to go over our doodles," I tell her. "We haven't compared in a while, and some of mine are really good."

"Definitely. Are you still doodling at 9:04 p.m.? I am."

"Even when you're sleeping at Cami's?" I make a face at her.

"Well, no. On those days, I do it earlier." She glares at me. "But I don't sleep at Cami's that much, you know."

"I know. I'm just kidding." I draw a tiny little heart in the corner of my paper. "OMG." I look at Kaylan and hope she can read my mind.

"What?" she asks.

"Big P. It just happened."

"Right now?" She clenches her teeth. "Really? How do you know?"

I nod. "I just do." I hoist my backpack up off the floor and stand up to head to the bathroom. "Come with me. Please."

She shakes her head a little. "But Mr. Gavinder will be here any minute! And I'm already doing so badly in this class."

"Kay. Please. I've never gotten the big P in school before." I grab her hand. "Come on."

Thankfully she follows me, and we head to the single-stall bathroom by the main entrance.

"Wait outside the door," I instruct, in case anyone tries to come in.

"On it."

I have a little Ziploc bag of big P supplies in the inside pocket of my backpack, so I take out a pad and thankfully I caught it early enough that I don't need to change my undies.

Girls have it so hard, dealing with this on top of every-thing else. Bleeding at random times and random places?

If you explained all of it to aliens from outer space, they'd be seriously freaked out.

I wash my hands and leave the bathroom. I'm so grate-ful to see Kaylan there waiting for me that I hug her tight. "Thank you, thank you, thank you," I whisper.

"Welcome, but we gotta go." She pulls back from the hug. "Come on, we can make it if we run."

"What are you doing this weekend?" I ask her as we're running to class. "Want to sleep over?"

Kaylan hesitates a second before answering. "Um, what's this weekend? Oh yeah, I can't. My mom is insist-ing on family time."

"She is?" I ask.

"Yeah. I don't know."

We get to class just in time and take our seats. I don't have much time to dwell on the big P or Kaylan's family time since Mr. Gavinder starts class right away.

"Who would like to come up to the board to show us how they arrived at the solution from last night's homework?" Mr. Gavinder asks.

Keisha Brown raises her hand, and so do Isabela Gomez-Wright and Owen Tefli and Kenny Youn.

He calls on Owen.

After that, he asks if anyone wants to come up to the board to complete the geometry proof?

Isabela raises her hand, and Kenny and Owen and this boy who just moved here—Rafa Agedob.

He calls on Rafa.

Isabela's sitting right next to me, and it seems like every time she raises her hand for a question, Mr. Gavinder doesn't even notice her.

She looks crestfallen, like math is her main passion in life and she's not getting to live up to her potential. She does love math. And she's so good at it. She was the one who started a Mathletes club last year.

As we leave class, I whisper to Kaylan, "Isabela Gomez-Wright is basically a math genius. Sometimes I watch her working to see her skills. Is that weird?"

"Um, I don't know. I spend the whole class in a cold sweat, furiously trying to copy down whatever Mr. Gavinder writes on the board."

"Well, whatever. Maybe we can get Isabela Gomez-Wright to tutor us."

She thinks for a second, and then laughs. "Why do you call Isabela by her full name?"

I laugh for a second. "It's just that kind of name."

"I guess."

When we're all seated at the lunch table, digging into our sandwiches, I ask the table if anyone else has Mr. Gavinder for math. I know he teaches a few sections of honors and a few sections of regular, so it's possible. I need to get to the bottom of this weird only-calling-on-boys thing.

"I had him last year," Amirah says.

"Did he ever call on girls?"

"Um." Amirah bites into her apple. "No clue, actually. I don't remember."

"I was in that class, too," Kira says. "He really never did. Once in a while, but he usually called on boys."

"So I'm not crazy!" I sit back, feeling a little bit better about this. I still don't know what to do about it. But at least Kaylan and I aren't the only ones who've noticed.

"When are they announcing clubs?" Sydney asks. "Did I tell you guys I decided to add a club? Cheerleading! We can totally cheer for the soccer games."

The whole table goes silent then.

"OMG. Genius," Cami says. "I want to do that!"

"You do?" I recoil.

"Yeah. Why?" She peels her clementine.

"Just seems, so, like, antifeminist," I say.

"Why?" Cami asks again.

I sip my water and say, "Well, do the boys put on matching outfits and cheer for the girls' volleyball games?"

"Um, no," Cami says, and everyone starts laughing. "But for real, since when are you such a feminist?" Cami asks.

"I don't know. I'm not sure I even realized I was." I laugh then, but everyone else has gone silent, even Kaylan, who's spreading cream cheese on a bagel with a plastic knife.

It feels like all the cafeteria noises are getting louder and louder in my head, and I can't take it anymore. Like it's all crashing down on me, and I'm going to end up covered in tuna salad.

I stay quiet after that, finish my lunch, and think about swimming and sunshine and the way the air at Camp Silver smelled right after it rained. I think about mud sliding and making Cup-a-Soups with the bathroom sink water and the way that Alice was able to climb through the tiny space above the rafters that connected bunk nineteen to bunk twenty.

"Earth to Ari!" Kaylan says. "Lunch is over."

"Oh, okay, duh." I laugh, recalling my bad habit. But

then I wonder—is it really such a bad habit? I like to daydream. I like to think about happy times when I'm not feeling 100 percent happy where I am.

I wonder if it's possible for a bad habit to be the tiniest bit good, too.

THIRTY-TWO

"YOU GUYS ARE GOING OUT?" I ask my parents on Saturday night. I'm in the den with Gemma, and we're watching some old show on Nick at Nite when I see my parents all dressed up, coming down the stairs and putting jackets on.

"We are," my mom says. "A potential job opportunity for Dad. And they invited us to Vintage 25 for dinner."

Vintage 25 is this super-nice restaurant downtown near the library. It's known for its steaks, but they have fish too, and lobster, and fancy pastas. But they're most known for their twice-baked potatoes. Seriously, some people go there just for that.

Who even came up with the concept of the twice-baked potato? Did it just occur to someone one day that one baking wasn't enough?

I watch my parents put their coats on, and I perk up in a way I haven't perked up in months. My whole body feels lighter—the troubles are just floating off into the atmosphere somewhere.

"That's so great," I say. "And you guys look so nice. Don't they, Gem?"

"Yeah, you look great." She doesn't even turn around from the TV. Doesn't she understand what a big deal this is? They haven't gone out in months.

In the past I might've been annoyed that they just assumed I would babysit, not even asking me. Not that I've been babysitting Gemma for that long—just since last year. But I don't even care that they didn't ask me because they're going out! Together! To a nice restaurant!

And a possible job, too?

I feel like I've won the lottery.

Too bad Kaylan isn't free to sleep over—this would have been the perfect night for it. A 100 percent guarantee that there would be no parental arguing.

"Be good, girls," my mom says.

"Call if you need anything," my dad reminds us.

After I hear the door close, I turn to Gemma and say, "This is such a good night. Isn't it?"

She doesn't respond.

"Gemma! Mom and Dad seemed happy, didn't they? And they're going out together on a Saturday night." I clap. "To Vintage 25!"

I wiggle my feet excitedly on the coffee table.

"You're so weird getting this excited about Mom and Dad's plans. What is wrong with you?" Gemma asks.

"You don't get it," I mumble. "Never mind. I'm going to order pizza."

I guess nine-year-olds don't really understand the whole job-loss thing. But she has ears—I'm sure she's heard them arguing.

Oh well. She's in her little fourth-grade bubble, and I guess I'll let her stay in happy land for a little bit longer, before the realities of middle school come crashing down on her.

I walk into the kitchen to get the number for Mario's Pizza off the magnet Mom keeps on the refrigerator. They have a new texting system where all you have to do is text your order. It's outstanding.

Ari: 1 large pizza with extra cheese
  1 order of mozzarella sticks
  2 bottles of pink lemonade

I know we should probably be saving money, but Mom and Dad are out for the night and everything feels sparkly and twinkly all of a sudden, so I splurge for the mozzarella sticks and the lemonade. It's good to splurge every now and again.

After I text the order in, I sit down at the kitchen table

scrolling through my email and then checking out Instagram.

And then I see it.

And my sparkly feeling evaporates into a thick cloud of dusty smoke.

My whole body feels like it's been plunged into the giant pizza oven at Mario's. My ears are singeing and the echo of whatever Gemma's watching on TV pounds in my head.

Right there, on my phone, is a picture of Cami. And June. And Lizzie. And Amirah. And M.W. And Sydney. And Kira. And Marie.

And Kaylan.

Arm in arm at Lizzie's bat mitzvah.

All of them.

Everyone.

Together.

Lizzie is wearing a turquoise spaghetti strap dress with sequins on the top. Kaylan is holding some inflatable microphone and June and Cami are wearing matching hot-pink top hats.

They're having the best time together.

Without me.

Five minutes later, Kaylan posts another picture with the group—this time with Jason in the back spreading his arms out over their heads.

I look up at the top of the screen and see all of their Instagram stories.

So many of Kaylan's—everyone dancing, drinking Shirley Temples, Lizzie held high in the chair.

How could she do this to me?

They were all invited. Kaylan didn't even tell me about it.

And then she posts about it? Posts on Instagram where she knows I'll see it.

I mean, the least she could've done was not post, not rub it in my face that they're all having a great time and I'm not there.

This stings like someone poured rubbing alcohol on my head.

It's worse than over the summer when this happened with the ice cream, because now Kaylan is there, too. And she lied to me about what she was doing over the weekend.

I scroll through the stories, and I can see everything that's happening at the party. It's like I'm peering into someone's window, shivering cold outside in a blizzard, but I can see the warm fire blazing in their fireplace.

I can see what I'm missing. I can see that a good time is going on.

I know I'm not part of it.

When the doorbell rings fifteen minutes later with the

pizza, mozzarella sticks, and lemonade, I plop it all down on the coffee table in the den, in front of Gemma.

So much for the splurge dinner. And the sparkly feeling.

I can't eat a thing.

THIRTY-THREE

IT'S THE NEXT MORNING, AND I'm still seething from the Lizzie bat mitzvah Instagram incident. And I have to babysit Gemma. Again.

My parents need to go meet with a lawyer to rearrange my grandma's finances. Whatever that means. I don't know.

My grandma lives close to us, so we see her all the time, and she always needs help with everything. And Bubbie and Zeyda live kinda far away, so we don't see them as often, but when we do, it's super special. And they never really need any help, or at least I don't think they do.

"Ari, please make sure you do all of the homework. When Ms. Fineman called to say you forgot the last page of the history packet last week, it was very concerning."

My mom holds her head at the kitchen table. "And to be honest, the scores on your last few science quizzes haven't been ideal, either. I know it's harder this year, so it's going to take a little more effort. Up until now you've been able to sort of scoot by. But this is seventh grade. The real deal here, and I . . ."

I tune out the end. There are only so many times I can hear this.

"I know, Mom. Got it."

When my parents leave, I do my homework, little by little, taking breaks to watch TV with Gemma.

I keep my phone visible and on ring so I'll be ready when Kaylan calls or texts. I don't know what I'll say to her, but it'll come to me.

"Ari, can you please make us some popcorn? I'm starving," Gemma says, tucking her legs under herself. "Please."

"Fine." I grumble. I get up and scan the pantry for the popcorn. Usually it's right in front, but I don't see it today.

I'm moving stuff around to find it. I look behind the cereal, near the boxes of pasta. I get on my tiptoes to see the top shelf where my mom keeps the sugar and the flour and other baking stuff. I kneel down to look on the bottom shelves—near the paper towels and boxes of tissues.

No sign of popcorn.

I scan the middle shelves. I take out the peanut butter

and the jars of jam my mom and dad got as a wedding favor last summer to see if it's hiding behind there.

Nope.

I'm pushing aside the pesto and the vodka sauce when two entire glass jars of marinara sauce fall to the floor. They crack on the Italian tile my mom was obsessed with when we redid the kitchen a few years ago.

The sauce splatters all over the kitchen floor, onto my gray leggings. Some even gets on the walls.

At first I'm so shocked that it even happened, I just stare at the mess, not even quite sure how to pick it up. I don't yell or anything—I'm literally speechless.

"Are you okay?" Gemma yells from the den. "What happened? And where's my popcorn?"

"Hold on a minute!" I yell back.

I take a deep breath and attempt to clean up the mess.

I sweep up the shards and spray the floor with our grapefruit countertop spray. I think I get everything.

And then I keep searching for the popcorn.

I scan the cabinets, wondering if my mom moved the popcorn somewhere else. Nope. Not in the cabinets, either. So I go back to the pantry. And when I open the door, it half falls off.

Literally.

"Oh my God!" I scream. "What is happening?"

How does a door even fall off? I'm not sure. It comes loose from a hinge, and I have no idea how to put it back on. So I just leave it there, half hanging off.

"Gemma, there's no popcorn!" I scream.

"Yes, there is! Mom left a bag on the kitchen table."

When I spin around, I see it. Right there. On the kitchen table.

Rolling my eyes at the world, I put the bag of popcorn in the microwave, and right next to it is a letter addressed to my parents in the most beautiful handwriting I've ever seen.

I know I shouldn't open it, but when you see something like this, you almost have to. It's staring at you. You don't have a choice.

Dear Mr. and Mrs. Nodberg:

My name is Eve Bowlin, and my husband and I have been searching for a house in Brookside for quite some time. As you know, the market is competitive. We are expecting twins early next year, and we have our hearts set on your home. You probably have no intention of selling. But when we first drove by and saw the big bay window and the hammock and the porch swing—we just fell in love. We would love to raise our family there, and we are prepared to make you an outstanding offer.

Please give it some consideration.

All our very best,

Eve and Anthony Bowlin

I stop reading because I'm so furious—they include their email and their phone number and a zillion ways to contact them, like my parents are even going to give this a second thought.

Is this a thing—people just writing letters to other people they don't even know, saying they fell in love with their house? This cannot be normal. Eve and Anthony Bowlin—whoever they are—are clearly crazy. I don't care about them or their twins. This is my home. That is my bay window and my porch swing and my hammock.

I crumple the paper in my hands, as forcefully as possible, until it's a tiny ball. Forget you, Eve and Anthony. Find another house.

I shove the ball in my sweatshirt pocket, pour the popcorn into a bowl, and walk out of the kitchen.

I try to ignore the pantry door hanging off and the light bulb in the hallway that needs replacing.

I keep walking.

And then I step on a shard of broken tomato sauce jar.

"Everything is broken!" I scream. "Everything! Every little thing is broken!"

"Ari?" Gemma runs in, staring at me like I'm standing there wearing a bikini and a fur coat doing a tap dance.

"Everything is broken," I repeat. "I swear, everything is broken!"

"What's going on in here?" My mom storms in, carrying

a stack of file folders. "What is happening? Why is there tomato sauce on the wall?"

"Everything is broken!" I scream again.

"What's gotten into her?" my dad asks. "I've never seen her like this."

"Me neither," my mom says softly.

Gemma takes the bowl of popcorn out of my hands and walks into the den. I hesitate a second, and then I follow along behind her.

Kaylan was right—it's not possible to stay chill when everything is falling apart around you. I've tried. I've tried for so long.

I just can't anymore.

THIRTY-FOUR

KAYLAN DOESN'T CALL OR TEXT me all weekend. And I don't call or text her, either.

At the bus on Monday, I wait for her to say something. I know she knows I saw her Instagram story.

She doesn't say anything. Well, she does, but not about that.

"Jason and I are on again, by the way."

"Oh, cool."

"I told him how I feel. Again." She laughs. "So I JHHed that one. Again."

I force a smile. "Nice, Kay."

We're quiet after that, and for the rest of the ride, until we get to school, and then I can't take it anymore.

"You lied to me, Kaylan, and you're just, like, pretending everything is fine," I say to her, stopping to talk outside the main doors before we go into the building.

She stares at me.

"About Lizzie's bat mitzvah. You said you couldn't sleep over because it was family time with your mom. You lied to me. And then you posted about it!" I hiss, feeling all the blood start circling around my brain. I take my jacket off because it feels like the earth is three thousand degrees right now.

"I didn't tell you because I didn't want to hurt your feelings that you weren't invited," she explains. "Remember that talk we had on visiting day? TH or PF? You said you're PF sometimes!"

I nod. When Kaylan first mentioned the whole thing, it seemed sort of silly. But it popped into my mind more often than I expected it to.

She goes on, "Anyway, I was lab partners with Lizzie last year, and then we all hung with her at the pool while you were at camp, and so, like, it just sort of happened that we all became friends. She actually invited everyone else kinda last minute."

I glare at her. "Well, why did you need to post about it? When you knew I would see?" I'm talking so fast that I accidentally spit on my shirt and have to wipe it away.

"Everyone was posting, and we were having so much fun," Kaylan says, looking at the grass. "I didn't think it was such a big deal."

"So? You knew I would see it! That's not PF at all! It's,

like, the opposite of PF! Do you know how bad that makes someone feel? To see everyone they know out doing something fun, and to know they're not a part of it?" I choke back tears.

"Ari, you really never cared about this stuff before." Kaylan looks into my eyes. "I can't believe how seriously you've thought about this!"

"Well, I care now! And I am serious about it. It hurt me so bad, like someone put out a candle on my arm. That's how much it hurt. Worse, even!"

The rest of the lunch table girls walk by and almost stop to talk to us, but then Kaylan waves them away.

"I honestly didn't think you would even notice." Kaylan takes her backpack off her shoulders and puts it on the grass. "Camp is all that matters to you! Camp this and camp that. And Alice and Golfy and whatever. You don't care about these girls, Ari! Just admit it." She pauses. "Camp is all that matters to you."

"Not true," I say softly. "You know I check Instagram all the time, so you knew I would notice. And besides, obviously you matter—I've been working so hard at keeping our friendship strong!"

"So have I!" Kaylan yells. "That doesn't mean we're only going to hang with each other. You can't have your camp friends on the side but then expect me to only be friends with you. Weren't you the one who invited Marie to do the list with us last year?"

"That has nothing to do with it!" I yell.

"Yes, it does. Now, come on. We're going to be late." She picks her backpack up off the grass and walks into school.

"You're not coming in with me?" She turns around when she's almost at the door.

I shake my head.

"Let's just take a break from each other, okay?" she yells back. "It doesn't matter if we're trying. Our friendship isn't staying strong, and I think we need a break before it totally falls apart."

"Fine! Whatever you say!"

I lean against the brick building and cry, wiping my tears on the sleeve of my fleece-lined jean jacket.

I take the list out of my bag and rip it to pieces, shoving them all in the front pocket of my backpack.

Barely any of it even makes sense to me anymore.

I don't need to tell a boy how I really feel. I need to tell Kaylan how I really feel. And I did. And my bad habit isn't daydreaming. It's the fact that I keep everything bottled up, that I never tell anyone what I'm feeling.

Well, I think I just broke it. I spoke my mind.

And keeping our friendship strong—forget about it.

It's impossible.

We're too different, and too much has happened.

I ask my guidance counselor if I can switch into Marie's Japanese class so I don't have to eat lunch at my usual table, but I'm told I have to wait until January to do that.

So I sit at our table in the cafeteria, and everyone talks around me, and I pretend I'm not there.

"Guys, we didn't officially decide on Halloween costumes," Cami says. "And are we doing the town parade and then trick-or-treating? Or just going to Jay Yeung's party?"

I look up from my chicken salad sandwich, and Cami says, "Literally the whole grade is invited. Check his Insta. It says it right there."

I'm not sure if she's saying that to alert the whole table or just me, but even though it really means nothing, it feels nice to be included along with everyone else.

"Let's go to Jay's and then leave early for some end-of-the-night trick-or-treating," Kira declares. "We're not too old."

"I agree," Amirah replies. "I like this plan."

Everyone else says, "Me too," so I offer a smile like I'm in, even though it feels weird to be in on something with Kaylan when we're in a not-speaking-to-each-other, in-a-break kind of fight.

"And costumes?" Cami asks. "We need something for—" She looks around the table and counts everyone. "Nine, or uh, eight, I guess—depends on if Ari's coming. Marie already said she is, so I counted her. And Lizzie said she's not dressing up this year."

She raises her eyebrows at me. "Are you doing Halloween with us?"

"Sure, um, I hadn't thought about it, really." I look over at Kaylan, but she's not paying attention, on purpose, I think.

Cami shrugs. "It'll be weird if you and Kaylan aren't speaking, but . . ." Her voice trails off.

"Let's all be different candies," Sydney suggests. "I saw these costumes online. They're like candy dresses. Super cute and easy. And there are definitely at least nine."

"Or Starbucks cups!" Amirah squeals. "How awesome!"

Cami considers that. "But then we'd all be the same."

"Crayons!" Kaylan yells. "Kind of like a throwback to our younger days. It would be so cute."

They keep talking about this, and I just sit there and listen and eat my lunch.

I really hope Kaylan and I are speaking by Halloween. Not only for the costume situation, but for the list situation and the general day-to-day life situation.

It's never fun to be in a not-speaking, on-a-break kind of fight.

THIRTY-FIVE

AFTER SCHOOL, MY MOM PICKS me up because I have a bat mitzvah lesson.

I don't bother to text Kaylan that I won't be on the bus ride home. I don't think she'll care either way.

"Eleanor Feldman says this same thing happened to Ashley when she was your age," my mom says, turning down the music in the car.

"Huh?"

"I stopped in to talk to her today." She looks over at me, but I don't make eye contact. "I was concerned about what I saw when we got home yesterday."

"So you talked to the executive director of our temple about it?" I shriek. "Mom! That is so humiliating."

"Why? She's lovely, she's a mother, and she's very wise, Ari."

I don't respond.

My mom continues. "And it's a lot happening at once—big changes. Not only at school, but hormonally, and your body has to keep up, and it's a lot. I mean, Ari, look at how much you've devel—"

"Mom!" I scream. "Stop! Ew! This is so inappropriate! Stop. You can't just go talking about me to a woman I barely know. I am humiliated. Now how am I going to even look at her? Uch. How can I even walk into the temple and see her? This is madness."

"Ari."

"Stop saying my name!"

"This is so unlike you," she says. "I've never seen you so worked up so often."

I roll my eyes at the windshield. "Well, probably because I always try to keep calm because you and Kaylan are always freaking out! So I am forced to be the calm one."

It only starts to make sense as I say it. It's not only about staying chill when things are chill. It's about needing to stay chill because no one else is.

"That's not true," my mom mumbles.

"It is true. You know it. I'm the one who always has to calm everyone down!" I yell. "And I'm over it!"

We get to the temple, and I pray a thousand times that I don't run into Eleanor Feldman on the way to the cantor's office.

I'm so glad the temple administrator knows all the details about my body.

Gross.

I walk into the cantor's office, and who do I find sitting there on one of the chairs facing her desk?

Eleanor Feldman.

Thanks, God. Clearly you didn't answer my prayers. Maybe you didn't hear them.

"Hello, Arianna," she says, all cheery. "I just saw your mom earlier." She gets up from the chair. "Have a good lesson."

"Thanks."

I sit down and take out my bat mitzvah folder.

"How are things?" Cantor Simon asks.

I think back to the list, and what I just told my mom in the car, and the whole fight with Kaylan. "Eh, could be better," I say.

It feels like I just took off a tight wool scarf that was itching me and choking me, and now my neck can finally breathe again.

"Yeah? How come?"

"Well, I guess it all started when I went away to camp this summer," I begin, and then I pretty much tell her everything—about the list, and Kaylan and the lunch table girls and the Instagram stories from Lizzie's bat mitzvah, and how Kaylan thinks I'm obsessed with camp, and my parents, and my dad's job, and the bagel bat mitzvah plan. It feels like I talk for a really long time.

"Wow. That is a lot for one person to handle," she says.

"And I'm still a kid!" I remind her. "For a few more weeks, at least."

"That's true." Cantor Simon smiles, pausing to think. "You know, the bar and bat mitzvah party as we know it today is kind of a new phenomenon. It wasn't always like this. Yes, we are celebrating an amazing life cycle event. However, bagels and music and good company is certainly a lovely celebration."

"I know, but everyone goes crazy here. It feels depressing to just have bagels at the temple—no offense—when everyone else has these amazing parties." I look at her, almost regretting my words. "Is it wrong to admit that?"

"Not at all. And I understand how you feel," she says. "The feeling of wanting to keep up and needing to keep up is very real and very difficult. At all ages."

I nod.

"And it's hard to go away for the summer and come back and find things to be a little wobbly," she tells me. "I remember there was always a transition period when I got home. And my friends would seem really different. And I would feel different. It was tough."

"Exactly." I close my eyes and tilt my head back against the chair. "So what should I do?"

"Well," she starts, and clears her throat. "Like everything in life, as we've been discussing, it takes time. I think you can tell Kaylan how you feel, though. That you love camp and your new friends, but you love her, too. And that you do care about being friends with the lunch table girls." She laughs. "That's what you call them, right?"

I laugh too. "Yeah."

"I'm glad you felt comfortable enough to share all of that with me." She sits back in her chair. "Do you feel better that you told me? Or worse? Or somewhere in the middle?"

I think for a second. "Somewhere in the middle. I liked being the kind of person who listened to everyone else's problems, and helped, and cheered them up. I liked being the chill one who never really needed to talk things out or vent or whatever. But I guess it's not always possible. I guess we're not all the same thing all the time."

"That is a perfect segue into your Torah portion . . . and I know you're still figuring out your speech." She smiles. "Are you struggling with it still?"

I nod. "Yes. Definitely. I've scrapped three drafts already."

"So I think this may help. As you know, your portion is called: *Chayei* Sarah. The Life of Sarah. It's called the Life of Sarah, even though it's also very much about her death. Let's discuss."

"Okay." I smile, letting my shoulders relax. "I think that's why I like learning about Judaism so much. There seem to be so many similarities between our biblical ancestors and us today. It's like we kind of have a guide-book to follow. And, like, it's something to lean on during hard times."

"Ding-ding-ding! Are you planning on highlighting that in your speech?" she asks.

I laugh a little. "The thing is, it just feels so important. And every time I start to write, I get a different idea of what I want to say. Like, my feelings about everything Judaism related are still kind of evolving."

Cantor Simon nods. "I see. That's understandable."

I scrunch up my face. "And I know I'm running out of time."

"Right. Eventually we'll have to get some words down," she says. "But I think discussing the Torah portion more in depth will help you."

It's kind of amazing to me how Cantor Simon has so many bar and bat mitzvah students this year—like fifty at least—and yet she makes me feel like I'm the only one, devoting so much time and energy to my spiritual journey.

I think that's another example of a good leader. Making the person you're talking to feel like the only person in the world.

Later that night, after my homework is done, I'm still thinking about my bat mitzvah lesson. I text Alice to check in.

Ari: how r u feeling bat mitzvah wise?

Alice: um like I still have tons to do

Ari: no I mean like r u loving the prep stuff?

Alice: loving it nahhh but it's ok

Ari: how is ur gma?

Alice: she's better. not much going on here. so much
hw

Alice: ack! just got in soooooo much trouble

Alice: gg explain l8r

Ari: ok xo

Ten minutes later, my phone dings that I have an email.
From Alice.

> OMG. Phone confiscated. For texting during
> homework time even though my mom told
> me a million times not to. UGH. I shouldn't
> be emailing this, but I told her u would worry
> if I just disappeared forever. Pray for me.
> XOXOOXXXOXOXOXXOXOXO AIKAI

I didn't even have a chance to tell her about my fight
with Kaylan, and who knows when she'll get her phone
back. Maybe I should just write her an old-fashioned letter. It may be the fastest way to communicate now.

THIRTY-SIX

MY BREAK WITH KAYLAN GOES on for a few more days.

We don't talk or text or FaceTime or anything. We see each other at school and I still sit at the lunch table, but we just sort of exist near each other.

I think about what Cantor Simon said, and I do want to talk to Kaylan about it. But everything just feels too fragile to bring it all to the surface again. It's easier to bury it for a little while. Not forever. Just for a little.

And the only time I really see Kaylan, other than lunch, is during math. She changed her seat and seems way more focused now. I'm not sure if that has anything to do with me or not. But there's not really a time for us to talk about it.

"Good morning. I'd like to highlight everyone who got a one hundred percent on the pop quiz the other day," Mr.

Gavinder says, starting class. "These peers are an example for everyone. Good work Rafa, Owen, Kenny, Daniel, and Seth."

Owen stands up and starts clapping in an over-the-top jokey way, and Mr. Gavinder tells him to sit down. "Now, please now turn to page seventy-three in the textbook and take out a pencil and some lined paper," he tells us.

Isabela turns to me and shows me her paper. "I got a hundred, too."

"That's so weird," I whisper.

She shakes her head. "I don't get it."

"Isabela, you need to tell him," I insist.

She shrugs. "Whatever, it's fine. I'm sure he just forgot."

"You need to tell him," I repeat. "It's not right. Also, he never calls on you. You raise your hand for every question!"

She shrugs again and then focuses her attention on the board.

I look over at Kaylan, sitting in the front row now with her glasses on, copying down every number that's written on the board.

After class, Kaylan and I walk out at the same time, but it's not exactly like we're walking together. We're just sort of going down the hallway at the same pace.

We pass Isabela, sitting on the wooden bench in the main lobby.

"Are you okay?" I ask her.

"Stomachache. Going home early."

I scrunch up my face. "Feel better."

Once we're far enough away that Isabela can't hear us, I catch up to Kaylan and say, "Okay, I know we're not really talking, but I just had an epiphany. For our list. And it involves Isabela."

Kaylan looks at me, confused.

We duck into an empty classroom, and I whisper, "For *help someone else shine*. She is already shining, and Mr. Gavinder isn't noticing! We need to make sure he notices."

"Um, how can we do that, though?" Kaylan looks up at the clock. "I got a sixty-seven on that quiz, by the way."

I ignore the fact that Kaylan seems to be changing the topic. "Isabela is never gonna stand up for herself," I explain. "We need to do it."

"Ari, I'm on board," Kaylan says, looking right at me, putting her hands on my shoulders. "I just don't know how to do it."

"Well, let's be thinking," I say. "We have until my bat mitzvah to fix this, and to help Isabela shine."

Kaylan nods. "Yes."

She starts walking ahead of me, but then I touch her shoulder and ask, "Can we talk later? For real?"

"Sure." She shrugs. "I didn't think our break would last forever. Duh. That's why it's called a break."

I laugh for a second. Kaylan can always make tense situations feel funny, at least for a moment or two.

"Come over after school, okay?" I shake my head up and down, hoping she'll agree.

"Okay."

Kaylan and I take the bus together and then walk over to my house. It's a funny feeling to know you're about to have a big conversation, so you just kind of stay quiet until it happens. It feels like the few moments that pass between walking into the examining room at the doctor's office and then waiting for the doctor to come in with your shots. You know it's coming. All you can do is wait.

When we get home, I find another one of my mom's famous kitchen table notes.

Hi, Ari,

Gemma is going over to Sally's after school. Dad and I have an appointment. We'll all be home for dinner. Please do your homework, practice for your bat mitzvah, etc.

Empty the dishwasher if you have time.

Thank you.

Love, Mom

"Does she realize that you have a phone and she can just text you?" Kaylan asks me, scanning the pantry for a snack. "What happened here?" She points to the broken door.

"Oh, it fell off the hinge a few weeks ago. Be careful of the crisper drawer in the fridge. That's broken, too."

"Noted."

We grab a few mini bags of pretzels and little bottles of iced tea and head up the stairs to my room.

"I see you've redecorated since I've been here last," Kaylan remarks, noticing my camp pictures all over the walls.

"You're represented, too." I show her the bulletin, aka the shrine of Kaylan and Ari through the years.

"Good." She kicks off her sneakers and goes to sit on my bed. "So what's up?"

I laugh for a second. "Um, well, I wanted to talk to you, because—" The phone rings. "Oops, hold that thought."

"Hi, Bub," I say, answering the phone.

"Hi, doll. How are you? Just wanted to check in."

"I'm good. Kaylan's over now, can I call you back?"

"Of course. Talk later."

I go back to the bed and start the Kaylan conversation again. "So, um, as I was saying. The thing is, I still really want to keep our friendship strong. Do you?"

"Obviously. But what does that even mean, really?" she asks. "We never really said when we made the new list, so . . . Like, did that mean not having new friends?"

In a way, it kind of feels like she's attacking me, but I

don't want this conversation to be like that. I want it to be calm, and relaxed, and thoughtful. "No, of course not. And it didn't mean skipping fun and new experiences just because the other one wasn't a part of it, right?"

She shakes her head. "No."

"So . . ."

Kaylan leans back against my pillows. "So . . ."

"I'm sorry if I made you feel that I only cared about camp," I tell her. "So not true. I care about you a zillion percent."

"And what about the lunch table girls?"

"I care about them, and I want to be friends with them. But can I be honest?"

She nods.

"They're kind of mean sometimes. They made me feel bad about my bat mitzvah party changing, and I don't know—sometimes they're a little intense. They all just follow Cami, and I wasn't sure they even really wanted me around."

"They can be intense, sometimes, yeah," Kaylan says, scratching her eyebrow. "But not all the time. And I think they do want you around. I'm sorry if I made you feel like you weren't included in stuff, also sorry I posted those Instagram stories."

"I think the bottom line is that we need to stay strong while also realizing that our friendship won't totally stay the same," I tell her. "Ya know? And you hate change, obviously. But you're also much better with it now."

"I am?" Kaylan shrieks.

"I think so." I lie back next to her. "And you barely freak out anymore. You can totally JHH that bad habit."

She hops up off the bed and JHHs by herself, but then runs over to high-five me.

"I think you were right about my bad habit," I tell her. "I started telling the cantor how I really feel about stuff, and it was a relief, in a way. I really have been keeping things bottled up."

"And you can lean on me, too, ya know . . . and the lunch table girls." Kaylan sits up and rests her head on her palm. "I mean, we're here for you. It's way harder to get through all this stuff on your own."

"I know. I'm gonna try. It's just that you get used to being one way for so long, it's hard to change. . . ."

"Hello! You're telling me this? Duh. I know!" She rolls her eyes. "You can do it."

I stand up and scroll through my phone for a good summer song. I turn it on and then jump off the bed, grabbing a handful of pens from my desk for the microphone.

I start snapping with my other hand. *"Havana ooh na na!"*

Kaylan says "hey" at just the right time and hops off the bed to join me.

"Ooh ooh ooh," she sings into her fist.

I burst out laughing and then we sing through the chorus together.

At the end of the song, we fall back onto the bed. "No one dance parties like we dance party," I tell Kaylan.

"No. Definitely not. We are dance party champions. Forever."

I add, "And ever."

THIRTY-SEVEN

I FEEL BETTER ABOUT THE Kaylan fight, but I still barely sleep that night. I'm tossing and turning and trying to figure out what we can do about the Isabela thing, and my mind keeps going back to that leadership program at camp. Helping someone else shine is a key part of leadership.

She should be shining.

One day she will stop raising her hand, and Mr. Gavinder won't even notice. She'll lose all her confidence in math. She'll stop caring about it. And she won't even really know why or how it happened.

The next morning, I'm half-asleep at the kitchen table, sipping my orange juice, when my mom asks my dad what's on his agenda for the day. She does this every morning. And that's the exact moment they start arguing.

It usually goes like this: If he says nothing, or "applying for jobs" in a short kind of way, she gets annoyed. And then he criticizes her for not being supportive. And then they look at me all sad and pathetic. And I try to pretend I haven't heard them arguing and that all is totally fine, and I'm strong and happy and school is great and I'm thrilled about an only-bagel bat mitzvah.

I guess I still have more work to do in terms of keeping feelings to myself. I'm midsip of my orange juice when it occurs to me.

I can't keep pretending that everything is fine.

The boy I need to *tell how I really feel* is actually my dad.

And I need to do it soon.

"I just have one question," I say to my mom's back as she's scrambling a few eggs for Gemma and me. My dad has left the kitchen and gone upstairs to stare blankly at his computer. I've seen him do it, and it's pretty scary—those empty eyes, the brightness of the screen. It's like he's entering an abyss, and I don't know when or if we will get him back.

"Yes?" my mom asks, forcing her voice to be cheerful.

"Remember when you were obsessing over the party favors for my bat mitzvah? And you wanted to design a logo and stuff? And then you decided on a hoodie?" I pause, waiting for my mom to chime in. She doesn't. "I just wondered if you ever ordered them or if you canceled it or whatever." I pause again. She's still silent.

"People at school were asking me."

She finally turns around and pulls out a chair to sit down at the kitchen table next to me.

She looks at me for a few seconds, like she's debating what to say. "I was waiting to order them, Ari. I wanted to see who was coming so we could get them personalized. I wanted a little embroidered name on the corner of each hoodie." She rolls her lips together, and a few tears trickle down from her eyelids. "Dad's promotion was supposed to come through. None of this was supposed to be an issue."

"I'm kind of sad about this, Mom," I tell her.

"I know. I am too." She's quiet for a few seconds and then she says, "Have you seen a letter around here? It was kind of important. Someone wanted to get in touch with us. It was right on the counter, next to the microwave. And now I can't seem to find it."

I look at her, straight in the eyes. "I have no idea what you're talking about."

I was kind of hoping she'd come up with some alternative plan for the giveaway, like buying a ton of white T-shirts and ironing something cool on them. But she doesn't. She's lost in her own world and isn't willing to improvise.

I walk up the stairs and crawl back into bed. I have ten minutes before I need to leave for the bus, and I'm not hungry for breakfast anyway.

I feel a little guilty for lying to her about the letter. But not that guilty.

When Kaylan and I get to school, all the lunch table girls are hanging out on the floor by our lockers.

"I told everyone we made up," Kaylan whispers as we walk over there. "Just FYI."

"Oh, um, okay." I start unpacking my books and lining them up on the top shelf of my locker.

"And I told them you're going to start opening up and stuff," she continues. "Like leaning on us, and we'll all feel like real friends."

"Kay." I crack up so hard I can't talk. "Did you leave anything for me to say?"

"Um, yeah, that's all I said to them. . . ."

I hug her for a second and then sit down in front of my locker.

"So glad you guys are talking again!" Cami puts her arms around Kaylan and me. "Seriously. So, so happy."

I pull back after a few seconds. "Me too."

"And you can talk to me about anything at any time," Cami says. "You know that, right?"

I nod, forcing myself not to laugh. This girl is way too much, especially for this early in the morning.

"They're announcing the clubs this morning!" Cami says loudly so everyone can hear, doing a little shimmy. "Get excited!"

I look at my watch and realize the first bell will ring in approximately nine minutes. "When?"

"Before first bell," Cami declares.

I take out my notebook to start reviewing my Spanish vocabulary words. The girls keep talking all around me, but I try to tune them out. Even Kaylan is going on and on about what the comedy club will do, and how they can have a comedy showcase at the end of the year and maybe even some famous comedians will come.

Even though I feel great about the Kaylan stuff, I have this slimy feeling about that letter from Anthony and Eve Bowlin, and an even slimier feeling about how I lied to my mom. I start to wonder if selling the house would really save everything. Maybe I should dig it out and give it to her.

Abuelo—grandfather

Abuela—grandmother

Hermana—sister

I look at my watch again. "Guys, first bell is literally going off in a minute. Where is this announcement?"

Cami looks around. "She said she was announcing! I am so confused. I really thought that—"

She's cut off when we hear the chime signaling that an announcement is about to start. We all look at one another, tense expressions on our faces. I didn't expect this to become so hectic. I didn't even think most people would suggest clubs. Now it's like we're in some kind of competition we didn't plan or want or even know we were in.

"Hello, Brookside Middle School students! Good morning on this bright and sunny day! I am thrilled to announce the new additions to our outstanding after-school clubs roster. We had many more entries than we ever expected, and all were incredible ideas." Ms. Bixhorn pauses and clears her throat. "If your club wasn't picked, don't worry. We will accept more submissions midyear when we have a better sense of everyone's interests." She pauses again.

"OMG, she is so slow," Amirah whines.

Kaylan shushes her.

"The selections are: Krav Maga, Israeli self-defense . . ." The girls and I stare at one another. "Ultimate Frisbee, Social Action Task Force, Dance Team, Cooking Club, Debate Team, and last but not least, Mindfulness Club. Thanks to everyone who entered an idea. Please get to first period calmly and quickly and have an outstanding Brookside Middle School day."

Cami shakes her head at all of us. "I don't get it. Advice is, like, the main thing we all need now. . . ." She walks ahead, not waiting for us, still shaking her head like it's all our fault.

Amirah and June and some of the others try to run

and catch up to her, but I stay back.

"And coloring club is like mindfulness, Arianna!" M.W. says forcefully. "We should have joined forces!"

"Oh, yeah, I didn't think of it." I smile. "But don't worry, there will be other chances."

She shrugs and hoists her backpack over her shoulder and walks away.

Soon it's just Kaylan and me at the lockers. I don't know what to say to her.

"You crushed it," Kaylan says softly.

"Thanks," I say. "I didn't exactly do anything, though. I just suggested it. I'm sorry comedy wasn't picked."

"I'm bummed, but it's okay," she says. "I can still pursue it outside of school, and maybe, like, go to local comedy clubs and see if they want to have some kind of kids in comedy night or something?"

I nod, super enthusiastic. "That's an amazing idea! And you can have kids from other schools, too!"

"Totally," she says, still seeming a touch defeated. "Plus for the list it just said pursue a passion, not finish it. . . ."

"True," I say. "We're still totally on track for the list. And can I be honest?"

"Of course."

I play with the zipper on my hoodie. "I think I may have more than one passion. And I think that's okay?

How can I narrow it down to just one?"

We start walking together. Kaylan says, "That's true. I mean, we just said pursue a passion and find one . . . but we didn't say *only* one."

"Exactly!"

"Oh wait!" She stops in the middle of the hallway. "I wanted this to be for *Make our mark*, too!"

I clench my teeth. "Um, well, you still can! Like you just said with the kids' nights at local comedy clubs . . ."

"But what if I run out of time?"

"Well, we still have some time!"

"I guess. Maybe I need to think of something else for *Make our mark* now." She shakes her head. "Ugh! This isn't going like I expected."

I put an arm around her. "Don't stress. Honestly. You still have a really good idea."

We walk quietly the rest of the way to class with our arms linked.

"We could JHH now for pursuing our passions because we totally are," I suggest. "Would that make you feel better?"

She nods. We go into the single-stall bathroom near the main office and make sure the door is locked. We put our backpacks on the hooks on the back of the door.

"Ready?" I ask.

"Yup!"

Jump in the air. High-five. Hug.

"I think we needed a good JHH," I tell her.

She hugs me again. "I totally agree."

During study hall, I decide to email Alice. How long can she possibly be without her phone? I don't even know how she's surviving.

> **Dear Alice,**
>
> **Did you get your phone back yet? I miss you! I feel like we haven't talked or texted in forever. So much to update you on! They picked my Mindfulness Club idea at school. I'm so excited.**
>
> **Kaylan and I were in a fight, but we made up. So much to explain.**
>
> **I miss you soooooo much! XOXO Ari**

Later that night, I'm out on my front porch in the wicker rocking chair, staring at the falling leaves and trying to ignore my parents fighting inside when my phone rings.

I jump, immediately thinking it's Alice.

But it's Golfy!

"Guess who is going right near Brookside tomorrow for his great-uncle's ninetieth birthday party?" he asks.

"Um."

"Me. Can we hang?" he asks.

"Did you just find out about this party?" I laugh. "It's literally tomorrow."

"Kind of, yeah. No one ever tells me anything . . . sorry it's last minute." He pauses. "Are you free?"

Every part of me wants to say yes, of course, let's go for a long walk and then go sit somewhere near a pretty view and talk all about life and the meaning of everything. Golfy has a good perspective on things. Maybe he can help me sort out the drama with my parents. Now that I know how good it feels to open up to people, I kind of want to do it all the time.

"Are you there?" he asks again.

"I'm here," I say. "I'd love to hang. But where? My house is kind of chaos right now."

"I can handle chaos," he says.

"Your family is perfect, Golfy."

"No family is perfect," he replies. "Anyway, we don't have to hang at your house. We can go bowling or something or mini-golf, or out for ice cream sundaes."

"All of that sounds amazing."

"Okay, then it's set, and you can't back out," he instructs.

"What makes you think I'll back out?" I laugh a little, putting my feet up on the wicker ottoman. The air feels crisp and cool—the epitome of fall. I smell a fire blazing in a fireplace somewhere close to me. I just want to curl up under a cozy blanket and eat some cider donuts. It may not be summer anymore, which is sad, but when the air smells and feels like this, I think you just need to lean into fall and accept and embrace the coziness.

"I just have a weird feeling you might." He laughs too now. "Oh, did they pick your club? You never told me."

"They did! I just found out. I'm so excited."

"That's awesome, Ari!" He stops talking for a second. "Did you hear me clapping?"

"Um, kind of. I'm outside, and it's a little loud out here. The man next door is playing catch with his grandsons, and they keep screaming."

"Well, I'm pumped for you."

"Thanks," I say.

I think I could talk to Golfy for twenty-four hours straight and not get bored or tired or run out of things to say.

I don't know what it is about him. But to me, he is the greatest.

I don't really care that no one else sees it; I see it, and that's what matters.

"I'll call you in the morning to firm up the plans. Okay?"

"Okay."

"Nighty-night, Nodberg."

"Nighty-night, Golfy."

"You can call me Jonah. You know that, right?"

"I know." I laugh for a second. "But is it okay if I call you Golfy?"

"Sure. I was just saying."

"Cool. Good to know."

THIRTY-EIGHT

THE NEXT DAY, I'M GETTING ready to meet Golfy at the Ice Cream Shop when I think I hear Kaylan's voice coming from my kitchen. But she told me she was going shopping with her mom today, and I told her I was seeing Golfy. So I have no idea what she's doing here.

I open my door a tiny crack—just enough so I can hear what's going on down there but not so much that it makes the loud creaking sound and everyone in the world will know I'm listening.

"I have it all figured out," Kaylan says in her quiet voice, which is actually still pretty loud. She can't help it. She just talks in a loud way even when she tries not to. "It's all set."

"Are you sure, Kaylan?" My mom sounds worn out.

"Seems a little hard to organize and a lot for you to take on."

"I'm sure," Kaylan replies. "I got this."

"I don't know. I need to discuss it with Marc."

"You said your brother's done stand-up in LA, right?" Kaylan asks. "I'll definitely need his help. May I have his email, please?"

I'm guessing this is about the kids' nights at the comedy clubs. Since her club didn't get picked, I feel like she'll become even more hard-core about pursuing comedy. Like she literally won't take no for an answer.

She could've just asked me for Uncle David's email.

I try to eavesdrop a little more, but they leave the kitchen and go into my dad's office and then I can't hear them anymore.

By the time I'm finished getting dressed, Kaylan is gone. My mom is still searching all over the house for that letter, and with each day that passes I feel a little more guilty that it's a crumpled ball at the bottom of my desk drawer.

"Was Kaylan here?" I ask Gemma. She's sitting in the den with her feet up on the coffee table watching an old *Full House* episode.

"No clue," she replies. "When was this show on for real? It seems really old."

"No clue," I mimic her. "Where's Mom?"

Gemma shrugs. "I dunno. Somewhere."

She's a lot of help.

"Mom," I say to her back. She's taking every book off the bookshelf in the living room, searching. "Mom," I say again when she doesn't answer me.

"What, Ari?" She finally turns around. Her hair is in her face.

"Was Kaylan here? I thought I heard her."

She ignores my question. "Are you sure you didn't see a letter anywhere? Your father is about to kill me. I misplaced something very important."

"He's about to kill you?" I recoil. "Come on, Mom."

"You know what I mean." She turns around again, hands on her hips. "Let me know if you see a letter. It was in a pale-green envelope."

"Why is this letter so important?" I ask. "I don't get it."

"I can't get into it now, Ari." She pauses. "Have fun with Golfman or, that's not it . . . whatever it is you call him."

"Golfy, Mom."

"Okay."

I wait for her to say more, but she doesn't. It's sad my own mother doesn't take more of an interest in me or my new boy-friend or boyfriend or who knows what he is, but at the very least, he's someone very important to me.

I feel like she'd be all excited about this, wanting to know every detail, so much so that I'd end up finding it annoying.

But no—she's just not herself lately.

I walk to the Ice Cream Shop, and Golfy's already there when I arrive. He's at one of the tables outside, under the purple umbrellas, reading a library book.

"Hi," I say sheepishly. It's been a few weeks since I've seen him, and I think he looks different—his hair is shaggier, he's not wearing a baseball cap, and somehow he looks older in a way, or more mature.

I don't know any boys from my school who would sit alone in a public place reading a library book. But Golfy looks totally natural doing it.

"Oh, hey!" He jumps up and gives me an awkward hug and the sides of our foreheads crash a little bit. "How are you, Noddie?"

"I'm good." I sit back down because it feels strange to just be standing there after a hug. "How are you? How was your great-uncle's party?"

"It was so fab," he says. "He taught everyone how to do this really old-fashioned dance? The fox-trot. He literally led a dance class at his own birthday party. I mean, he's ninety but he's still got it. It was the funniest thing ever."

"He sounds so awesome."

"He really is. My parents are still at his house looking through old photos. He has boxes and boxes. They're trying to make sense of them."

"Oh, that's so nice." I smile. "So? Ice cream."

"Well, duh." He stands up and so do I, and we walk

inside. "What's good here?"

"Well, the espresso cookie is my favorite. But the peaches and cream is also really good. And so is the cookie dough." I shrug. "Basically every flavor is good."

He stares at the flavor list on the wall. "What about the shakes?"

"Also good." I laugh.

"Hmm. This is so hard to pick." He turns around and faces me. "What should I do?"

I shrug. "Get a shake. And I'll get a cone. And we can share?"

"Perfect."

After we have our ice cream and our shake, we go back outside to the tables. He asks, "So what's new? Talk to me."

I take a sip of the chocolate peanut butter shake. "Actually, I kind of have a dilemma," I start.

The whole walk over here, I was debating telling him about the letter situation. I think I need to. It's weighing on me, and my shoulders feel so heavy—I need to discuss this with someone.

"Spill it," he says, taking a bite of the cone.

"So, there was this letter," I start, already feeling my body relax that I'm opening up and talking about this. "And it was so weird. Like, someone drove by our house and decided they needed to buy it and would make any offer." I take another sip of shake. "And I got so mad when I saw it. Like, what the heck? This is our house. And yeah my dad lost his job, but we don't need to sell our house! Not yet! Right?"

"Right . . . I mean, I don't really know, but I guess." He looks at me, waiting for me to continue. "And?"

"And I hid the letter. And my mom is looking all over for it. And she's super stressed. But I just don't think we need to sell our house," I explain. "But now I feel so bad. Should I tell her I have the letter?"

He bites his lip and looks up into the sky like maybe there will be some kind of divine intervention or answer or something. "Noddie . . ." He smiles a nervous kind of smile. "I think you should give back the letter. Just say you found it under a pile of laundry or something. Don't say you stole it. Ya know? And just, like, let it unfold how it's going to unfold."

"Well, there's one other problem . . ." I look down at the table. "I crumpled it up, and it's kind of a mess now."

He nods. "Hmm. Okay. Well, again, the laundry theory works. It got crumpled under some really heavy clothes!"

"But I don't want to move," I whine.

"Ooh! But what if these people are like billionaires and they're willing to pay ten million dollars for your house and then you can buy a gigantic house with a pool and home movie theater and then your dad won't be stressed, and it could be really great?" He does a pretend mic drop. "Huh? Right? Maybe it even has some kind of outdoor kitchen with one of those cool pizza ovens."

I roll my eyes. "Um. That sounds kind of doubtful. But maybe. I like your optimism, Jonah Malkin."

"Well, it could happen," he reminds me. "That's all I'm saying."

We stay at the ice cream place way longer than anyone really should. But no one else is waiting for our table, so I figure it's okay.

Finally at around five in the afternoon, my mom texts me.

Mom: Where are you? We are eating at 6. Tacos.

I write back:

Ari: Be home for dinner.

Thankfully, she doesn't write anything else after that. "What time do you need to be back at your great-uncle's?" I ask Golfy.

"Probably now," he replies. "But no one has called me, so . . ."

"I need to be home by six for dinner," I tell him.

"Let's start walking over to your house," he says. "My parents can pick me up there. I won't come in. Don't worry."

"Okay. Thanks. And sorry."

"Nothing to be sorry for," he says.

We walk quietly for a few minutes, and then Golfy

takes my hand. We're both a little sweaty, but I don't really mind. Holding someone's hand may be one of the simplest, nicest feelings in the world. It's this sense that you're going somewhere with someone else. You're not in this alone. There's someone there, someone right next to you, and that someone makes you feel safe and secure.

The person is saying *it's going to be okay* without saying anything at all.

It's the universal symbol for *we got this*.

THIRTY-NINE

"THAT'S IT. I CAN'T TAKE it anymore," I tell Kaylan after math.

Today's a B schedule, so we have math first period, and it's the worst way to start the day. "He didn't even acknowledge that Isabela was the only one in the whole class to get a hundred on the test." I shake my head. "The only one! His whole thing about highlighting success! It's not true. He only highlights the boys' success!"

"I know." She side-eyes me. "But you're yelling!"

I try to quiet my voice. "We're writing an anonymous note. We'll say we're concerned students and Isabela Gomez-Wright is clearly the strongest one in our math class, and we want her to get recognition. Also, does he know she tutors elementary school kids in math every week?"

"Shh, Ari, you're still yelling," Kaylan says as soon as we get to our lockers.

"I'm really upset about this."

"I know." Kaylan puts an arm around me. "Okay. Okay. We'll write the note. But maybe we should talk to Isabela first? Inspire her to write the note?"

I consider it for a second.

"I think that will make it even more powerful," Kaylan suggests. "Let's talk to her at the Halloween party!"

"Maybe. But I don't want to bring up a bad subject during a fun time. . . ."

"Well, we won't spend the whole time talking about it," she reminds me. "Anyway, I gotta go check the extra-help schedule. See you at lunch, dahling."

"Of course. Ta-ta, dahling."

At the lunch table, the girls are deciding what club to join.

"I'm definitely not doing Krav Maga and definitely not doing mindfulness meditation, no offense, Arianna," Cami says, still obviously disgruntled from her club not getting picked. "I would've done the adult coloring, though." She shoots M.W. a look. "I may just stick with gymnastics outside of school and my cello lessons, and that's probably enough. I mean, we have so much more homework in seventh grade."

"Yeah, she's right," Kaylan adds, putting mayo on her turkey sandwich. "And I think it's going to get even worse. Ryan had tons of homework last year. Not that he ever really did it." She laughs. "But he did have a lot."

I crack up, too, and steal a chip out of Kaylan's bag.

"Want to trade my pretzels for your chips?" I ask her.

She contemplates that a minute and then nods in agreement.

"I'm joining Mindfulness, by the way," M.W. tells me. "It seems really good."

"Thanks. And also, today is just the trial day. If you don't like it, you can totally switch."

Kaylan rolls her eyes. "I'm not joining anything, but I'm staying after school to use the computer lab and email some of the local comedy clubs."

"Did you find any funny people in this school?" Amirah asks. "You can still recruit them for your comedy nights."

"We probably do," Kaylan says defensively. "They'll come out of the woodwork. You'll see."

"What does that expression even mean?" June shrugs. "Like, what's woodwork?"

No one answers her.

"Okay, guys, for real, can I just say that I am so glad we decided to be crayons for Halloween?" Cami claps. "Kaylan, your idea was fab."

"Thank you, dear."

"So we're all set for tomorrow? We're going to meet at Jay's house at five when the party starts, stay for a little, and then trick-or-treat around there?" Cami asks, going over the plan for the millionth time. "Are we dressing up for school?"

"Yes!" Kira yells. "Of course. Everyone does!"

"They do?" M.W. asks. "I don't remember last year."

"Me either," I whisper to her.

Kaylan says, "I'm in," and then reaches across the table for one of Sydney's mini chocolate chip cookies.

The rest of the day crawls by until we make it to after school.

Ms. Bixhorn says over the loudspeaker that the room assignments for all the clubs are posted on all of the bulletin boards.

I race right over to the one closest to my last-period class and discover that my club will be meeting in the astronomy classroom on the third floor and Ms. Yarden is the faculty adviser.

She's Israeli and she teaches Earth Science, and I think we're going to be the perfect team. Plus if there's downtime she can help me improve my Israeli dancing skills—four weeks at camp was only enough time to really learn the basics.

I get to the astronomy classroom, and six kids are there already. Then Ms. Yarden comes running in. Her glasses are on the top of her head and her frizzy brown curls are flying all around.

"Hello, hello, my lovely students," she says, putting down her piles of folders and taking a deep breath.

"Hi," I say quietly.

I don't know most of the other kids in here, but they all seem to be on the shy side—just sitting at the desks, not really talking to one another.

"Arianna," Ms. Yarden says from the desk at the front of the room. She calls me over with a curved finger.

I walk over to her, and she says, "Would you like to introduce the club? Explain what we'll be doing? That sort of thing."

I nod. "Sure. I'm just getting the hang of this myself, though," I admit. "So do you have any experience with this? I figure you do, and that's why you're the faculty adviser, but . . ."

"I do. Don't worry." She smiles. "It will be great."

I walk over to the group, and we all move our chairs in a circle.

"Let's go around and say our names, our grades, and our favorite ice cream flavor," I tell everyone. Two more kids come in at that point, and I motion for them to take a seat.

It's not like I really planned this or anything, it's just kind of coming to me. At this very moment, I really feel like a leader. One hundred percent. And it doesn't seem like a struggle or a wobbly start—I feel pretty natural about it.

"I'll start. I'm Arianna, but a lot of people call me Ari. Either is fine. And, um, I'm in seventh grade, and my favorite ice cream flavor is chocolate milk and cookies. It's very specific and hard to find, but it's basically cookies and cream but with chocolate ice cream."

"Hi, I'm Anya, I'm in seventh grade. I'm new this year, by the way. And my favorite ice cream flavor is rocky road."

Anya has a super high-pitched voice and her hair is in pigtails. She's wearing overalls with a faded gray T-shirt underneath.

There's something about her that seems easygoing and calming.

The rest of the kids go—a few sixth graders, a few eighth graders, and three seventh graders I don't know.

"Okay, so we're going to start slow," I tell everyone, kind of feeling like I'm channeling Pres from Camp Silver right now. "We're going to do these three-minute meditation exercises that I found online to start, and then every meeting we will increase it by a minute. And it's okay if your mind wanders. You just have to let it wander and then let it come back."

Ms. Yarden nods. "Yes, wonderful. And then if there are people who want to lead any exercises that will be great, too. But we will get there. We have all year."

When she says that, I let out a deep breath.

It feels like Kaylan and I are rushing and cramming to

get everything in by my bat mitzvah—our list deadline.

But this club isn't like that—we really do have the entire school year.

And that feels great and reassuring.

"The first exercise we're going to try is called Concentration Meditation. It's basically just focusing all your energy on one thing." I pause. "And today we'll focus on breathing."

Everyone looks at me.

"Ready?" I smile.

They nod.

And I know we're at the start of something magical.

FORTY

I WAIT FOR KAYLAN OUTSIDE the gym because we planned to take the late bus home together.

We're only a few days away from the deadline. And maybe more important—a few days away from our birthdays and my bat mitzvah.

It's already ten minutes after the clubs have ended, and she's not here.

I start to get a wrangly feeling in my stomach, like she got a ride home with someone else and forgot me.

Not this again.

I'll have to call my mom for a ride, but who knows if she's even home. And what if I call and my dad is there, and he has to pick me up? I hate to be alone with him since he's so depressed and worn-out looking.

There's like nothing to say to him anymore. I don't know how that happened.

Ever since the job-loss thing, it's like there's this glaze of sadness covering my whole family. Like when you buy a picture frame, and there's that slim sheet of plastic you have to peel off before you can use it.

We're all covered in a slim piece of sadness plastic.

I need to talk to him and get all of this out in the open. Not only because I still need to tell a boy how I really feel, but because I want to get rid of this giant slimy alien tension that seems to always be creeping around.

I keep looking behind me to find Kaylan, and after another ten minutes of that, I can't take it anymore. I try to do a quick meditation exercise, focusing on my breathing to calm myself down.

It kind of works.

I decide to walk around the school and look for her. Maybe she's stuck talking to a teacher or something.

I hoist my backpack over my shoulders and start searching. For a second, I feel like some wilderness explorer with a heavy pack, hiking through tall grass in search of some nearly extinct wildlife. But truthfully, I'm just walking on linoleum, carrying a mildly heavy pack, looking for my best friend.

I turn down the C corridor and peek into the computer lab, and there she is—staring at a screen, typing furiously.

"Kaylan? What's happening? You know it's time to go, right?" I look at my watch. "Actually, I think we already missed the late bus."

"Oh, really?" She jumps up and then leans over to sign out of whatever she was doing on the computer. "Sorry, Ari." She makes a silly smile at her rhyme.

"I don't get it—what were you doing? Still researching comedy clubs?"

She hesitates a second. "Yeah. Exactly."

"There aren't that many near us." I look at her sideways, waiting for her to tell me the truth, but she doesn't. I get that wrangly feeling again, like something is up.

"Why are you being shady again?" I ask her.

"I'm not. I promise." She leaves the computer lab and comes over to me. "We can call my mom to pick us up. She told me she was taking the afternoon off. Mental health day or something."

"Oh, like a massage? Mani-pedi?" I ask, suddenly feeling jealous of Kaylan's mom. Maybe I need a mental health day.

"I think so. She's seeing Robert Irwin Krieger this weekend." Kaylan wiggles her eyebrows up and down. "They're kind of in love, I think. How easy was that? Like, too easy, right?"

"I guess," I say. "We're just good matchmakers. Maybe that can be our career one day."

"OMG." Kaylan stops in the middle of the hallway and

eye-bulges at me. "Yes! BFF matchmakers! How amazing?"

"Amazing," I say, still a little uncertain about what Kaylan was doing on the computer for so long.

Kaylan calls her mom, and she says she'll pick us up in fifteen minutes; she's just waiting for her nails to dry. We sit outside on the curb in front of the gym.

"How was Mindfulness Club? Were you extra mindful?" She giggles.

"It went well," I tell her. "Definitely not a million people. But the few that showed were pretty into it."

"That's all you need," Kaylan replies.

"I got to lead an exercise! On the first day."

"For real? That's awesome, Ar."

"Sorry to brag," I say, kicking around a pebble on the pavement in front of me. "It was just so cool. I had to tell you."

"Arianna Simone Nodberg." Kaylan looks deep into my eyes, and we try as hard as we can not to laugh. "I'm your BFF. BFFs are for bragging."

"That has a fab ring to it." I crack up and repeat, "BFFs are for bragging."

FORTY-ONE

"HOW COME YOU GOT TO be the purple crayon?" Gemma asks me when we're eating breakfast. She decided to dress up as a bowl of popcorn. Of course. "Was it because of that book *Harold and the Purple Crayon?*"

I laugh. "Um, I don't know. I just said I'd be purple? And no one else wanted it."

"What color is Kaylan?"

"Green. She loves green. I think it has to do with the Irish thing," I explain.

"Do Jews have a color?" she asks me. Seriously, how is she so chatty this early in the morning? I don't get it.

"Um, blue or white, I guess. For Israel." I pour some Cheerios into my bowl. "You have a lot of questions, Gem."

"So?" She glares at me.

I finish chewing. "Just saying."

When Kaylan and I walk into school in our costumes on Halloween, the whole world feels like it's lit up. I don't think anyone is ever too old for Halloween—the excitement, the candy, the chance to dress up and be someone or something else. It's pure magic and a nice break from the stress of all my other days.

The only slightly wiggly thing on my mind is that my bat mitzvah is in four days. Our deadline is in four days. I think I've lost track of how much we still have to accomplish, but I don't want to bring it up now.

We find the rest of the girls at our lockers.

"Picture time!" Cami squeals. She hands the phone to Mrs. Divar, the hallway monitor. "Thanks so much."

"After this picture, the phone goes away, Cameron." Mrs. Divar looks at us through the bottom of her glasses. "Doesn't matter that it's Halloween. Rules are rules."

Such a shame that she can't get into the holiday spirit.

We all stand together, arms over one another's shoulders, and a content, satisfied feeling washes over me. Yeah, these girls aren't perfect. Yeah, they're not my soul mate Camp Silver friends. But they're not the worst, either. I mean, they put a lot of thought and effort into the Halloween costumes. They picked something that could include everyone.

I think they can grow on me. They already kinda have.

"Attention, students, first period is canceled today. Please make your way to the auditorium for the social action assembly. Thank you."

I turn to look at Kaylan. "It's a B day. No math!"

"Hallelujah!" she sings.

"I'm talking to Isabela at Jay's party tonight. Okay? Don't argue with me." I put my backpack in my locker since we don't need it for the assembly. "Like you suggested."

Kaylan nods. "Sounds good, but can we discuss this later? I don't want to ruin my happy Halloween, no-math-today good mood!"

"Of course." I link my arm through hers, and we walk to assembly together. "Let's write the note to Mr. G after lunch, okay?"

The rest of the day flies by because everyone (except for Mrs. Divar, apparently) is in a happy mood. Even my super-strict honors block teachers let us watch movies and hang out. In library class, we don't have to do any database or catalog exercises—we get to sit and listen to a group of teachers do a spooky reading of Edgar Allan Poe's "The Raven."

All in all, it's a great day, and at five o'clock on the dot, the Crayons get to Jay Yeung's party.

"Guys, we are going to be the cutest people at this party," June says as we walk in.

"No doubt about it," I reply.

"He has this every year?" Kira asks as we walk up the long path to his front door. "We didn't go last Halloween."

"No, this is his first year doing it," Cami explains. "They moved to Brookside last year, but they built this house from the ground up and it's so huge and the backyard is pretty much a golf course, so his parents said he could have a Halloween party and invite the whole grade."

"Wow," Amirah says, adjusting her orange crayon outfit.

"How do you know all of this, Cam?" M.W. asks. "Like, for real? You're like a Brookside encyclopedia."

"Um, yeah I am." She holds out her hand for everyone to high-five her. She's too much, as always, but tonight it's not bothering me the way it usually does.

We go inside, and Jay's mom (at least I think she's Jay's mom) is dressed in a witch costume. We all take a red drink off of the platter she's holding.

"Um, there are eyeballs in here!" Kaylan yelps. "OMG."

We go through the kitchen to the backyard, and it's set up like a crazy-spooky haunted house. Skeletons everywhere. Dangling heads. Spiderwebs. Some sound system that makes the creepiest sounds—like people screaming and doors creaking and ominous cat sounds.

"This is intense," I whisper to Kaylan.

Jason and his friends are over by the snack table, so

we walk over there to say hi. There's a spread of the usual stuff, like pizza and pigs in a blanket and mini egg rolls. But then there are also creepy Halloween snacks. Rolled bread in the shape of severed fingers with almonds as the nail and jelly on the edges. A cheese dip made to look like a giant eyeball with a green olive in the middle. A Jell-O mold in the shape of a brain. And then a big bowl of spaghetti that really and truly looks like worms to me.

Part of me wonders if they hired some kind of party planner and caterer for this. Would anyone really do that for a kids' Halloween party? And then I wonder—should I have Jay plan my new bat mitzvah?

"Everyone having fun?" Jay comes over to us, taking out his fangs and interrupting my train of thought. "Sorry, didn't want to spit on y'all."

"This party is sick," Jason says.

"Yeah, such an awesome party, Jay."

He gives us all two thumbs-ups, and we take plates of food and go to sit near the very large half-decapitated coffin man by the swimming pool.

I'm in the middle of some of my eyeball cheese dip when I see Isabela Gomez-Wright coming in with a few of her friends.

"Be right back, guys." I get up from the table and walk over to her. A few minutes later, Kaylan comes to join us.

Good. We need to do this together.

"Isabela, can we talk to you about something?" I ask her, after I gush about her amazing *Where's Waldo* costume.

"What? Why? Is my costume messed up or something?"

"Oh no. Nothing like that. It's okay," I reassure her.

We go to sit on the hammock, and I say, "Listen, I don't want to make this long because we're at a party obviously, and we're here to have fun, but . . ."

Kaylan jumps in, "Mr. Gavinder never calls on you. Or any GIRLS." She yells the last part. "And we want to change that. And, um, help you shine."

Isabela laughs. "Wait, what? This is weird, guys."

"No, for real," I say. "We're going to write him an anonymous note. But we wanted you to know about it. We want you to be noticed for your efforts. And your brilliance. You're amazing at math, Isabela."

She shifts to the edge of the hammock. "Thank you. I mean, it has been bothering me. Math is, like, my thing. And he never notices me. At all."

"Exactly!" I yell, grateful that this party is so noisy that no one can hear me. "That's not right! Are you okay with us writing the anonymous note? Do you want to write it?"

Isabela laughs for a second. "Um, you can write it, I guess."

"Okay. It's seriously messed up," Kaylan says, shaking her head. "We want to help."

"Thank you, guys. This is really nice."

One of her friends calls over to her. "Isabela, come check this out!"

"I gotta run." She smiles.

Kaylan and I discuss the note for a few seconds, and I write down a few things on my phone.

"I'll write it when I get home tonight. I mean, type it, so he can't recognize my handwriting or anything, okay?" I ask Kaylan.

"Sounds great. My heart is pounding right now. Is yours? I feel like we're really going to make some actual, like, real change."

"I know! Me too!" I laugh. "About the heart pounding and the change."

We go back to the Crayons, and we keep snacking and hanging out. My insides feel foamy like the soap Mom buys for the downstairs bathroom. Helping people is definitely one of my passions.

There was literally no way to narrow it down to just one.

I found a few passions. And I'm pursuing all of them.

I make a mental note to check that off the list and JHH when I get home.

After trick-or-treating, I get home, text a quick selfie of my Crayon costume to the camp girls, and then I get into pajamas and crawl into bed.

Alice: ari u look so good!

Ari: thank u! How was every1's Halloween? Fab times here. 4 real

Alice: so fab here 2. My friends & I dressed as fairytale peeps. I was little red riding hood

Hana: amaze. Every1 came to my house and we handed out candy for the little kids. Fun!

Zoe: did bldg trick-or-treating, town houses, stores, etc. Halloween in NYC is BONKERS

Ari: love u guys so so so so much

When I can't fall asleep, I group text the Crayons about what a fab Halloween I had and then I write out Kaylan's birthday card.

Kaylan never complains about her birthday being the day after Halloween. It's a funny day to have for a birthday because there's, like, no buildup to it. Everyone is pumped for Halloween and then bam—birthday time.

I think the fact that mine is the day after hers makes it better—like we're in this weird birthday zone together.

It makes it easier and also more celebratory.

FORTY-TWO

"HAPPY BIRTHDAY TO YOU!" I scream into the phone. "So sorry I won't be on the bus, but I'm getting a ride to school because I need to talk to Ms. Yarden about Mindfulness Club."

"Uh-huh. Whatever." She laughs. "See you soon, Ari."

She totally knows I'm lying, but she doesn't fight me on it.

Our birthdays are a guaranteed ride-the-bus-alone day, which is sad because, duh, it's our birthday. But it's essential.

Birthdays mean locker decorations. And that requires getting to school early.

And today is Kaylan's thirteenth birthday. Real teenagerhood.

And that means the best locker decoration in the history of the world. That's the goal, at least.

I meet Cami and the rest of the girls by the main doors so we can decorate together before Kaylan gets to school.

"Ooh, this was such a good idea," I say, standing back and admiring everything. Cami cut out pictures of all these different famous comediennes—Ellen DeGeneres, Amy Schumer, Tina Fey, Wanda Sykes—and people like Lucille Ball and Betty White.

"She's going to love it!" M.W. squeals.

"Did you bring the glitter streamers?" Cami asks me, and I nod, and we spend a few minutes pulling it off the rolls and taping it to the top and bottom of her locker.

"I picked up the Harvey Supreme Sandwich," Amirah says, running in with Sydney and June by her side. "And I got some iced tea, too."

"Fab!" Cami and I say at the exact same time. We high-five each other and go back to decorating.

"I think we're good, guys," Kira says, surveying everything, hands on her hips. "Oh, the buses are rollin' in! Quick! Everyone sit."

We all plop down in front of the lockers, acting all chill and nonchalant. Kaylan comes in a few minutes later and yelps, "Oh my God! Guys!" She does a little tap dance right in front of her locker. Then she carefully admires everything. "This is amazing."

I whisper in Kaylan's ear, "I know it's your birthday, but can we go a few minutes before first period, so we can drop off the note?"

She nods. "Come on. Let's go."

Dear Mr. Gavinder:
We are students in your seventh-grade honors
math class. We think you're a great teacher;
however, we have realized that you call on the boys
way more than the girls. You pretty much never
call on the girls. Maybe you don't even realize
you're doing this.
Also, do you know Isabela Gomez-Wright tutors
elementary students in math? She is the strongest
math student in our whole grade. Maybe even our
school.
We think you should notice that.
Sincerely,
Anonymous

We check to make sure the main office is empty before we put the letter in his mailbox. Then, when we're on our way to first period, Ms. Yarden stops me in the middle of the hallway.

"Am I in trouble?" I ask her, scanning my brain for anything I could've possibly done wrong with the Mind-fulness Club.

"Oh no. Don't be silly." She smiles. "But can we talk for a second?"

I nod. "Can Kaylan come, too? It's her birthday."

"Sure," she says, and we pop into the computer lab.

"So," she says quietly. "I was at a meeting with other middle school teachers from our county this morning, and we were sharing extracurricular ideas, and I told them about your suggestion for the Mindfulness Club, and they were in love with it." She claps. "Really, truly in love. They thought it was brilliant."

"Really?" I squeak. "That's so awesome."

"Ari! Go you!" Kaylan yells, and then tones it down to a whisper. "Sorry, it's my birthday."

"It is awesome," Ms. Yarden agrees. "And they want to start one at the other schools, too. And eventually we may make it some kind of countywide program."

I lift my eyebrows. "Wow. I can't believe it."

Ms. Yarden shifts her weight from foot to foot. "I just wanted to tell you. We're in the early stages, but I'll be getting back to you about how you can be involved and what the next steps are."

"Yay! I am so excited." I almost reach out to hug her, but it doesn't feel quite right. Hugging a teacher is always kind of awkward.

"Me too. Congrats, Arianna." She smiles. "Okay, now we must get to class, yes? And happy birthday, Kaylan."

"I just need to stay here for a second, and make sure I printed out my English essay."

"Okay, Arianna. Have a great day."

My cheeks are still up high, tight into a gigantic smile.

"Ari! What! This is huge!" Kaylan spins around and puts her hands on my shoulders once Ms. Yarden has left the room.

"I know! I'm JHHing right now. I think a countywide mindfulness initiative counts as *Making our mark*." I wait for her to reply. "Right? I mean, right?"

"Totally. Go for it."

After I JHH, I quickly look over the list and check off *Make our mark*.

Kaylan and I walk to our next classes together, and I say, "Kay, it's your birthday. Mine is tomorrow. My bat mitzvah is in two days." I clench my teeth. "We are so close to the finish line."

"Crushing it," she says. "Totally crushing it."

1. Keep our friendship strong. ✓
2. Drink enough water (for a glowing complexion). ✓
3. Make our mark. ✓
4. Master the art of mac and cheese (from scratch!). ✓
5. Perfect our handstand. ✓
6. Help someone else shine. (in progress)

7. Stay up long enough to watch the sun set and rise. ✓
8. Find the perfect man for Kaylan's mom. ✓
9. Draw a doodle a day. ✓
10. Tell a boy how we really feel.
11. Pursue a passion (first find one). ✓
12. Break a bad habit. ✓

After school, my dad drives me to my bat mitzvah lesson. My mom is finalizing the order for the balloons at Get Ready to Party, the store in Carlton Park, the town a few miles away from Brookside.

At least I'll have balloons in the social hall. That'll make it feel different than any regular after-the-service luncheon. Balloons make a big difference; they're basically tangible happiness.

"How are things?" he asks, when we're stopped at a red light.

It's now or never, Ari. Time to do this. Your bat mitzvah is in two days. The list deadline is looming.

"Um, well, not the best. Not the worst," I start. "But I need to talk to you."

He keeps staring at the road, straight ahead. "Okay . . ."

"I feel like this job-loss thing has been really hard and you've been really distant, and everyone expects me to cheer everyone up," I start, feeling small puddles of tears forming behind my eyes. "I can't always cheer everyone up. Or calm everyone down. Mom is always freaking out."

"I know," he says softly. "It's been a tough time. And you've been handling it really well."

I wait for him to say more, but he doesn't. Is that all he can offer? Grown-ups should be able to do better than that. They should be capable of explaining things and making tough times make sense.

I look at him even though he doesn't make eye contact with me, and I wipe my tears away with the sleeve of my corduroy jacket. "I wasn't sure if you knew it was tough for me. Everyone always expects me to be the calm one, because that's how I've always been. But it's not possible to be that way all the time."

"I know." He pauses. "I see how hard you're trying. But also how much you're hurting, too. And I'm sorry. About all of it."

We get to the temple, and my dad says, "I'm glad we talked. And, uh, have a good lesson. I'll wait for you out here."

I get out of the car, and I can't tell if that conversation was what I expected or not. He didn't really say anything. He listened, I guess, so that's good. But he didn't have any explanations or solutions or anything, really.

Maybe there's not always an answer or a way to fix anything. Or maybe it takes a while to figure out if there's a solution.

"Hello, Arianna!" Cantor Simon says when I get to her

office, as cheerful as can be.

"Hi." I sit down in the leather chair and take out my folders.

She puts a finger in the air. "Oh wait! This is your last lesson. We need to practice on the bimah, imagine that there's a whole congregation out there in front of you!"

I follow her out of her office and down the hall toward the sanctuary. It's strange to see it empty, dark without the lights on.

She flicks a light switch and the whole place lights up.

"Sorry it's so cold in here," she says.

"I have layers on," I reassure her.

"It'll be warmer in here on your bat mitzvah day. I promise."

We walk up the steps and then I stand there, in front of the podium, looking out into an empty sanctuary.

"Imagine this whole room full of people who love you." She smiles.

We start going through the prayers in the early part of the service. My Hebrew is sparkling, all the pronunciations come out perfectly, even the words I stumbled on during our lessons.

Cantor Simon takes the Torah out of the ark and moves the wooden rollers to get it to the exact spot. And then I stand there, ready to read from this scroll that thousands and thousands of people have read from before me. And now it's me doing it.

My turn. My time.

It's hard to believe it.

"Are you ready?" Cantor Simon asks me. She hands me a long, skinny silver pointer thing. It's called a *yad*, which means "hand" in Hebrew, and it's used to help keep your place as you move from word to word.

"I think so," I say.

"You are." She smiles. "I know you are."

I chant from the Torah—my portion—the Life of Sarah. And as I'm chanting, it hits me. All of it. Everything that led to this moment—all of my questioning, and soul-searchiness, and even the drama with the lunch table girls and my parents.

Judaism—its teachings and its community—was always there for me to lean on. It was something to fall back on, something bigger than myself and my problems.

This whole experience wasn't about fulfilling obligations and milestones that are set out for you.

It was about religion being there for me, during the hard times and the good times and everything in between. Religion gives us a guide to follow when nothing makes sense.

Religion is there for us, no matter what.

It's having faith in what you cannot see.

"Arianna, that was outstanding," Cantor Simon says when I'm done chanting. It felt almost like an out-of-body experience since my mind was wandering so much while chanting, but somehow that made it even more meaning-ful. Because I had that beautiful epiphany. And I finally figured out my speech!

See—a bad habit isn't always bad.

Nothing is ever one thing.

Everything is multilayered and messy and compli-cated and blurred.

That's what life is.

The Life of Sarah.

The life of Arianna, too.

"Ready for your speech?" she asks. "I know you've been struggling, but I just have a feeling you'll nail it."

I swallow hard. "I need to redo it. I promise it'll be ready for my bat mitzvah, though. I mean, I don't have a choice, right?"

She laughs a little.

"I got this. I promise." I smile. "I finally figured it out, like literally, just now."

Cantor Simon raises her eyebrows. "A little suspense is always good, I guess." She puts her hand on my shoul-der. "You sure you don't want to discuss anything else? Give me a little taste of what's to come?"

I shake my head. "You've taken me this far, but I need to do the rest on my own."

FORTY-THREE

I STAY UP UNTIL MIDNIGHT working on my speech, so I expect to be super tired when I wake up on my birthday morning. But the thing about birthdays is that adrenaline always kicks in. So even if you're tired, you don't feel it.

The best night of the year to stay up really late is the night before your birthday.

My phone alarm goes off, and I already have birthday texts from so many people, even Cantor Simon.

Cantor Simon: Happy birthday almost bat mitzvah girl! Yay you! ☺

Alice: happy birthday to you, happy birthday to you, happy birthday dearest girl in the world Arianna

Nodberg, happy birthday to you! see u in 1 day!!!!!!!!!
XOXOXOXOXOXOXOXOXOXOXO

Hana: Ari, it's your birthday and I love you and you're the best girl ever. mwahhhhhhhhh

Zoe: HAPPY BIRTHDAY, ARIANNA SIMONE NODBERG! I LOVE YOU!

Jason: happy bday 2 u

Cami: happy bday!!!!!!!!!!!!!!!!!!!!!!!!!

Golfy: did u think I wld forget ur bday? Obv not. Happy bday, ari <3

I kind of love how he doesn't even bother with emojis; he just tries to make a heart symbol on his own.

When I get down to breakfast, I find a spread of banana nut muffins (my mom got the recipe from Kaylan's mom), bagels with lox and cream cheese, fresh-squeezed orange juice, and a platter of fresh fruit.

"Happy birthday, Ari!" my whole family yells at the same time.

"Thank you," I say, sitting down at the table.

"I'll drive you to school today," my mom says. "No taking the bus for the birthday girl."

I smile and cream cheese my bagel.

"How does it feel to be thirteen?" Gemma asks, picking a strawberry off the platter. "A teenager."

"Feels normal. So far."

The phone rings as I'm checking my teeth for poppy seeds.

"Ari, it's Bubbie," Gemma yells out.

I take the phone from her and say hello.

Bubbie and Zeyda start singing right away.

"Thanks, guys. You're good singers," I tell them.

"Only the best for you, our darling girl," Bubbie says. "We're singing from the airport! And we get to see you so soon! How lucky are we?"

"I can't wait," I say. "But I gotta get to school now. See you later! Love you!"

"Love you more," they reply at the same time.

I get to school, a little relieved to see that my locker has been decorated, too. There was a tiny part of me that wasn't totally sure.

"Heart sunglasses all over!" I clap. "Guys! I love it! Where did you even find this?"

"It's wrapping paper!" Marie says, putting an arm around me. "I actually found it last spring, and I've been saving it for your birthday locker decoration. Can you believe it?"

"Not really!" I giggle. "Guys, this is awesome."

"Look inside, look inside," Kaylan says. When I open

the door, I find about fifty of those spiral lollipops I love—the big ones you can only find at specialty candy stores. They take like a day and a half to eat.

"Kaylan! Did you spend your whole life savings on these?"

"You're worth it, dahling." She pulls me into a hug.

The first bell rings, and we all gather our stuff. Kaylan puts her arm around me as we walk to math.

I say, "Do you think Mr. Gavinder is going to say anything about the note?"

"I don't know," she says. "I still want to switch out of his section, whether he makes a change or not."

We get to class and take our seats, and Mr. Gavinder is at his desk, not looking at anyone.

"Do you think he knows it was us?" Kaylan asks. "Or that Isabela was involved?"

"Shh," I say.

Class starts, and he takes attendance. And then, when he asks for volunteers to complete the geometry proof on the board . . .

My heart beats furiously.

The moment of truth.

Owen raises his hand. And Kenny. And Rafa. And Daniel.

And Isabela.

I don't raise my hand because I seriously don't know how to do it. Neither does Kaylan.

Plus what girl wants to do a geometry proof in front of the class on her birthday?

Not me. That's for sure.

"Isabela, please come up," he says, half smiling, not looking at anyone in particular.

Isabela smiles at Kaylan and me as she walks up to the board.

She completes the proof perfectly and sits back down, still smiling.

"Excellent job, Isabela," he says. "Now, let's take out our workbooks. Please complete pages seven and nine, and then we'll go over our processes."

Kaylan scribbles me a note.

Ari,
I feel so great. We will JHH this at home. XX K-K
P.S. Rip up this note when Mr. G isn't looking and throw it away after class.
P.P.S. AMAZING BIRTHDAY PRESENT FOR YOU (and me too ☺ LIST IS COMPLETE!!!!!!!!!!!!!!!!!! And don't you think this Isabela thing also brought us back together?)

I smile for the rest of the day, not only because it's my birthday. I smile because I keep thinking about Isabela and how the note worked and how Mr. Gavinder has realized his mistake.

He sees Isabela's genius now. And hopefully he'll call

on girls as often as he calls on boys. Maybe more. Who knows.

I feel like we really did something—as good friends and good leaders—and I've never felt so proud of anything in my whole life, I don't think.

Golfy calls me after school and sings me happy birthday. Once in English and once in Hebrew, the way we sing it at camp.

"Great singing, Golfy. I didn't know you had such a good voice." I'm only half kidding; his voice is actually pretty good.

"Thank you. And also, your bat mitzvah is tomorrow," he says. "Just wanted to remind you."

"Thanks. I don't think there's any way I could forget."

He laughs. "Not to change the subject, and sorry if you don't want to talk about this on your birthday, but I've been meaning to ask you—what ever happened with that piece of paper and the millionaire who wanted to buy your house?"

I pause and get up to close my door, quickly listening out to make sure no one is close enough to overhear.

"I put it back in the kitchen, but under a pile of paper. So, like, I did the right thing, but not necessarily the best thing." I wait for him to say something, but I think he's waiting for me to continue. "Anyway, it was where I found it pretty much, so it seems normal, like it just got shoved in a pile. And hopefully my mom won't notice the crinkles."

"That was the right thing to do," he tells me. "So whatever happens, happens."

"Yeah," I reply, leaning back against my pillows. "I talked to my dad about stuff, and how I was feeling."

"And?"

I untuck my legs. "He listened, basically. He didn't say much."

"Maybe he needed time to think about it," he offers. "People don't always know what to say in the moment."

"Yeah. I guess. It was kind of disappointing, though."

"Changing topic for a sec. Did I ever tell you about the time this kid Wyatt hid in the garbage cans in my garage?"

I crack up. "Um, no. I don't think so."

"Okay, so it's this crazy story. He got into a fight with his brother, who's a twin by the way, and then his mom was telling them they had to separate and then . . ."

I listen to what he's saying pretty intently, but more than that I listen to the sound of Golfy's voice and the way he tells a story. I don't even know if there's anything truly special about it, or if it's just special because it's him.

"Golfy, I have to tell you something," I say, looking over

the list and feeling the need to make a quick change, an addition, a double JHH because I'm going to do one list item twice.

Plus, it's my birthday—the one magical day of the year when I can do what I want.

"Yes?" he asks.

"I like you," I say. "I mean, like, like. Like a lot of like."

He cracks up. "A lot of like. I like that." He pauses. "And you. I like you, too. Also a lot of like."

I put the phone on speaker and rest it on my night-stand, and as he's talking, I do a quick JHH on my own.

He probably already knew how I felt about him, but I said it out loud. I said it, anyway.

Talking to my dad counted as telling a boy how I really feel. But he's a man, so it was kind of like cheating a little, even though it was important.

And list or no list—I still wanted Golfy to know how I feel about him.

After that, Golfy keeps telling me random stuff, like how his BFF from camp, Eli, who's, like, two inches shorter than he is, is trying to get everyone to call him Miniature Golfy next summer.

I crack up. "OMG, that's hilarious. I love it."

"So now get everyone else on board, okay? We need this to catch on."

"Okay. But why did it take so long for him to think of this? I mean, you've had the nickname forever, right?"

"Yeah." He laughs again. "No idea."

My mom yells from downstairs that it's time to get ready for dinner.

"I gotta go, Golfy," I tell him.

"See you tomorrow, AT YOUR BAT MITZVAH," he yells through the phone so loud I have to move it away from my ear a little.

After he hangs up, I sit there on my bed, staring at the photos on my bulletin board, still cracking up about the Miniature Golfy thing.

FORTY-FOUR

IT'S KIND OF FUNNY TO have your birthday the day before your bat mitzvah. My family and I celebrate and stuff—and it's a bigger celebration than normal since the relatives that live far away are already in Brookside for my bat mitzvah.

We don't have a fancy dinner or anything, the way my mom originally wanted, but the people at Antonucci Café, the Italian place close to the beach, let us use their back room for no extra charge.

So it's festive and fun, and they even bring out a yellow cake with chocolate frosting and everyone sings me "Happy Birthday."

We're getting ready to go when Bubbie pulls me aside. "You're so beautiful. Do you know that?"

I smile.

"You don't know how beautiful you are," she tells me.

"Um." I never know what to say to that.

"Listen, I have a surprise for you."

I expect jewelry or something and I look at her hands for a shiny, nicely wrapped box. But they're empty.

"I was going to wait and tell you tomorrow, but it's going to be too crazy." She pauses. "Zeyda and I decided . . . you know, we're getting older, and we miss you and Gemma, and you're getting older, too, and . . ."

"What?" I ask, impatient.

"We're moving closer to you! We found an apartment ten minutes away and there's lots of stuff going on in the community and it's going to be great!"

"What? This is the best news ever." I stand up on my tiptoes and wrap my arms around her neck. "This is seriously the best bat mitzvah gift in the world, Bub."

She smiles. "I had a feeling you'd be excited about it."

After we get back from Antonucci Café, we all change into pajamas and my mom and I sit at the kitchen table and finish the place cards. Originally we were going to have the calligraphy lady do them, and she was going to calligraphy the invitations, too, but that was another bat mitzvah thing left in the dust.

"I'm not sure we still need these, really, since it's no longer a sit-down meal, but it's always helpful to know where you're supposed to sit, isn't it?" she asks me, eating her third mini Snickers of the day. We are hitting the Halloween candy pretty hard this year. "We'll ask the custodians at the temple if they can put them on the right tables before the service ends."

"It's good to have them so nobody feels excluded. I loved how we had assigned lunch tables in elementary school."

"Exactly." My mom finishes writing *Eleanor and Steven Feldman* on a card and then she looks up and smiles at me.

Oh God. I don't even want to imagine all the weird details Eleanor Feldman knows about me.

"What?" I ask after a few seconds of my mom sitting there and staring at me with that weird mom smile.

"I'm just so proud of you." Her voice catches. "The way you handle everything, and look on the bright side, and you're just so wonderful."

"Thanks, Mom." I look down at the stack of place cards and the list of people attending my bat mitzvah. It's kind of amazing how far people will travel just to be here with us. "And I don't know if Dad told you this, but I can't be that way all the time. I can't always be calm and positive. It doesn't work or make sense. It's probably not even healthy!"

"I know," she says. "I'm sorry it's been so hard on you. I'm sorry it took me so long to say sorry. It's not your job to cheer everyone up or calm anyone down. It was never your job."

The phone rings, startling me and taking me out of this emotional moment. "Hello?" my mom answers.

She always nods while the person on the other end of the line talks. It's kind of funny since the other person can't see her.

Nodding. Nodding. More nodding.

And then my mom says, "Oh yes, nice to hear from you. I'd lost your note for a while, and then just recently found it under a stack of papers. Things are a little hectic here with my daughter's bat mitzvah coming up."

"Uh-huh. Uh-huh," my mom replies to whatever the person is saying. "How about we wait a little while? This weekend we're very busy. So I guess next weekend would be okay?"

She nods again. "Great. Touch base with me the day before." She smiles. "Oh, I'm glad."

When she hangs up the phone and comes back to the table, she turns to me, sighs a deep sigh, and then gets back to the place cards. I wait for a few minutes to see if she's going to explain what happened on that phone call.

She doesn't, though.

And I obviously know what it's about. But I still need to ask.

My heart pounds a little bit. Sometimes it's hard to

ask a question if you're not really sure you even want to know the answer.

"What was that all about?" I unwrap another mini Snickers.

"Nothing, really," my mom says, writing out the place card for *Zoe Krieger*.

"Well, it was obviously something," I press.

She sighs her deep sigh again. "Some people fell in love with our house, and they want to buy it. But I don't think it's for sale."

"So how can they buy it if it's not for sale?"

"They can't." She looks up at me again. "We'll let them come and look, and maybe make an offer, but I don't think we're going anywhere. This is our house. We belong here."

I wait for her to say more, but she stays quiet after that, writing all the place cards for the camp friends table.

I like that I have a camp friends table. That I have a whole group outside of school that I care about, and that cares about me.

"Are things any better with Dad's job situation?" I ask her, all hesitant.

"Not yet. But they will be." She looks over the list again. "I don't want to jinx it, but I think good things will come through. I really do."

I wonder if it has to do with that dinner at Vintage 25 they went to a few weeks ago. Maybe it was the magical twice-baked potatoes everyone talks about.

I get what she means about not wanting to jinx things, so I don't ask anything else. Sometimes you just need to trust the universe that things will work out. It kind of ties into my bat mitzvah speech a little bit, but there are certain times in life where faith is really super important, I think.

And this is one of those times.

We continue with the place cards, and I wonder if I should tell her that I stole that letter from the people who want to buy our house. That I crumpled it up and hid it.

But I don't think I need to. I put it back where I found it. And maybe it was a good thing that I hid it in the first place. If they had called right away, we might've sold the house, assuming that things were only going to get worse.

My Bubbie always says that everything happens for a reason, and to be honest, I usually roll my eyes when she says it because it just feels like an easy way out.

But now I'm kind of realizing that she may be onto something.

It can just take us a long time to figure out what the reason was.

I don't have time to think about this anymore, though.

Speech brainstorms keep coming to me, and I need to quickly add them in.

There's something exciting about the down-to-the-wire

moment (whatever that means), crunch time and deadlines.

The feeling of making something perfect just the way you want it to be, right before it's going to happen.

I guess I'm not really a plan-ahead type of gal—I think back to my mac and cheese method.

But I do make things the best they can be, right when it counts.

FORTY-FIVE

THE MORNING OF MY BAT mitzvah, I wake up and it feels different than every other Saturday.

My alarm goes off at six, and my mom is already up. We rush around, eating breakfast (but I can't eat) and getting ready. When we're all in our temple clothes, we drive over there and attempt to do some family photos before the service starts.

Random cousins that I've only met once or twice come up to me saying things like "you're so tall" and "the last time I saw you, you were missing your front teeth!" and "what a beautiful young lady you've become."

I'm not going to lie—being called a young lady is just as creepy as being called a woman.

I still want to be a girl. I think that's okay.

After a zillion photos taken by my uncle Scott, who is

actually a professional photographer and offered to help out for the day, it's time for everyone to take their seats in the sanctuary.

My parents, Gemma, and I stand by the door for a few minutes greeting more people, and the longer I stand there, the more my stomach rumbles. Time is moving in slow motion. I need this service to start already. I need to feel like I've done okay with all the prayers and the Torah portion and my speech and everything.

After most of the grown-ups have arrived, the kids finally start coming.

"You look so amazing," Marie says, squeezing me into a tight hug. "Did you get your hair done?"

I shake my head. "My mom curled it with this new curling iron she found online."

"It looks profesh," M.W. adds. "Like, hard-core pro-fesh."

I laugh. "Thanks, guys."

"Okay, we're going to sit," Cami says, and blows me a kiss. "You are very chill today, Ari. Like, you don't look nervous at all."

"Thanks, Cami."

Kaylan comes in a second later with her mom and Ryan.

"OMG, I am so sorry we're late, Ari," she says, sort of out of breath. "You look like a model. A bat mitzvah girl model."

"Thanks, Kay-Kay." I reach over to hug her, my heart pounding.

This is really happening. Like now. Right now. I have to step outside myself for a minute to observe this scene as someone else. I want to be mindful of all that is taking place—breathe it in, pay attention, really notice everything.

My bat mitzvah. Today. Now. All of it.

Ryan head-nods in my direction, and Kaylan's mom kisses me on the cheek and tells me I look beautiful and to break a leg.

Then the camp girls start coming in, and Alice sprints down the hallway and lifts me up and twirls me around. "Ari, my lovieeeee," she squeals. "OMG, I missed you beyond!"

"AlKal, I missed youuuuu beyond," I reply, as she puts me down.

Zoe and Hana walk in at the same time, and they pull Alice and me into a group hug, and we all start swaying together and squealing and then it feels like everyone in the sanctuary turns around to stare at us.

"Guys, okay. Stop." I try to break free. "You're crumpling my dress!"

They finally pull apart but squeal a few more times. It feels like the puzzle version of me is almost complete again.

"Is Golfy here?" Zoe mouths.

I shrug. "Haven't seen him yet."

My throat starts to get tight and scratchy, and I get a bubbly, fizzy feeling when I think about seeing Golfy. It's kind of like the feeling right before you're about to get a present you're really hoping for, or the moment when the roller coaster you're on is about to do the downhill part.

The best kind of nervous feeling.

This receiving line is kind of nice because my parents are so busy talking to people that come in that they can't overhear my conversations with my friends.

As I'm walking with my parents up the aisle to go sit on the bimah, I feel someone tap me.

Golfy.

"So sorry we're late," he says. "Traffic. Duh. You look amazing. You're going to crush this. You're my new favorite person. Okay, go. Bye."

I laugh behind my hands and smile my whole way up to the bimah.

FORTY-SIX

WHEN I LOOK OUT INTO the congregation at all my family and friends there in front of me, I swear it feels like my heart swells a little bit. Even the lunch table girls look mildly interested in the service, way more than they did on Rosh Hashanah.

Rabbi Oliker and Cantor Simon welcome everyone and say "Shabbat Shalom" and they introduce me, saying that I'll be leading most of the service. And when I'm reciting the prayers in Hebrew and English, my mind isn't wandering at all. I'm all in. I'm not even thinking about anything else.

I'm 100 percent mindful, in the moment.

I read the English parts, and then the congregation reads their parts responsively.

And I smile when I get to my favorite passage: *"Standing*

on the parted shores, we still believe what we were taught before ever we stood at Sinai's foot; that wherever we go, it is eternally Egypt; that there is a better place, a promised land; that the winding way to that promise passes through the wilderness. That there is no way to get from here to there except by joining hands, marching together."

I think back to all the metaphorical marching together—as a Camp Silver community that really brought Judaism to life for me, Kaylan telling me that I could lean on the lunch table girls when things were hard, reaching out to my camp friends, too, even though we were far apart. Golfy helping me sort out the drama with that letter.

And when it's time for my Torah portion, different family members—my parents, Bubbie and Zeyda, Grandma, my aunts and uncles—come up to chant the Hebrew blessings before each part of the portion. They're pretty much thanking God for everything, especially for giving Jewish people the Torah.

When they finish, they all give me a smile and a squeeze. And I think the main amazing thing about this whole experience is that yes—it's my day. But so many people are part of it, too. It really feels like a community in here.

Like we are all together—to celebrate happy times and get through hard times—and if we remember that and stay true to that, it will all be okay.

We are a community here, together, today.

Again, the only way to get from here to there . . .

The service goes on, and soon it's time for my speech. It took me months and months to figure out what I wanted to say. But I finally did.

"Good morning, everyone. Shabbat Shalom. And thank you so much for coming out to share my bat mitzvah with me.

"My Torah portion is called Chayei Sarah. That literally means 'the Life of Sarah.'

"Big stuff happens in this portion, and there's a great deal to discuss here—especially about marriage, and family, and legacy. But I don't have time to get into it all, so you'll just have to trust me."

Everyone laughs. I give myself a metaphorical pat on the back and keep reading.

"The aspect that interested me most was highlighted in the name of the portion and in the first line—'the Life of Sarah.' The portion also tells us that Sarah lived for one hundred and twenty-seven years and then says, 'Such was the span of Sarah's life.'

"At first glance, this seemed kind of redundant to me. But then, after discussing this with Cantor Simon, I realized that it's meant to be repetitive. And it's meant to make us think about life.

"How moments, days, months, years all add up to the 'span of our lives.'

"I think it's also there to tell us that life is long, but there will be ups and downs. For Sarah, this meant leaving her homeland

with Abraham and struggling for many years to have a child. Eventually, she does have a child (Isaac), but she's very old at that time.

"Life is tricky. We have to muddle through the hard spots, hoping that they will pass quickly and that we will gain some understanding and perspective, and be better equipped to handle them the next time they come around. And then we strive as best we can to appreciate the great times while we are living them.

"Like Sarah, I have had some struggles. Of course, hers were way harder."

Everyone laughs again.

"But I've also had some amazing times. And in many cases, I had to go through the struggle to get to the amazing.

"This past summer, I spent four weeks at Camp Silver in the Berkshires, and I had no idea what I was getting myself into. I'd never been to camp before, and I was leaving my family and my best friend behind.

"Spoiler alert: it was the best summer ever. No offense, family and BFF Kaylan."

I look out into the congregation and make eye contact with her. She gives me a thumbs-up.

"At Camp Silver, I learned how to be mindful. How to really be in the moment. How to appreciate everything that's right in front of us, even when things are difficult. And that has carried me through some really hard times. I started a Mindfulness Club at school, and it may even be a countywide thing pretty soon.

"It was at camp that I realized the importance of community

and how important it is to lean on that community when times are hard. I had to be reminded of that a few times after I came home, too, and that's when I realized I had community right in Brookside.

"I'm proud to be an adult in the eyes of my people now. I'm honored to be able to stand up here before you, and lead the service, and pray with all of you. I hope I can keep up with everything and fulfill all the commandments and be a great Jewish adult.

"I know that in the days and years ahead, I will face more struggle, and I will face more wonderful. And hopefully I will be as blessed as Sarah was—to live a full life.

"Maybe even one hundred and twenty-seven years."

More laughter from the congregation.

Maybe I should take this speech to one of Kaylan's kids' nights at the comedy clubs. Maybe I'm funnier than I'd ever realized. Who knows?

"The best realization of all is that Judaism has given me a guidebook to follow when nothing makes sense. And a community to lean on when I'm struggling. And I hope that I can be there for others, like people have been there for me.

"Joining hands and marching together, like I just read earlier. It's the only way.

"Thank you all so much for being here with me on this special day.

"Extra thanks to Cantor Simon for helping me figure everything out."

After my speech, there are a few more prayers, and Rabbi Oliker makes some announcements and offers me a blessing, and then that's it. The service is over.

I sort of expected to feel some sort of relief, but it's not really that. It's a little bit of relief, but also a sense of sadness. Like the end of your birthday. You've waited so long for it, and it was great, but then it's over.

It's like the minute after you take a final, you just want to go back and look at your flash cards again. It's so hard to put that feeling away.

And this is sort of like that feeling to the extreme. Because I worked so hard and learned so much and then it's just done.

I walk out into the lobby to meet my family and greet everyone. We'll all go down to the social hall for the bagels and it'll be fine. What people don't tell you is that you feel so great after your bat mitzvah service, you feel such a sense of pride and accomplishment, that the party is actually the last thing on your mind.

At least for me.

"Ari, you are amazing, amazing, amazing," my mom says, pulling me into the tightest hug in the history of the world. "Now come on, let's go."

"Let's go where?" I ask. "The social hall is this way."

I start walking.

"No, come with me. This way. Come on. You'll see," she says.

I look around and the crowd has already dispersed, and I feel this sense of doom like I may have entered *The Twilight Zone* even though I've never really seen that show, so maybe I don't know what I'm talking about.

"Wait. What?" I turn my head to the side to sort of see down the hallway. Where are my camp friends? Where are my school friends? I look out through the big glass doors and into the parking lot, and everyone is getting into cars. Are they all going home? Did my parents cancel the bagels, too? Are we going to Fleetwood for some kind of small celebratory brunch, just family, no friends?

"Just come." She pulls me a little bit, and my head is spinning with questions.

"I don't get what's going on," I say as we walk out into the parking lot. "Seriously, this is freaking me out. What about the place cards?"

Gemma sits in the backseat with me, silently, pursing her lips together as tightly as possible, like a smile is about to squeak out at any moment.

"What's going on, Gem?" I whisper. I know I can get this out of her.

She shakes her head side to side. "Can't say. Won't say."

I try to figure out where my dad is driving, what direction he's going. It seems like we're going home? Oh no, not a backyard barbecue with everyone at our house. We just did that a month ago.

"Dad, where are we going?" I ask.

For the first time in so long I hear emotion and feeling in his voice. "I am so beyond proud of you, Arianna Simone."

That chokes me up; I'll admit it. But it doesn't really answer the question.

FORTY-SEVEN

"THE POOL?" I SQUEAL. "WHY are we at the pool?"

I see people walking in, still in their temple clothes, all dressed up. It makes me laugh out loud—to see all of these people going to the pool, of all places, in fancy outfits.

"You'll see," my mom says. "You'll see."

We follow the path alongside the pool fence, and soon we're in the brand-new building that took way longer to remodel than anyone ever expected it to.

Joey is out front guiding people, welcoming everyone and helping assist with the place cards.

"Mazel tov, Arianna Nodberg!" he yells out into his microphone, the one he uses for Freeze Dance all summer. "Our guest of honor is here! Our bat mitzvah girl has arrived!"

To be honest, I've never seen Joey so excited.

The double doors to the brand-new building open wide and then everyone yells out "MAZEL TOV." It really means *good luck* in Hebrew, but people say it like *congratulations*.

It's kind of like they'd yell out at a surprise party, and I guess they could still yell *surprise* in this case since I seriously have no idea what's going on.

But inside the giant room in the newly remodeled pool building is everyone who was at my bat mitzvah service. And the tables have red-and-white-checked tablecloths like you'd see at a barbecue. And there are two giant speakers and "Hava Nagila" is playing and everyone is joining hands and dancing in a circle: a very enthusiastic hora.

The walls are decorated with giant pictures of Camp Silver—I think Kaylan printed them from the website and had them blown up.

The centerpieces are mini campfires made from tissue paper and sticks and modeling clay and each one has a fake lit-up candle in the middle.

"Talk to Kaylan." She smiles and leans in to kiss me on the cheek.

I don't have to walk very far, because a second later Kaylan runs up to me and hugs me super tight, so tight she even lifts me in the air a little bit and I have to make sure my dress is still down and people aren't seeing my underwear.

There are a zillion conversations spiraling around us.

"Kaylan," I say, hopeful sounding, waiting for her to explain.

"Arianna," she replies, mimicking my tone.

"You did all of this?" I ask her.

She nods. "Well, Alice helped, too. Thank her for all the pictures of Camp Silver and the silver streamers, especially."

"You guys worked together on this?" My cheeks start to hurt from smiling so much.

"You're right—once you give Alice a mission . . ."

"Exactly." I hug her again. "But seriously—this was all your idea?"

She nods. "I told you I'd make my mark."

"Loyal to the list," we say at the same time.

"But how did you do it?" I ask her.

She puts a finger on her chin. "Worked with Joey, and he let me have the space. I emailed all the guests about the change in venue. Alice helped with all the Silver stuff. Literally. Golfy and Jason helped me with the playlists. Golfy added all the Jewish/hora/Hebrew songs, obviously. My mom and I made the centerpieces together . . . um." She pauses. "I told your mom I was handling everything, and she sort of believed me, and then backed off, but I don't think she did trust me completely because she'd call me freaking out like every other day."

"I can't believe she let you do this," I squeak.

She shrugs. "Deep down, she knows I have everything under control."

"I guess so." I hug her again.

"So can I do a quick JHH for me making my mark and then can we hora together?" Kaylan asks me. "That's not really something I ever thought I'd say."

"It has a good ring to it."

We walk to the side of the room and JHH behind the food table—which is completely covered with subs from Harvey Deli.

"I am guessing Cami helped you with this?" I ask.

She nods.

"She's not that bad, I guess." I smile.

Kaylan looks around the room for a second. "Oh, and Mr. Wainscott handled the mini hot dogs." She bursts out laughing. "They were essential. Obviously."

"Obviously." I crack up. "Listen, I can't let you JHH alone, even though I already did make my mark, and this is clearly your moment . . . so can we JHH together?"

She nods. "Okay."

It's the highest we've ever jumped, the hardest we've ever high-fived, and the tightest we've ever hugged.

"Kaylan Terrel, you've definitely made your mark as my BFFAE."

"Arianna Nodberg, you have, too. You crushed that service, and you're a woman in the eyes of your people now."

I crack up again.

"We need our bat mitzvah girl," my dad yells into Joey's pool microphone. Joey is dragging some chairs over so they can lift me up. "Arianna Nodberg, it's hora tiiimmme."

Everyone joins hands and dances in a circle, and soon I will be in the middle of it. Lifted up on a chair, high up so I can see everyone and all this joy around me.

"You gotta go," Kaylan says. "I think I'm going to be a party planner when I grow up, now. FYI. It's my passion. My new passion."

"You already JHHed the comedy thing, though."

"I'll JHH this one, too, at the end of the party. Double JHH. Oh yeah." She smiles. "You were right. We can definitely have more than one passion. And pursue them all."

"Arianna Nodberg!" my dad yells out again. And then Golfy gets on the microphone, "Arianna Nodberg. Where are yooouuu?"

"Okay, you really gotta go," Kaylan says. "Your dad and Golfy are sharing the mic."

"Come on." I grab Kaylan's hand. "I need you with me out there."

Kaylan smiles and whispers in my ear, "When should

we start our next list? Should we wait until summer again?"

I shake my head. "No. Let's start right away. We're teenagers now, we can do things differently."

"I like it," Kaylan replies.

We walk into the center of the room, hand in hand. Alice blows me a kiss and Bubbie and Zeyda and Grandma clap to the beat and my mom and dad hold hands and bounce on their toes.

I scan the crowd, and a happy, content, warm, filled-up-like-a-cup-of-cocoa feeling washes over me.

The words I read an hour ago echo in my head: *There is no way to get from here to there except by joining hands, marching together.*

I wonder why it took me so long to figure out my speech and everything else, really.

The answers were right in front of me this whole time.

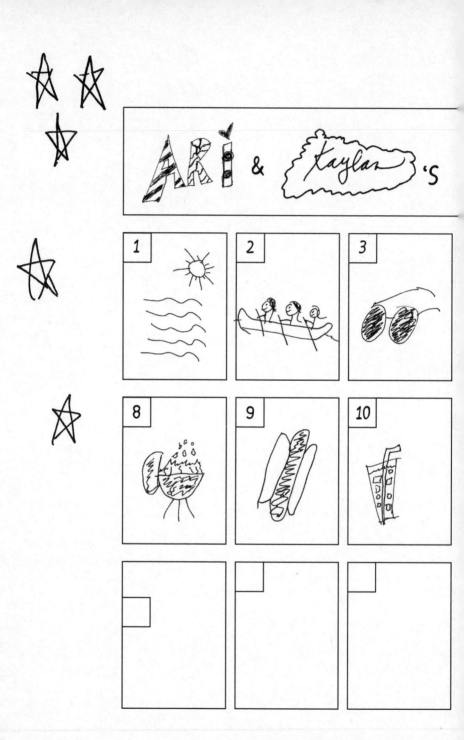

13 BEST DAILY DOODLES

ACKNOWLEDGMENTS

Dave, Aleah, and Hazel—you're the lights of my life and my marching partners. I could write an entire book expressing my gratitude for the three of you and it wouldn't be enough.

All the Greenwalds and all the Rosenbergs—thank you for the love, enthusiasm, and support.

BWL Library & Tech team—you are superstar coworkers.

Caroline Hickey and Lisa Graff—my fab writing retreat partners and awesome friends. I am so glad the New School brought us together.

Alyssa Eisner Henkin—I am endlessly grateful for all your guidance and encouragement.

Maria Barbo—I want to JHH nonstop for all the thought, care, passion, and dedication you put into this book.

Stephanie Guerdan—you get countless high fives for your brilliant ideas, organization, and patience.

To the fabulous people at Katherine Tegen books: Katherine, Ann, Aurora, Amy, Gina, Ro, Emily, Mark, Kimberly, and Vanessa—you're the best, best, best in the biz and I feel lucky every single day that I get to work with you all of you.

Aleah, Alexander, Daphne, Emma, Gabbi, Lindsay, and Sophia—thanks for doodling.

Last but never least, to the kids who have read my books and to the kids who have emailed me and written me letters—I love you! Keep reading!

Ari and Kaylan's friendship continues
in Friendship List #3:

13 AND COUNTING!

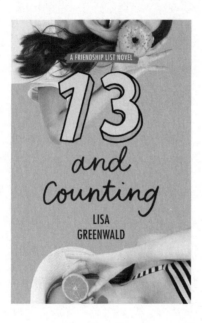

More great books by
LISA GREENWALD!

The Friendship List

TBH